ADOBE GOLD

Stone Justice
Book I

by
Robert C. Mowry

PRAISE FOR ROBERT C. MOWRY

"This was a wonderful book and a hard one to put down. I kept reading into the wee hours of the morning just so I could find out what happens next."
—Barbara Rhoades, on *Fugitive Father*

"I give high accolades to the author for clean language and no scenes that have to be screened for sensitive readers. Thank you from the bottom of my heart! Fugitive Father was an excellent read and I would highly recommend it to all those who enjoy thrillers. I gave this book five stars out of five."
—Kathryn Svendsen, on *Fugitive Father*

"Mysteries, conspiracies, crazy people, good people, family–this book has it all."
—Barb Johnson, on *Fugitive Father*

"The writer, deftly and with a light touch, injects religious faith and belief in God into the narrative...If you like a fast paced thriller with clever twists and turns, on top of an intriguing subplot, which are neatly knitted together into a credible culmination, then this book is for you."
—Sinohey, on *Fugitive Father*

"This book holds the reader's attention without skipping a beat. It is well written and the characters and scenes are well described I found I couldn't let go of the book. It was so interesting and the struggles the people met were so well described, you felt you were right there. These type of things happened day in and day out as the soldiers faced struggles while fighting in the Civil War. This is an excellent read for anyone who loves history and stories of the wars that took place."
—Gayle Pace, on *Smoking Springs*

"This story is consistent in its adventures and fight for survival. It is well written, the characters are well described and these struggles keep the story intense and the reader glued to the book as these almost-impossible-to-overcome new challenges occur almost every day. This is no fairy tale. There were soldiers during the Civil War who faced such challenges and this author did an excellent job of putting them down on paper. I recommend this book for anyone who enjoys war stories during the time of the Civil War, especially in the New Mexico territories."

—Joan Adamak on *Smoking Springs*

OTHER BOOKS BY ROBERT C. MOWRY

Smoking Springs

"Ain't gonna die," Judah Ward repeats over and over. The surgeons want to amputate his festering, wounded foot. He's been shot in the shoulder by one of his own officers. Then too, his skull is ravaged by shrapnel. Frostbite and sheer exhaustion plague even the healthiest of these Confederate soldiers after their invasion of New Mexico Territory has been ingloriously halted at Glorieta Pass and they forge a hasty retreat out of this rugged wilderness.

"Ain't going back to Texas," Judah also often asserts. "Hate you, Pa-- your God, too," he bitterly proclaims. But for the tenacity of his cousin, Sam Houston McCoy; the affection of Ramona, a kind-hearted Mexican girl and her trader uncle; the help of Bones, a semi-free slave; help and protection from some fellow Confederate deserters and a troop of compassionate, Union spies; and especially for the aid and wisdom of an outcast, Apache woman he names Red Bear who uses the healing of the steamy, mineral springs and other indigenous remedies, Judah wouldn't survive.

Fleeing his mountain sanctuary, now all alone, his body is on the mend. But, what about his confused mind and tormented soul?

Fugitive Father

He Can Prevent A Terror Attack, Or He Can Save His Son-But Can He Do Both? He has taken his son and he is on the run. The FBI wants him. Homeland Security needs him. The Santa Fe police chief fears him. His ex-wifes cult wants to kill him. With Dr. Alex Vincent having the hard drive from his Los Alamos National Lab computer in his pocket with encrypted data fom a known terrorist, it is no surprise security there haunts him also. As you read Fugitive Father you will feel as though you are right there with Alex and Tucker as they face fear, anger, shame, discouragement, and even happiness. Author Robert Mowry will keep your fingertips on the page, ready to turn asking the questions: -Is Alex to evermore be branded a traitor? -Can he crack this terrorist code and emerge as the man who saves his country? -Can he become a real father, or will he be relegated to being an underground one forever?

CHAPTER 1

The figure that paused in the shadow of the darkened doorway triggered an alert in Tyrone Rafter's melancholy mind. There, with his right hand grasping the doorpost, a gaunt, ashen-faced Padre stood as if unable to cross the threshold and step into this smoky, raucous den of iniquity. Rafter sensed this out-of-place man's eyes peer intently, yet cautiously, through the open doorway into the crumbling Mexican cantina.

Through bleary eyes, the dusk of heavy tobacco smoke, and with only a few meager candles lighting the room, Ty Rafter glared at this unwelcome intruder. Rafter watched the old man's eyes wander across each of those seeking solace in the cantina's decadence and decay.

Though it was hard for him to tell for sure from where he sat slouched on a banco in the darkest corner of the room, Ty Rafter sensed that when the man's eyes reached him, they stopped and stayed fixed. With his left hand, Rafter pushed aside his now empty glass as his right hand slid under the table.

Slowly, methodically, as if advancing through ankle-deep mud, the old Padre forced one foot ahead of the other. The room went deathly silent. All eyes were on this boney, little man as he advanced toward Rafter. As the Padre passed by the end of the scarred and stained wooden bar, the cantinero grabbed hold of the Padre's peasant robe.

"Padre, por favor, 'ees El Pata Fantasma," he whispered, tilting his head slightly toward Rafter.

The Padre weakly nodded his head, made the sign of the cross, then trudged slowly forward.

With each advancing step, Ty Rafter became more enraged. When the Padre was but four or five steps away, Rafter drew one of his large Walker-Colt pistol with his right hand, and with his left grabbed the whiskey bottle from the table, then smashed it across the table's edge, leaving the jagged bottle neck protruding from his fingers.

The Padre stopped for a few seconds, then forced himself forward again. Rafter kicked over the table.

"Come any closer, you old fool, and I'll send you off to meet that God you always talk about. I don't need you, or your God. You can't save me from Hell—I'm already there."

The Padre again hesitated, then, with quivering lips, praying to God for intervention, he took the last few steps until he was only inches from the enraged Rafter. With his gun hand, Rafter reached around the old man, then pulled his head down as he thrust up his left hand until the jagged bottleneck pushed ever so slightly into the flesh of the Padre's neck.

A small trickle of blood started down the quivering neck of the old man as he opened his eyes widely. He swallowed hard, then whispered.

"Señor, I pray the peace of God over you. I bring you no harm, only word that the one you cry out to in your sleep, she is no more with us. Sí, this one whom your mind torments itself over night and day no longer walks among us on this earth, but is with the saints above at the feet of the Holy Father Himself. However, your son, Señor, now is the time to be his father, as your heart so desires, and as he so needs you to be. Time—time is now your friend. Vaya con Dios, Señor."

Rafter then let loose his grip, and the Padre slowly straightened up. Through several seconds of silence, the Godly and the Godless stared deep into the other's eyes. Then, the Padre made the sign of the cross, turned, and with soft, short steps he disappeared into the solace of the blackened village street.

Not a sound was made by any of the few patrons inside the cantina. None dared to look at this crazed gringo they knew as El Pata Fantasma— the wooden legged ghost—whose fits of rage had for years plagued much of this border area with brutal acts few cared to remember.

Rafter closed his eyes and leaned back against the wall. He let the broken bottleneck fall to the floor. Loneliness, an old and often visitor, flooded the depths of his soul. Laura was dead. That was his fault. He could have stopped it.

He rose, holstered his gun, picked up his cane, then hobbled toward the door.

I swear by anything holy. If there is a God, I swear by him. I'll make things right with little Buck.

Tyrone Rafter crouched by the small pool of water that had formed among some rocks along the bank of the Rio Grande—the American bank. Looking north from the river, he reminisced how he'd last crossed near here about eight years ago, a few months after he'd escaped from his long and brutal captivity in Mexico City. The pain he'd suffered hobbling, and even at times crawling, back to Illinois was nothing compared to the pain that stabbed his heart when he learned his beloved Laura, believing as did all others that he was dead, had by then married another.

With her new husband and Rafter's son, little Buck, she'd moved to Texas. He'd found them, watched them from a distance for a week, and wrestled with the idea of telling Laura that he was very much alive. More than once he'd yearned to kill her new husband. One time, when well hidden behind a boulder some fifty yards away, he'd even drawn a bead on this other man's forehead, but failed to pull the trigger.

Looking past his pride and facing the truth, Rafter acknowledged that he was no longer the man Laura had known and had married. He so feared she wouldn't want him back. She'd married Colonel Tyrone Rafter, the United States Army's top espionage agent. His foray into Mexico, his capture, his loss of a leg and his long imprisonment had, by the time he'd made it back to the States, left him merely a crippled shell of that man—and a dead hero to the masses. He'd kept asking himself: What would he do if he approached Laura and she rejected him for this new man she'd found? Unwilling to risk her possible rebuff, he'd retreated back across the river and into a life of self-pity, hate and violence.

Now, here at the shimmering little pool along the river, Rafter looked down and stared at his image. He hadn't taken time to do that for years. Who was this rough, old man looking back at him? He reached up and touched his face, then he ran his fingers through his shaggy hair. In anger, he then fiercely struck the water with his fist.

Time was now his friend, the old Padre had said. To Ty Rafter, it seemed time had been his enemy—one very cruel enemy.

He rose, then again looked north. To find Buck, and face this son who believed him to be dead for fifteen years, he needed to muster up some dignity. First, he had to get sober, then he'd have to get cleaned up. He'd have to stay free from those demons in the bottle, too. He needed money. One man could help with the money part. This same man owed him the new start in life he now craved. The debt was old—but never collected. Now was the time.

———

Ty Rafter stepped out of the barber's shop and stood on the plank sidewalk. He leaned his cane against the vertical, red and white striped, signpole by the doorpost. He glanced at the advertised prices posted above the door: shave 17¢, haircut 33¢, bath 60¢... Since they were worth 40¢ more than the bill for his services, the barber had gladly accepted the last dozen reales Rafter had in his pocket.

Earlier in the day at the boarding house, then again at the dry goods store, he'd learned his Mexican money wasn't legal here anymore, though, still commonly accepted. With his pockets now empty, Rafter no longer had a money exchange problem.

The breeze felt good as it filtered through his new, ready-made suit down to his freshly bathed and still slightly damp body. He ran his fingers across his now short beard, then back through his closely cropped hair. As he slid his index finger around the stiff collar of his new boiled shirt, he remembered how much he'd loved the pomp and flair of the military in his old days. Through his mind flashed the times when he would put on his dress uniform and crowds cheered and honored him.

With his mind far adrift, Rafter was startled when his cane slipped from its rest and dropped to the walkway. As he awkwardly tried to retrieve it, a young woman walking nearby stepped over to him and smiled.

"Allow me. My grandfather uses one of these. I imagine you hate it as much as he does."

Ty closed his eyes for a second and took a deep breath.

"Thank you," he said as he took the cane from the young lady. "You're very kind."

"My father taught me to show respect to my elders," she said with a smile, then moved on.

Ty slowly nodded his head. All memories of those former days of pomp and flair slipped far back into his mind.

He surveyed the building up the street, the one with the compelling dome still under construction. He'd check that out later, along with many other unfamiliar things, to assess the progress of this city, thus the nation, in the last fifteen years.

With a push of his cane, Rafter started across the walkway, then across the street, off to Lincoln's office. It took some time, but he finally reached the stairway leading up to the massive doorway.

About halfway up the steps he stopped. This was somewhat to catch his breath, but more so to get up his nerve. His hands trembled. His throat was dry. Water would do, but whiskey would surely be better. He took a deep breath, then slowly exhaled. He did this several more times before he continued up the remaining steps.

Once through the outside doors, and past the initial guards, Rafter walked straight to Lincoln's office. With anger, fear and uncertainty pushing him, he awkwardly strode right up beside the guard who stopped him at the doorway.

"Lord have mercy." Lincoln said when he looked up to see what had caused the commotion. "I face the presence of a ghost. Have mercy on me. For what reason have you come to torment me?"

"I'm no ghost, you lanky old lunkhead. It's me, in the flesh. What you see is all that's left of me—however, it's more than you ever expected to see again." Rafter pushed on his cane, then moved right up to Lincoln's desk as the president waved away the guard.

"This ain't no social call, Abe. No sir. You think back deep in that mind of yours, Abe Lincoln, and you'll recollect well that you owe me. Reckon you can't give me my lost years back, but I do expect my back pay, and a pension for all my time in that hell-hole prison in Mexico. Then, too, I want my name back. I want to walk out onto any street and announce to the

4

world that I'm Tyrone Rafter, and I'm alive. No thanks to you, Abe, or my country, but I'm alive.

Rafter straightened up a little as he shifted his weight from his cane to his good leg. "Time's come that I've gotta find my son. I plan to do it with as much dignity as I can muster up, and you're gonna help make it all possible."

Lincoln rose, walked around his desk, got his face close to Rafters, then stared into the other man's eyes for a moment without speaking. He slowly reached up and touched Ty's face.

"You're dead," Lincoln finally said. "The whole world knows your dead."

Rafter grabbed his old friend by the collar.

"Listen to me. I'm tired. I'm angry. Maybe tomorrow I'll feel like being your friend again, but right now I don't care about any of that. Tomorrow, you'll start telling the whole world that I'm alive. You'll tell them that our government sent me into Mexico to bring back a scoundrel traitor who they'd made into a hero. But then..." Rafter broke off his rant, then let loose of Lincoln's collar.

"No one ever ca—came for me," Rafter said. "Why, Abe, why?"

"We got word that you were dead and—"

"And everyone just believed it?"

"Mercy, Ty, forgive me. I—"

"Laura's dead. My Laura's dead. Now, I've got to find Buck. You're the only one I can turn to, Abe. You've got to help me."

"Why now? I don't need this, not now," Lincoln said. "This war... We're breaking apart at the seams. Families split right down the middle..."

There was silence for a moment, then Lincoln spoke again.

"I'll do what I can, Ty. There's just—well, you understand. Come back tomorrow. I'll see what I can do. I'm sure I can use your talents in some job—"

"A job! Look at me. Take a look at me, Abe. I'm not the man you remember. I need help, justice really, for all I gave this country. It's not easy, but I'm begging, Abe. Ain't never begged in my life, but I'm begging now."

"If I had ten men such as you, I'd win this war in no time," Lincoln said.

"You're not listening, or seeing. Don't make me get on my knees."

"I'll make you a general..."

"All I want is colonel's pay for those seven years I spent in that Mexican prison, and a pension for the future. I deserve that. I earned every cent of that, and more."

"Well, with money what it is now—I'll work on something. Come back tomorrow. *General* Tyrone Rafter. Has a nice ring, doesn't it?"

5

Ty shook his head, then turned and started to leave. His cane tapped harshly on the marble floor.

"Wait, Ty. Where are you staying? You say you need money—here." Lincoln reached into his pocket and took out a ten-dollar gold piece as he quickly stepped to Ty's side.

"From me. For old time's sake."

Ty looked at the coin Lincoln held out to him for a minute, then reached out and took it.

"Yeah, for old time's sake. I'll be back tomorrow, Abe. Ya gotta help me."

Shortly before noon the next day, Ty Rafter again showed up at Lincoln's door.

"Slept nary a wink last night," Lincoln said. "After seeing you, Ty, why I couldn't get you off my mind. I'd close my eyes and you were staring at me. I could see the hurt in your eyes, hear the thump of your cane... Then, I thought of Laura, and I remembered how much you adored her, and... Ahhh..."

Lincoln cleared his throat. "I've re-instated you to full colonel. Your pay starts today. About that pension you want, and well deserve, well, that's going to take some time. The back pay... With this war and all, well, you know how things work.

"Here, look at this." Lincoln handed Ty a letter, as he lowered his head. "Tell me what you think," he said, then he walked over to a window.

Ty took the letter and read it. It carried no signature, and was addressed from Santa Fe, New Mexico Territory. "...in excess of two hundred fifty thousand dollars American, in gold ingots awaits the treasury of the Union War Department," the letter read. "Send an agent, using the code name of the Blue Eagle, and meet me at the abandoned, Methodist Church in Santa Fe, New Mexico Territory on the eve of Christmas of this year..." Rafter handed the letter to Abe, who'd walked back over to him.

"It's probably legitimate. It would be a very odd thing to make up. I'd surely follow up."

"I knew you would. I knew you couldn't resist this challenge. You're just the man for the job. Think of this for your cover—"

"NO! Don't be a fool. You know I didn't mean it that way. Look at me. I'm but a wisp of the man you remember. My body's gone. Some days my mind is, too. I just want to find my son, then have some peace in my life. Listen to me, Abe Lincoln. You owe me some peace and comfort in my life. Straight and to the point, Abe, I am what I am today because of you."

"I owe you? Well, yes, I guess it was at my insistence that you were sent on that mission into Mexico. However, I was just a young congressman, and I knew you were the best man to get the job done. After all, you'd saved my…" Lincoln again walked over to a window.

"That's right, Abe. I saved your life back when we were rafting down the river. You remember—you have to. When the raft hit that rock and broke up, who risked his life and got you to shore? You were all bony arms and legs, flailing about the way of some frisky colt. I nearly drowned doing it, but I got you to shore. Without me, you'd be nothing but a wooden cross on a hill back home instead of where you are."

"Sure, Ty, sure. Just think of this. I've already requisitioned a thousand dollars to cover your expenses. There's more if you need it—all you need. I can see you can't do all the things you used to do. I really do understand that. However, this'll be as easy for you as stealing your mother's molasses drops out of that old cookie jar back in your cabin's little kitchen. Why, being the way you are now will be a natural part of your cover." Abe said as he returned to his desk. "Really, Ty, how hard can it be for you to play the part of a preacher? You truly do look the part."

"A preacher! Abe, I've never even so much as read a Bible and haven't darkened a church door since my wedding, twenty-one years ago."

The argument went on. Lincoln won, of course. Then he added another twist.

"While you're out there, put a stop to this westward expansion of those ever-aggressive Texans. Rumor is, they want to annex California, all that wasteland in between, too. I know it, Ty. I just know you still have enough of the old spy in you to pull off this preacher cover, get that gold in Santa Fe, and single-handedly stop those Rebel Texans from pushing westward."

Lincoln slumped into his chair. Ty sensed a crack in the take-charge persona Lincoln had presented. It was as if a cloud of fear and despair drifted through the room.

"You always were my hero, Ty. God sent you back to me in my time of need to do just this. I'll help you as best I can—but God knows I need your help more than you need mine."

CHAPTER 2

With the tap of his cane and the thump of his leg, Ty Rafter shuffled back the boot-heel and spur scarred aisle to the last row of seats. With no one yet laying claim to that part of this old train car, he dropped his bags to the floor off to his right, then eased his body down onto the horsehair-padded seat. With a push of his cane, he slid across the well-chafed cowhide seat cover to the window end.

With a yank and a tug, Rafter adjusted his leg, the wooden one, as he prepared to head west out of Washington. He closed his eyes as he leaned his head against the seatback and thought about these last several weeks.

The voices of several men entering the train car drew him back to the present. One man made his way to the back, then slid into the seat opposite his. Rafter nodded a greeting to him, but the other man never made eye contact, or in any way acknowledged his presence. Rafter then surveyed the others already on the railroad car.

Within minutes, two men who'd been talking together near the front of the car got up and came back his way. Rafter didn't look at them directly, but out of the side of his eye, he watched them sit in the rear-facing seat opposite the man who'd sat across the aisle from him.

"Name's Judge," one of the new men said to the first man. "I'll take up your invitation back at the depot to join you in a sporting game. This fellow here, Harley's his name, I sort of invited him in also. Hope you don't mind."

The first man, the silent one, just nodded his approval. He then broke out a deck of cards. Rafter knew he was a professional. These cards were his tools. The man introduced as Harley looked to be a farmer away from home on business. Judge then reached down into his valise and slipped out a bottle of Kentucky whiskey.

Harley stretched out his hand to the first man. "Didn't catch your name," he said.

"Tuck," the man said, ignoring Harley's outstretched hand as the cards danced back and forth in his fingers as he shuffled them—or rather, set them up as he wanted.

Rafter was sure Judge and Tuck weren't the strangers they pretended to be. They'd found an easy mark in the unaware Harley, and Rafter had little doubt that the jingle in this farmer's pocket would soon pass into theirs.

The engineer blew the boarding whistle. In minutes, the now sizzling hot boiler sent out bursts of steam that started forcing the big pistons back and forth, very slowly at first, then progressively faster. Thus rose the pace of the clacking of the large, iron wheels across the well-worn rail joints.

With an inquisitive scan across the car, Ty Rafter observed that most of the couples, and several of the men who appeared to be traveling on business, sat in relative stillness, absorbed in quiet conversation, the pages of the morning's local newspaper, or were engrossed in some other personal activity.

Seeing the three men in the card game across the aisle pass the whiskey bottle from one to another, the thorny old Colonel's mouth became sticky dry. His body yearned for its lips to encircle the neck of that bottle, while his soul cried out for its contents to fill his veins, thus influencing every part of his being.

Rafter closed his eyes to shake away those thoughts, but then his mind, as it had been doing a lot lately, slipped into the depths of his ordeal in Mexico. It had indeed been the young congressman Abe Lincoln who proclaimed to his fellow law-makers: "If you want to see Captain Kanter again, send Colonel Rafter. He saved my life once, so he did. He can straighten out this mess with Mexico better than any man alive." Ty remembered how his protests after that were futile. The war department caved to Lincoln's congressional pressure.

Rafter now wiggled around in his seat as his mind left Lincoln for a moment, but stayed in Mexico. He remembered that whole scene well. Even now, fifteen years later, it came to him often in his dreams.

It always started with that young private, a boy in his late teen years. Always, he could see the horrid fear in the bright blue eyes of this boy and he still heard his frantic cry.

"Colonel! We've been ambushed—double-crossed. I'm the only one lef..." The voice trailed off as a sniper's ball split the back of the young man's skull, dropping him instantly at Rafter's feet. So real were these dreams he often woke up and looked at his feet to see if the young man's blood was splashed all over them as it had been that day so long ago. The daytime, conscious memories were just as vivid.

As the dreams, and times of remembering, would continue, Rafter would then see himself as he'd leapt from his cover and ran for his horse. He'd hear the shot cut the air from behind him, and he'd feel his leg collapse at the knee. He'd see, and feel, himself falling forward, burying his face in the loose sand. Then, as he lay there stunned, helpless, he'd sense several men standing over him, but though he'd be trying with all his strength, he couldn't get his face out of the sand to see who was there.

He'd then hear the voice of an American. That voice was forever etched in his mind. The man spoke Spanish, but was obviously from an

American southern state. Ty knew the words he spoke meant to leave him there to suffer a slow death, not to finish him off. When the men walked away, Rafter had forced his head up enough to see the blue trousers of an American army officer amongst those walking away. Over and over he'd hear the words in Spanish this American traitor spoke. He often wondered if he'd hear this man speak in English, would he recognize his voice?

Always in the dreams, and often in the memories, as it had been for real, the next scene is waking up in a foul prison with a man standing by his side. A woman, appearing to be a nurse, is washing off his shattered knee. Reaching in a tattered, black bag, the man then retrieves a long knife and swiftly cuts back a flap of flesh above the knee. Then he swiftly slaps a saw into the gash and starts sawing. Only the nurse is there when Rafter next awakens—often to screams, sweats and pain.

"Hey, Preacher," Judge suddenly said. "You are a preacher, right? No one else would wear that get up, except maybe a hangman and that kind usually rides alone on some old mule up the back trails, and the like."

Stone looked at Judge, then nodded to answer his inquiry. He couldn't bring himself to say the words: *Yes, I'm a preacher.*

"You don't mind us having a friendly game, do you, Preacher?" Judge asked. "I'd invite you in," he continued, "but I 'spect my even suggesting your participating in such a sinful sport would be an affront to you—you being a God-fearing gentleman, and such."

Preacher? God-fearing gentleman? How will I ever pull off this cover?

"You fellows throwing a little paper, and drawing on that bottle over on your side of the aisle won't corrupt me in the least," Rafter said, flashing a smile toward his fellow travelers. He rapidly glanced at each one. Only the one face stirred his mind; the one with the long scar—the talkative gambler—the one who'd called himself *Judge.* He'd seen this face before, most likely many years ago, probably before that scar. Maybe it had only been in a photographic picture, or painting, but, somewhere he'd seen this face. This was someone he should know.

Rafter closed his eyes and laid his head back against the seat. The last two weeks had been a whirlwind. Now that he'd actually stepped into this new mission, his mind was tormented more than ever. Could he stoke up the old fire and tough up the needed grit to pull this off? Was there still enough ice in his veins and calluses on his old heart to hold himself together when he faced-down torture to his mind or body?

It wasn't that living a lie would be new for Ty Rafter. He hadn't used his own name for the last seven years—and not for much of the time before that. However, that was all before he'd met Elias Crump.

"No man should try to fool God," old Elias Crump had said multiple times every day for the last two weeks. As a friend of Lincoln's, this retired seminary teacher and preacher had been commissioned to pound the basic ways of Christianity, and the preaching of such, into the skeptic mind and the infidel soul of Colonel Tyrone Rafter.

"I don't fancy being any part of this foolin' folks about you being a preacher. It's cursed, I say," Elias Crump had ranted. "Sure as thunder follows lightning, God will strike you dead for this, Colonel Rafter. May He have mercy on me for my part in this charade. May He spare His judgment on me, I pray. Anybody but President Abraham Lincoln, anybody else and I'd have said never! Never! Never! But old Abe can be mighty persuasive. Might have persuaded me right into the fires of hell, so he might have."

A sudden burst of excitement from Harley in the card game across the aisle brought Ty's mind back to the present. "Yes!" Harley yelled. "You boys be mighty easy. You're gonna buy me the biggest nest in all of Missouri. I'm feelin' plumb lucky today. You fellas just keep those cards coming."

Rafter cast another glance that way. Who is this man with the scar?

"You're a good man, Preacher," Judge said, catching Rafter's glance. "I'd pass you the bottle and propose a toast to you, but I 'spect this old Blue Mountain shine wouldn't know what to do in your innards. I'll me a snort for you just the same, if you don't mind."

"Be my guest," Rafter said, flashing his tarnished teeth in a broad smile. "I promised my dear old grandmother many, many years ago I'd never touch the stuff."

A promise I never kept, Rafter reminded himself. What would his life be like if he'd kept that promise? Would he still have Laura and little Buck? The tremble in his hands worsened slightly at the sight of the drink being poured. He turned his head to the window, closed his eyes, then took several slow, deep breaths.

Moments later, with the crook of his cane, he reached down and hooked the worn, leather satchel he'd set on the floor beside him, then he drew it up to his side. He reached inside his coat and removed his spectacles from his vest pocket. He then removed a small, leather bound book from the case. He read the imprint on the book cover: Parson Justin Stone, Methodist Church. The imprint had been scuffed over to make it look as if it had been there for many years.

The Bible he then took out of the valise was truly old, well worn and full of notes made by its now-deceased, former owner. He held it sort of reverently, almost fearfully, in his hands. He'd just as soon it was a rattlesnake. If that, he'd know what to watch, where the danger was.

Rafter again turned to look out the window. He repeatedly stroked his beard in the way one would a pet cat, slowly running his fingers through its thick hair; now more gray than its former chestnut. A loud yelp from Harley brought him back to the present.

He looked down at the Bible on his lap. Actually, the preacher cover was a smart idea. Brilliant, for the right man. The few churches this Methodist organization had established out along the Rio Grande valley area were now empty, the pastors having been called back east to wait out the eminent Confederate invasion. Without any real support, posing as a man of the cloth could help one survive if he received some free meals and other things a preacher is often given.

Ty Rafter had done countless underhanded things before in his life. None had ever bothered his conscience. Now, for some strange and unsettling reason, the thought of his accepting things people thought they were giving to God, or doing for God, well, this stirred some deep down, buried fear in his soul. He kept hearing Elias Crump rant that, "...no man should try to fool God...."

Rafter again shuffled his body into a new position to ease his pain.

Parson Justin Stone.

He repeated this to himself again and again. This name appeared on the preacher's certificate, and other identification documents he now carried. Over and over he silently repeated his new name to his mind, knowing he had to become this person, in name and action, or he'd fail, and failure might well mean death.

From this moment on, until this mission was completed, in name and perception, Colonel Tyrone Rafter was once again dead.

When day passed into night, the creaking, trembling, old train car became filled with wisps of oily smoke from the lanterns giving meager light to all, including the ever-intensifying card game. Judge struck a match, then put it to the end of a cigar, adding greatly to the small area's thick smoke. The game had turned direction. Now, curses and accusations preceded, then followed, each play. Though he felt the tension between the players could well become physical, Parson Stone succumbed to his exhaustion and, with chin slumped to his chest, dozed into a shallow sleep.

Much later, while another hand of cards was being dealt, the engineer blew the whistle, then he eased off the throttle. They were approaching another town. Stone took out his watch: twenty-seven minutes before midnight. It was too late to take a chance on finding a fit room at this hour. Any decent innkeeper would be asleep. Still, he needed to get off the train for a few minutes to stretch his fatigued body. He gazed across the now sparsely filled car to the many empty seats up near the front.

"You're cheatin'. Been doin' it all day long," came the sudden cry from Harley as he looked at the pitiful mixture of cards he'd just picked up. "Ain't figured how, less'n both of ya be workin' this agin' me," Harley went on, first looking at Judge, then at Tuck.

"You," Harley pointed his finger at Tuck. "You ain't said but two words all day. And you," he said, pointing to Judge. "You ain't shut up. You said come join you, and we'd pick this fella in the back out of a bundle of cash. You said he'd taken it from others like me anyway, that he'd not really owned it. Said it wasn't really the fruit of his labor, and it wouldn't be stealin' to take it for our families and…"

Harley paused, then went on, "Work together with you, you said, and we'd split the till. Ain't been like that at all. You two's been workin' me. I should'a known no one would be on my side. Greed got to me. Thought I was in for an easy dollar. For once in my life, I thought I'd get me somethin' without workin' myself to the bone. Fool I was. You saw all that. You used me," Harley said, shaking his fist at Judge.

"Ain't no use in me goin' on to Missouri without any money," Harley continued. "If'n I had me a gun, I'd kill both of you right here and now."

"Don't threaten me, Harley," Judge said. "How can anyone be cheating you? If you think back, in the heat of the day, you had over two hundred of my money. Did I accuse you of cheating then?" Judge asked.

"You led me into this mess. You knew I'd play on, bein's I told you I'd be goin' all the way to Missouri. I should have figured this out before. There ain't no way I can win against a stacked deck, or stacked table." With that, Harley reached into his boot and pulled out a large butcher knife, then thrust it towards Judge.

With a move faster than Harley's, Parson Stone slapped the crook of his cane across the aisle, catching Harley's arm and jerking him out of his seat. Harley landed on his back, struggling to free himself from Stone's cane. The struggle quickly ended when Harley looked up and saw a pocket-pistol in Judge's hand. It was cocked and pointed right between his eyes—only a foot away.

CHAPTER 3

"Alright. Ya'll can have the money. Just let me up," Harley begged. "Oh please, let me up. I got a wife and—"

"Harley, you best thank this here preacher man," Judge said. "If he hadn't stopped you, your blood would now be dripping between the cracks in this floor. You played the game—you lost your money. Now get off this train and I don't ever want to see you again."

The train braked to a stop. Harley slowly rose from the floor. With shaking hands, he picked up his bag, then left the train without looking back, or saying anything else.

"Mighty fast with that cane, Preacher," Judge said. "Didn't catch your name."

"Stone." He cleared his throat, then expanded, "Parson Justin Stone."

"You saved me from having to kill that poor sap. Guess you've done your good deed for today, Preacher Stone. Fools such as young Harley just don't know when to quit. Their greed gets in my pocket every time."

You were cheating, Stone wanted to say. He'd seen the cards coming from the rigging up Judge's coat sleeve. He couldn't say anything, though. How would a preacher, a real preacher, know about such a thing? Such a crude setup would never work against any experienced gambler, but on a train such as this, and against players the likes of Harley, it was as good as reaching right into one's pocket and taking their money.

"Need to stretch a mite," Stone said. Rising slowly, he ambled off the train. Once outside, he saw Harley walking slowly toward a saloon. Something inside of Stone didn't settle with how Judge and his partner, Tuck, had plucked poor Harley. His mind went back to one time back in his youth when his father had lost all the family's money in a crooked card game. He hadn't thought about that incident in years. It was Abe Lincoln who got them justice then.

Abe had five dollars he'd saved up from doing day-work for area farmers. He flashed it around and got invited into a game with these traveling card-sharps. He brought another man into the game, too, the county sheriff who kept his badge hidden in his pocket. At just the right time, the sheriff called in his deputies, and they revealed the gamblers' cheating ways. After returning the sheriff's money, Abe's, and Mr. Rafter's also, the crooked players were given the boot out of the county.

That's one for you, Abe.

14

Outside on the plank walkway, Stone walked up to the front of the train and watched the men load on wood while the overhead, blackened, wood-slab tank flowed water into the hissing engine's tank.

Moments later, as Stone approached the steps of his car, the whistle sounded its departure call. Stone pulled himself up the steps and without talking to Judge or Tuck, retrieved his bags from the back, then found a seat near the front. He wiggled his leg off to the side to reduce the pain, then he leaned his head back and closed his eyes.

Two days later, Stone sat slicing his breakfast ham when someone put a hand on his shoulder and greeted him.

"Thought I lost you yesterday. You must have only taken a short break back there at Shadytown." It was Judge.

"Sometimes I have to get out of those torture boxes they call railroad cars," Stone said. "My well-used body can't stand to be in one place for very long, anymore. When we pulled into this little town at sundown yesterday, I got a room here and slept all night. Join me. Fine eggs and ham, if you've a hankering for a good feed."

"Don't mind if I do join you," Judge said. "I ate earlier, though. Could use a mite more coffee."

When Judge slid into a chair across from Stone, he bumped against Stone's wooden leg.

"Sorry about that. Didn't hurt you, did I?"

"It'd take more than a little bump to hurt this old door post," Stone said.

"If you don't mind my asking, how'd it happen?"

"Oh—sort of an accident."

"That's a shame. Is that when you took up the Bible thumping?"

"Well—not really."

"Where you headed?" Judge asked. Stone sensed Judge was trying to place him. It seemed that Judge also suspected he'd crossed trails with Stone at some earlier point in time.

"Texas, then New Mexico Territory," Stone replied.

"Texas? That's a real hotbed down there, let me tell you. Most of those boys are mighty anxious to leave the Union, but some of the big-guns, including old Sam Houston, they still want to remain loyal to the Union that got them out of their scraps with Mexico.

"Now that war in '46," Judge spoke quietly, seeming to be deep in thought, "that was quite a fight. Some derned good boys lost it all. Don't 'spose you had any part in that." Judge seemed to have slipped into the mind of someone else. Gone for a moment was the flashy gambler. Here sat the memory of something, someone, in Judge's past.

Stone didn't say anything. His mind was in turmoil about this man. *Who are you, really?* he so wanted to ask.

"Going back to Texas myself," Judge said. "Maybe I'll be seeing you. Frightful big place, though. Funny, something about you, nothing I can point to, but something makes me think we've been on the same path before. But then, I've never known anyone with a bum leg and I surely do my best to avoid any man of the cloth at all cost. You're different than most preachers, though. You were watching our game the other day. Not that you ever even looked our way, but, I believe you knew what was going on a whole lot better than Harley did. Then, the way you whipped your cane—I've never seen the likes of that move, anywhere. Makes me wonder if you might handle a gun the same way."

After a few seconds of silence, Stone pulled out his watch from his black, woolen vest. "I best get over to the depot. Train's supposed to depart in twenty minutes."

"I checked earlier," Judge said. "It's running a good quarter-hour late. If you'll allow me, I'll carry your bags. Mine are already on the dock."

———————

The train chugged rapidly across the flatland. The car was only half-full and the seat he sat in was the least uncomfortable of any of the cars Stone had been on yet. Judge spent much of his time trying to get any of several of the well-dressed men into a game of cards. Tuck sat in silence near the back. Every once in awhile, Stone sensed Judge staring at him.

Suddenly, the front door of the car burst open. Through it stepped a nervous-looking, young man, hand-in-hand with a flushed, freckled-faced, carrot-topped, even younger-looking girl. Eyes wide, the young man intently stared at each of the passengers—his eyes stopping on Stone.

"You're the pre—preacher?" the young man half declared, half asked. "The conductor told me you were here. Please, Mr. Preacher, you gotta marry us—me'n Lila."

Stone sat staring wide-eyed at the young couple who stepped up close to him. Nothing old Elias Crump had taught him prepared him for this.

Stone cleared his throat, swallowed, then responded.

"You want me to marry you?"

"Yes sir, Preacher," the young man pleaded. "Right here on this train, before we get to the next town."

"That's impossible. I mean—"

Like yoke from a dropped egg, tears oozed from the young girl's eyes as she slumped into the seat across from Stone. The young man put his hand on her shoulder to console her. For a moment, only the mechanical clatter of the train was heard. All eyes stared at the young couple, and

Stone. In a moment, the girl regained her composure. She reached over and put her dainty hand on Stone's.

"You must, Mr. Preacher. My pa will be waiting for me at the next town. I just know it. I *must* marry Charles before that. You're the only one who can save me. I can't go back home. Please understand."

"How will marrying Charles solve your problem with your father?" Stone asked.

"Pa has it all lined up for me to marry someone else. He sold me to some filthy old man. Pa ran up a debt he can't pay to that old redeye peddler, and I'm the payoff. It's just terrible. Me and Charles been a plannin' to get married for months now, anyway. Then came this marryin' that old man thing and, well I had to sneak out of the house while pa was drunk. It's so, so, it's just terrible. I'm to get married tonight to this awful, awful man and—" at that Lila turned her head and softly sobbed.

"You must help us, Mr. Preacher," Charles said. "If Lila marries me on the train before her father takes her off, we'll keep on going and never go back. You don't know her father. If you knew the frightful things he's done. If you knew—"

"How long to the next stop?" Stone asked while he pulled out his watch.

"Other than for fuel and water, the next town will be Hapsburg," Charles said. "It's about an hour, maybe a little less. That's where Lila's father will be. He'll cross the crick and take the shortcut. This train circles out around to that last town back there. That adds a couple of hours over what running a horse directly would be. He can beat the train to Hapsburg, I fear."

"Come back in a half-an-hour," Stone said. "I'll think about it until then. Go on now, leave me be."

"We'll be back, Preacher. I don't have much money, but I can give you a little," Charles said, while helping Lila to her feet.

"Money's not an issue," Stone said, waving them away as if chasing off a fly.

They started back toward their forward car. At the doorway, Charles stopped and looked back at Stone. Their eyes locked for a second, then Charles stepped through and closed the door.

Stone quickly took out the small book covering special services. With fumbling fingers, he opened it to the wedding section and frantically started reading. Old Elias hadn't even touched on this. Abe would enjoy this. He'd have a good laugh if he could see the fix Stone was in now.

Is this legal? Am I really a preacher?

He did have all those documents showing he was—of course, under his phony name. He'd been assured everything was legal. Legal maybe—but is it right? Was it something old Elias had said, or just the state of life he was in? Something in him now feared God—maybe it was just the *wrath of God* he'd always heard about.

Darn you Abe. Why couldn't my cover have been a drummer selling dry goods, or a horse trader, or anything—anything but a preacher?

———

"You're now man and wife," Stone proclaimed. He'd only stumbled once during the brief ceremony. The few passengers in the train car clapped and cheered. Charles and Lila clung to each other.

"Remember, Charles, you've given me your word, once off this train you'll go find the first preacher you can and have him do it all again, just to make sure things are all legal, and right. I don't know what the law is about marrying on a train, if there is such a thing. You'll most likely need to register at some courthouse, or such, to make it legal also. I don't even know what state we're in right now."

"I will, Parson, I will. 'Course nothin' could make me feel more married. I jist know Lila and me been all hitched up for good. You did it right and tight, Parson. It'll last forever. You have my word."

Stone nodded, then wearily slumped into the nearest empty seat.

"Good ceremony, Parson Stone," Judge said, moving up and sitting in the seat behind Stone. "That's about the last thing I ever expected to see happen on a train. It'll make a good story, though. This calls for a celebration. Surely, on a special occasion such as this, you'll let down and have a drink." Judge handed a nearly full bottle of rye whiskey to him. Stone took the bottle, closed his eyes, then nodded his head.

"A short nip to be sociable shouldn't offend the Lord at such a time of joy," Stone said. He tipped the bottle to his lips, allowing the biting liquid to burn freely down the depths of his throat. He swallowed, then swallowed again, then again.

———

The train hadn't quite reached the station when Lila screamed. "There he is! Oh, you've got to save me, Charles. I'll die before I go back with him!"

"Go to the back of the car and wait," Stone said. Judge got up and went back with them. There was silence among the few passengers. The train came to a stop. Suddenly, the car's front door was filled with a bedraggled man, a bottle in one hand, a large knife in the other.

"There ya be, Girl. Get up here now, I say. Got you a weddin' to get to, tonight."

"I ain't comin', Pa. Besides, I already got married. Got married right here on this train. Me'n Charles be goin' on west and startin' our own life. I hate you Pa. You hurt Ma and me so much, and—"

The man in the doorway leaned forward, and with a stagger in his step, he started back through the train car. Just before he reached Stone, the preacher stuck his wooden leg across the aisle, the man then clumsily tripped and fell face down in the aisle. He hit his head so hard he was knocked out, cold.

Judge and another man grabbed him by his ankles. They dragged him out the front door. Then, they threw him off to the side of the tracks.

The whistle blew. In seconds the train started slowly turning its huge wheels on the long steel tracks.

Then, just as it started moving, the car door flung open and Lila's father again stood in the doorway. This time he'd drawn his old, single-shot pistol and with the hammer cocked, pointed it back toward Lila.

"I'll kill ya 'fore I let ya go," he blurted out, then he took several steps down the aisle.

"Who was it?" he asked, his foggy mind started to remember what had happened a moment ago. He took several more rocky steps, then turned and pointed the pistol toward Stone.

"You!"

With a snap of his wrist, the hard-bound book of special services Stone still held went flying, striking the attacker square in the nose, sending him tumbling backwards to the floor. The gun went off, sending the ball scooting along the hard, wooden-floor. Judge again led the removal, tossing the fallen man off the now slowly moving train.

"Thank you, thank you, thank you," repeated Lila, who for the first time since Stone had seen her, breathed deeply, as if a huge weight had flung off her shoulders.

Judge sat down across from Stone.

"I've seen similar done with a knife, but never a book," Judge said.

"Just a lucky throw, I guess," Stone replied.

"No luck to it, Parson Stone. I'm thinkin' more and more that you and me have been on the same path, somewhere back in time. I just can't remember where, yet, Parson Justin Stone. If you got more than God on your mind, I'll figure that out. You best not be holding out on me, Parson. I don't give a flip about those old churches out New Mexico way. Something in my gut tells me you don't either."

CHAPTER 4

The calendar said late September, but apparently no one had told southern Texas that the heat of summer was to be diminished. Parson Stone removed his black hat, and with his large, white silk, kerchief he wiped the sweat from his forehead, then back across his thinning top. Meandering through the town streets, he let his team leisurely follow the wagon in front of it. Twisting again in his seat, he moved his leg for the tenth time in the last hour.

Stone knew well the danger of coming here, the possibility of his being recognized, yet he had to start at the beginning, and for him, San Antonio was the beginning. Here the massive recruitment of young men for the expansion of Texas—the Confederacy, really—was centered. More importantly, it was also his last known home for Buck.

The dusty train of freight wagons slowly passed the crumbling old mission, the Alamo, then went south to the commercial area of town. Stone parked his wagon where he was directed. He set the brake, tied off the reins, then he slowly pushed himself to the side of the wagon. He cautiously slid his good leg to the ground. The wooden one then struck the hardpan earth with a thud. Holding onto the wagon sides, carrying some of his weight on his shoulders until his hips could take the full load without too much pain, he stared at his wagon's large, single-crate load.

He heard footsteps behind him. With a slow twist of his stiff body, he turned to find one of the other wagon drivers, a man who'd been part of his train. This man had never spoken to Stone the entire trip. Now, he started a conversation.

"Never thought you'd make it, Preacher. When ya'll signed on up there in Saint Louie, I'd a taken all bets that you'd a never made it out of Missouri. Ya'll showed us what you're made of, for sure. I was against you, all around. Didn't want no preacher a frettin' and a harpin' at me for my habits and such, but ya'll never did. Every other preacher fella I ever did cross paths with just went on a condemnin' and a cuttin' at me night and day.

"All ya did was sit off by yourself a readin' that old Bible a mindin' your own business. Why, ya'll never even tried to take up an offering. Ya'll can pull freight with me anytime, Preacher. Name's Cole. Didn't tell that to ya back yonder 'cause I didn't want to be no friends with no crazy Bible thumper. You're just a regular fella, though. Be proud to call ya'll my friend, now. Goin' back to Saint Louie for another run?"

20

"No. Once was enough for me. I've got business way out in Franklin, then New Mexico. Want to buy a wagon? I need something similar to one of those little, coal-box buggies made to gently carry a man rather than a load of whatever it is we've been carrying."

"Franklin, huh," Cole said. "Mite rough 'tween here and there. Made that run twice myself. Mind if'n I speak my piece?"

"Please do. I've never been down that way, though I've heard plenty," Stone said.

"Keep your wagon, Preacher. Fill it with all the water barrels she'll hold and maybe some jerk meat and such. Them boys that be a walkin' them seven-hundred miserable miles will pay dear for a drink of water and somethin' for their belly once they get on out in that alkali dust.

"Out in Franklin, I come acquainted with one fine buggy maker," Mr. Cole continued. "Old German fella named Rumbaugh. He'll fit ya'll up in style, once ya'll get there.

"This here wagon of your's ain't worth but forty-, maybe fifty dollars here-a-bouts," Cole went on. "Look around. There's more wagons than horses to pull them. Out in Franklin, them merchants might pay ya'll five times that. That'd be what I'd do, Preacher. I'd make me some money along the way, then clean up big in Franklin."

"That's all sound reasoning, Mr. Cole, but I don't know if my back can take seven-hundred more miles riding this thing," Stone said.

"Sheepskin," Cole said. "Get ya'll 'bout three layers of thick fleece all laced up together. Nothin' on this earth better than that to pad a sore body with."

"Just where might I find such a pad of sheepskin?" Stone asked.

"I know just the place. Be my pleasure to get ya'll just what your old body be needin', Preacher. 'Spect it'll cost 'bout a dozen bits, but your old back will surely thank ya'll for it. I'll see you here 'bout this time tomorrow. Ya'll can pay me then."

"Much obliged, Mr. Cole. For now, I'm going to find a place with a bath and soak in that hot water for as long as they'll let me."

"Then just follow me, Preacher. These company fellas'll take care of them horses. They're gonna bill you for livery use tonight, anyway. Grab your bags and come with me. I'll grab one of them to help you. I know the place with the best bath and the best grub in town. Got the best of a few other things, too, but I don't 'spect ya'll be wantin' the likes of them."

"I do appreciate your advice and help, Mr. Cole. If you don't mind, I plan to wait for a spell until they remove this crate. I'm most curious about its contents."

"No sense in waitin'. Ya'll been haulin' the same thing most of us been a haulin'—lead. Big old bars of lead for the newly founded Confederate States of America. We're gonna whip them Yanks but good. Gonna take over old Californy and all them mountains and deserts in between. Then too, all that's north and south. Texas'll soon be bigger than that whole darned Yankee Union.

"The truth be known, most of us don't much give a dern about what them Carolinians and old Virginians does about startin' this new Confederate thing and whatever else," Cole continued. "Here in Texas, were fixin' to have us a takeover of western land like no critter's ever beheld."

The next day, Stone felt considerably better. He hung around the boarding house for a while, then moved off to a cantina for some coffee. Later, he checked on his horses and wagon, met with Mr. Cole who produced the sheepskin pad he'd promised, then Stone collected his pay for hauling the freight.

When the heat of the day broke, Stone rented a buckboard and rode out to a cemetery a few miles out of town. He figured he'd arouse less attention doing this rather than taking his team and wagon. He pulled up behind the old church to the little fenced-in, dirt patch with scattered stones and wooden placards shaped like crosses or headboards. He remembered seeing this place during his time here watching Laura, back eight years ago. He looked around, then he saw a small head-board, one of the newest ones.

Laura Roe, 1826 to 1861, was all it said. Stone put his hand on the little marker, then knelt beside it. After a moment of silence, he started to speak.

"I did you wrong, Laura—you and Buck. I know now, I should have let you know I was alive. I should have given you a choice. I thought I was protecting you, not fouling up your new life. That's what I thought I was doing. If I'd only—"

Alone in this desolate place, Stone let the tears flow freely.

"If I'd come to you, and we'd gotten back together—maybe—maybe you'd still be alive. Maybe I wouldn't be the mess I am, either. I thought you were being taken care of. Figured this fellow would do you better than I had, or then could. I was afraid you'd not want some broken-down cripple when you had a new, whole man. I didn't know he'd put you into this."

Stone knelt there, speechless for some time, his body convulsing in sobs. His breathing was short and choppy. His eyes were closed, oozing salty tears.

"I've never asked this of anyone before, never, but I'm asking you now, Laura. Forgive me for my mistakes. Don't hold what I did against me. I thought I did best by you—you and Buck. I thought I was the only one hurting. I guess I got my thinking on me and forgot about you—everyone else, really. When I did think of you, it was still about me. How much I missed you. How much I'd been hurt by it all. I hated the government for sending me to Mexico. I hated the Mexicans for how they treated me. I hated you for not waiting, even though you believed me dead. I hated—I guess I even hated God. Never knew much about Him—still don't. Guess deep down inside I still hate Him.

"Life ain't been real fair—with my leg and all. That's mostly why I didn't come to you. When I first got back from Mexico and found out you'd gotten married and moved to Texas and—well—as I said, I was afraid you'd choose to stay with your new man. I didn't think I could handle your outright rejection. I know now I should have given you the chance to decide. That's why I'm asking for your forgiveness."

Stone was silent for a moment, then went on.

"I'll find Buck. Somehow, I'll make things square with him." He paused again, then moved his hurting body around and sat on the sandy knoll. He rubbed his hands over the dry earth, the way one would brush a prize horse.

"I gotta go soon. Yeah, it's another secret government thing. Seems I always leave you to do something for the government. It's real serious this time. There's this war and—well, what it comes down to is this: I've got to help stop these Texans from expanding on west, and, well—there's a mess of gold some fellow wants to give to the Union, and I'm to meet him in Santa Fe come Christmas, and, well—"

He again paused. After a moment of deep thought, he went on.

"It's always something for the government, isn't it? It always was. I'm always the right man for the job. That's what someone always claims, usually that darned old friend of mine, Abe Lincoln, and I give in every time. I'll come back and see you, sometime. I promise, Laura. I'll be back."

Stone rose, then got back down on his good knee in front of the marker. He picked up a shard of granite with a sharp point, then marked an "X" across Roe. He scratched the name RAFTER above it.

"I'll be back, Laura." He said again, then rose and walked away into the sunset.

———

The next morning, Stone again rented the buckboard and rode out into the farm country, near by the cemetery. Stone rode up to a man working by a barn.

"Pardon my intrusion. Stone is my name. Parson Justin Stone."

The other man leaned against his fork, spit a stream of tobacco juice out several feet in front of him, then spoke.

"Know'd you was a preacher when I first laid eyes on you way down yonder. Ain't no one else who'd wear one of them upside-down, bell lookin' hats and even doctors quit wearin' them cape things around here. Never could figure why if'n God gives you preachers so much sense, why in thunder do you wear all that black getup in this heat? Don't matter none.

Just ride off down the road, Preacher. Ain't got no money for whatever it is your a wantin' it for. Times is hard."

"Didn't come for any money—nothing but some information. Over yonder, the old Roe place. Roe still own it?"

"What for you wanna know?"

Stone looked at the farmer, then said, "Actually I'm looking for the boy, Roe's stepson"

"Don't know what doin's a preacher got with that boy. The sheriff, maybe."

"I don't follow."

"Roe ain't there," the farmer said. "Got all busted up in a fight. Everyone says it had to be that boy. Buck, they called him. When his ma died, the boy got sorta real hot-headed. Then one day, old Roe was found near dead. That boy had taken off and joined the troops. Hightailed it west that very day. If'n he did in old Roe, can't say as I blame him much. Old Roe was meaner than a snake to that boy, his ma too. Seen her with bruises and such 'bout every time she showed up at the market. Often times she didn't even come. Had her arm in a sling once, too. She and that boy would be out a sweatin' in the fields while old Roe sat under a live oak suckin' on a jug.

"Always figured that boy would get his due when he got enough size and grit. That woman, though…" The farmer paused for a moment. "She seemed to be such a fine lady. Shame she died so young. Her first husband died, too, you know. The boy talked about him all the time, leastways when Roe wasn't around. Seems he'd been some army hero, to the boy anyway. That was all he had to hang onto, his pa's memory."

The farmer's words kept rolling through Stone's mind while he rode back to town. By nightfall, Stone had done some dickering at the mercantile, and he had his wagon full of water-barrels, one full of water. Beside the barrels were six big sacks of jerked beef. Due to the limited water and forage along the trail, the troops were being sent out in small groups, about a week apart. Franklin, Fort Bliss, El Paso del Norte, they were all right together on the Rio Grande at the far tip of West Texas—seven-hundred cacti and rock filled miles down the road.

Stone set out early in the morning, pushing his team hard in the cool air before the heat of the sun slowed everything to a crawl. He wanted to catch up with the column of men who'd left early the day before he did by the time he reached the haunts of the Comanches.

In the heat of the day, Stone pulled the team to a stop as the trail reached the top of a small rise. He looked around. His team seemed nervous—or was it just his imagination? He saw nothing, heard nothing, yet felt strongly in that inner sense that had guided him safely for years that something wasn't right. He licked his dry lips. Yeah, a stiff drink would be great about now—whole bottle even better. He shook the reins, nudging on his exhausted team.

CHAPTER 5

"Hey Rafter, Colonel Baylor wants to see you, pronto."

"Baylor? What's he want with me, Sergeant?" Buck asked.

"Told me to find you and send you over on the double. You'd best get going."

"Yeah, sure." Buck looked around Fort Bliss. With the afternoon heat waves wiggling off the blistering sand, no one seemed to be paying attention to what anyone else was doing. Buck was sure he could go saddle up a horse, then ride out without being questioned. But, how far would he get, and where would he go? He couldn't go back east—he was surely wanted there. He was afraid to go south into Mexico. His father had done that, and never returned. To the west and north was little but wastelands with Indians and Yankees.

"Hey Sergeant, am I in trouble?" Had what he'd done in San Antonio somehow caught up with him out here? If Roe never walked again, well, he deserved it. However, what if he'd died before anyone found him? Roe had goaded him into the fight and had actually thrown the first punch. But nobody else knew that.

"Trouble?" the sergeant asked. "What makes you think that? You hiding something out on me?"

"No, of course not," Buck said, rising to his feet.

It had to be something else that Colonel Baylor wanted. Maybe they were moving out into Yankee territory. He strode slowly to the officer's quarters, then stopped at the commander's door.

"Colonel Baylor, Sir. Private Rafter at your request, Sir."

"At ease, Rafter. Come in. Have a seat."

"Thank you, Sir," Buck said as he entered, then sat in a chair across the desk from Colonel Baylor.

"I've got a report here on you, Rafter," Colonel Baylor said, looking down at some papers on his desk. "It states here that you're the most fearless, most foolish and best dern storyteller of all the men in the whole fort. I'm told you can tell the biggest lie, stare a man down, and never crack a smile. I also hear that you could plunk a Yankee between the eyes at three hundred paces with that long barreled squirrel gun you shoot.

"I'm looking for the best," Baylor continued. "You seem to be one of them. But, I also hear that you've got a temper, burr under your saddle. Is that so?"

"Reckon so, Sir."

"Put that in a sack for now. The day's coming when you can take all your frustrations out on them Yankees. If that old man Sibley ever gets his tail out here, we'll have us a war. By golly, we'll win it too. Of course, by the time he gets here, though, who knows?"

"Be that as it may," Baylor continued. "I'm forming a new scouting unit, spies really, from the men here. We've been relying on the locals to be our forward eyes, those San Elizario boys of Captain Coopwood's from downriver. They do a crack job. They're dedicated to our cause—at least what pertains to Franklin and La Mesilla. When we move upriver, though, we'll need our own eyes out there, agree Rafter?"

Buck slowly nodded his head but said nothing. Baylor then continued. "Right now we've also got to keep a watch out west for those California Bluecoats. It's an important job. Think you've got what it takes, Corporal?"

"Corporal, Sir?" Buck asked.

"Sergeant real soon if you keep things up. I want to send you to Tucson to fortify our positions there. Most of this thing we now call Arizona is on board with us. Oh, I know some of these Mex locals don't hanker to being lorded over by Texans, but they'll have to get used to it. We're not leaving.

"Listen to me, Son," Baylor continued. "We're on the cusp of something big. Big, I tell you. There's gold and silver in those mines out by Patagonia, lead too. Colorado might have more gold than California. It's to be ours. All we have to do is march right up the Rio Grande, right into Colorado. I've got contacts in Utah who tell me those Mormons are just itching to break from the Union. Then nothing stops us from California. After that, we can lay claim to all of northern Mexico that we want.

"It's not only the gold, boy, it's the seaports," Baylor continued, his excitement rising by the moment. "Once we have ports on both oceans, and the Yanks don't, England, France and everyone else will line up to be our ally. Someday, even the Yanks will want to join up with us. Can't you see it, Rafter? Can you feel this down deep in your gut?" Colonel Baylor asked. "Someday we'll all be rich, and powerful. You move up to the top, now, Son, do all you can for the cause, then someday you'll have all you ever want."

Buck didn't say anything, but Baylor's enthusiasm proved infectious. Suddenly, San Antonio seemed a lifetime away.

"Report to my La Mesilla office this Friday," Baylor said. "I have a social planned that evening for my new scout recruits. You'll enjoy the local culture. The drink and the maidens from Mexico—aaah—they are to be savored. Join me Friday, Corporal Rafter."

Buck rose and saluted, unable to hold back a smile while he did.

"Rafter... Rafter? Something about your name... You look vaguely familiar, also," Colonel Baylor said. "You got kin I should know?"

"My father served in the Mexican War, Sir."

"Of course! Colonel Tyrone Rafter. I remember his story. Never met the man, but I saw his picture several times. Sitting around the campfire years ago you'd often hear tales of the exploits of your father, most highly exaggerated I'd 'spect. I'm honored to have you in my command, Corporal Rafter. I hope some of your father's blood runs in your veins."

"I believe it does, Sir."

"You must have been young when, ah—when your father, well, when he became a hero."

"My father rode off when I was three years old, Sir. I never did see him again ."

Baylor nodded. "War can be that way. I trust the one we're in now will be short. Once these Yankees are taken care of, then I can get back to eliminating those heathen redskins that have been giving me fits everywhere I send men. Lord knows that for years and years I tried to help them. But, I now know full well, they can't be helped. I dedicated my life to saving them. Then, they turned on me. Gotta exterminate them all. That's all we can do. Just gotta up and kill them all, or they'll kill us, so they will, " Baylor said, speaking slowly, as if he wasn't really sure of what he was saying.

Buck left Baylor's office with his chin up and chest out. He reached into his pocket and felt the tiny wooden horse his father had carved for him before he left on his last mission. He remembered back to when as a boy of three, and for many years thereafter, how he'd sit and watch down the road, believing his father would be coming home that day. Of course, he never did. His mother used to look at him and cry.

"You're the spittin' image of your father, Little Buck. When I look at you, I see him. If only I could touch him one more time." She would then hold Buck, and they'd cry together.

"You're looking a might smug, Private Rafter. Mind telling your sergeant what's got you so all happy?" His sergeant's curt approach startled Buck back to the present.

"*Corporal* Rafter, Sir." I'm joining a new scouting unit Colonel Baylor is forming, sir."

"A scout you say? Sounds important. No wonder you've got your head in the clouds. So, just when do you report to this new scout thing?"

"In La Mesilla, on Friday, Sir."

"Friday? This is Monday. That means I can have you cleaning stables and such for several days, yet, doesn't it?"

Buck bristled silently. He felt the old anger rise up in him. Though a good two inches shorter, and ten pounds or more lighter, Buck figured he

28

could hold his own against the sergeant. He doubled up his fist, and started to draw it back.

"Relax, Corporal. I know all about what's going on. I recommended you for the job. I'm just funnin' with ya. What do you say we cross the river tonight and celebrate?"

"I don't have any leave, Sir," Buck said, relaxing somewhat.

"I'll get you the leave. You been over to El Paso Del Norte, yet?"

Buck shook his head. "No, I've been trying to stay out of trouble. I'm not sure about Mexico."

"You'll love it. Loosen up some, Rafter. Have some fun in life."

"Yeah, maybe. But not tonight, Sergeant," Buck said. "Maybe some other time."

Parson Stone reined his team to a stop when they were about to cross a small, dry wash in the early light of the moon. His eye had caught sight of a small pond, a three-foot hole really, that some previous traveler, most likely the small company of soldiers who'd left the day before he did, had dug to collect water in the dry streambed. Water now shimmered in the moonlight, about a foot below the surface. Stone turned his team to it. He allowed them to drink their fill. They weren't very thirsty. It had only been an hour, or so, since he'd found a similar hole. He got down from his wagon, leaned over the side, then he slowly put weight on his stump.

Stone had really hoped to catch up to those troops ahead of him by now so he could camp near them. They'd left San Antonio a day before him with orders not permitting Stone, or any other civilian, to travel with them. Stone understood that reasoning, and didn't disagree with this maneuver. None the less, he wanted to get near them, very near, while in Comanche country. He figured that to be a little ways ahead yet, but wasn't really sure.

He had no proof—yet his senses told him that someone had been following him most of the day. Tonight he was experiencing something he rarely felt—fear.

In the darkness, he tried to examine the tracks at the crossing to determine when the company had passed through here. Many of the men were on foot, not owning their own horse and none being available for them by the start-up army. Given that, Stone was disappointed they still appeared to be well ahead of him. A few of the wagon ruts were still partially filled with water, though most were now dry, and several had even started to crack.

He'd rested well back in San Antonio, but the long, two days of driving his wagon had again stolen much of his strength. He looked around, then decided to make camp here. He'd start tomorrow off early. Surely, by nightfall tomorrow he'd catch up with the company of soldiers ahead. This company, as with most he'd seen back in San Antonio, came up short on men.

A mere seventy or eighty were in line when they'd proudly marched, or pranced their horses, out of town. Some were already struggling with the heat, yet proud to be serving their new country.

Their wagons contained abundant supplies, though not much water. That they'd get along the way, at least for the first part of the trip. Once they reached the rock-strewn, cacti-infested, grass-void, alkaline desert of the last one-third or so of their trip, they'd drink lizard blood to quench their thirst, if they had to.

Stone unhitched his team, then gave each a pinch of salt and a scoop of oats from a sack of each he'd brought for them. He hobbled them short, not taking any chances that they'd wander, off looking for grass. Ordinarily, the water would keep them close, but he figured these two were more in need of food than water. He'd let them forage some in the morning before they started on. He tied one end of his lariat to each hobble, then tossed the center of it over the area where he planned to roll out his blanket. Once he put down for the night, he'd slip his arm through a loop in the center of the rope. That way, if the Comanche tried to drive off the horses, he'd be awakened the second the horses stirred.

He decided against building a fire. No reason to invite trouble. He rolled out his blanket, then checked the caps in the .31 caliber, Baby Dragoon, pocket pistol he kept buried inside the valise with his books. He stuck the little pistol under the blanket by his right hand. He thought of the arsenal of weapons he'd left in Lincoln's care: his matched pair of Walker Colts, and his short barreled, double-twelve, scatter gun. Old friends from his border ruffian days. Old friends he wished he now had.

He opened a sack of jerk beef, took out a large strip, then took his bed roll and stretched out across it. With the earth still hot from the day's scorching sun, he'd need no cover blanket tonight—at least not until near sunup anyway.

———

Hours later, Stone stood in the light-void shadow of a live oak tree while he listened to the strange sound he heard coming from the trail ahead. He wasn't sure if it was some kind of wild animal, or worse. His horses had awakened him when they got nervous and tried to move away. He'd then led them away from the wagon, into the shadowy area of the oak trees and tied them solidly to a low branch. With his little pistol in hand, he slowly scoured in all directions.

What he knew of the Comanche ways didn't fit what was happening. Still, they could be causing a diversion up the trail, then attack from another direction. Maybe it was Lipan Apaches, or Tonkas. He knew little of the fighting tactics of those tribes.

After considerable time, he saw movement by the side of the moonlit trail. Something was slowly inching toward the waterhole in the dry streambed. Suddenly, a course, throaty growl of some animal cut the silence of the night. The horses tensed, one snorted and pawed the sandy earth. Then, Stone heard that strange sound again, the one he'd been hearing. This time it was much closer. It sounded human. It sounded like, "Hup… Hup me."

Stone listened intently. Was it what he thought? The animal growled again—then barked. A dog! Then it was someone calling for help.

"Who's out there?" Stone asked, in a soft voice.

"Hup… Hup me."

Stone strained his eyes and finally distinguished the form of a man. He was on his belly, slowly pawing and crawling toward the water hole now guarded by the dog. Stone moved to another tree where he could get a better look. The man slowly pulled himself to the water. He reached his hand into it, then slowly drew a handful to his mouth.

After taking one last look around, Stone stepped out into the light of the moon. The stranger heard him, slowly turned his head, nodded to Stone, then collapsed. The dog growled when Stone moved closer.

"Easy, dog. I'm not here to hurt you. What happened to this fellow? What did you two run into?" Stone rolled the man over on his back. He scooped water out of the hole, then splashed it on the man's face. Slowly, the man opened his eyes, reached up and touched Stone's face. Then he forced his lips open.

"Hup me… Ind—Indians… Me leg…"

Stone looked at the man's leg, what was left of it, then lifted the man's tattered and filthy undershirt where it was torn and soaked with blood. A broken shaft of an arrow protruded slightly from the backside of the man's left ribcage, dangerously close to his heart. He then looked closer at the man's leg. Bone thrust out through the skin and his blood soaked underdrawers a few inches below the knee. A huge gash in the flesh was probably made by a lance, though a war-club might have inflicted such a wound if the leg had been struck from behind. Stone shuttered at the sight of this. The last time he'd seen the likes of this was his own leg back in Mexico.

Stone knew he could do little for that leg except try to stop the bleeding. However, if possible, that arrow in the ribs needed to come out.

"Was it a war party, or a hunting party?" Stone asked the stranger.

"Bear teeth and horsetails on their shields. Didn't see no scalps."

Stone nodded. A hunting arrow should pull out with the head intact. It would have been made to be used over and over again. The flint, or iron, head wouldn't have barbs, and it should be tightly fastened to the shaft.

"You running away when they shot you?" Stone asked.

"Aye, mate. Fast as me legs could go."

Stone knew the typical hunting arrow would have a vertically mounted head. This was to penetrate between the vertical ribs of a buffalo, or other large animal. If this was such an arrow, with luck, its head would be wedged between two of this fellow's ribs. Since he said he was running away, his ribs would be horizontal, opposite a buffalo's.

However, if this turned out to be a war arrow, the head would be loosely attached. It would have barbs in the back to catch on flesh and bone, then tear loose from the shaft deep inside the body with any attempt to remove it. The head would also be attached horizontally to penetrate between an upright man's ribs into his vital organs.

More than once, Stone had watched doctors, and others, use a small, thin knife or bullet probe to enlarge the channel along the arrow shaft to allow for the extraction of the barbed, war head. Stone had no such tools. Besides, if this was a war arrow, it most likely would be poisoned with rattlesnake venom, or some type of putrid poisoning. This would mean this man would surely be dead by morning, no matter what was done for him.

Stone examined the exposed, short piece of the arrow's shaft. Nothing here told him what was inside. He took some water and gently washed away the dried blood and dirt from the wound. He had no light and wouldn't want to use one anyway with Indians nearby. Because of the oozing blood, he couldn't see any slices leading away from the central puncture wound to indicate which way the head cut through.

He reached down to the shaft, and, after gently pushing the flesh away, took hold of the exposed shaft stub. He then pulled with all he had. With a frightful moan, the man lapsed into unconsciousness, again. The arrow came out. Its small hunting head had penetrated only a couple of inches. Into what, Stone didn't know. The fact that blood didn't come gushing out told Stone it had missed the heart and all the major blood lines. The dog growled a warning as it paced back and forth near his master's head.

Whiskey—he needed whiskey to cleanse the wound. A good dose in this man's veins would help the pain, also. A healthy gulp for the man acting as a doctor might steady his nerves some too. Stone wrapped a tourniquet around the mangled leg, then pushed on his cane and straightened up. He stepped back to consider what to do next.

San Antonio was two days, hard ride behind him. Somewhere, out ahead camped a company of men. However, that was the direction this man crawled in from. That also meant that out that way were hostile Indians.

It only took Stone a minute to decide to head back toward San Antonio. He doubted if anything mattered, anyway. Stone didn't think this poor fellow had a chance in a thousand of being alive two days from now. How much blood he'd lost, Stone couldn't tell. He suspected lots.

Even knowing that most likely his efforts were in vain, something in him, maybe his memory of his own brush with death, something prodded Stone to do whatever he could.

He thought of that nurse down in Mexico. She'd saved his life, his sanity, too. He'd never thanked her. He was just too self-absorbed at the time. He probably never could, now. Until now, he hadn't thought of her in years.

He quickly hitched his team to the wagon. He then moved the sacks of dried meat up front with him and jimmied the water barrels around so he could roll out his bedroll for the wounded man. When he reached down to pick the man up, the dog came at him with vengeance, snarling with teeth showing.

"Easy you, whatever your name is. I'm trying to help your friend. How can I get that through to you? I don't want to have to kill you, but I will if that's the only way I can get this fellow to some help. So, just back up and shut up."

The dog still paced back and forth, growling nervously. Stone again tried to lift the wounded man. Frustrated at his failure, he admitted he couldn't get this done by himself. Going to the pool of water, he filled his tin cup, then threw the water on the man's face. Opening his eyes, the man slowly reached up toward Stone.

"I've got to get you into my wagon. You need a doctor and the closest one I know of is in San Antonio, about two days away. We might meet some troops on the road, sooner. Can you help me? If I lift you up, can you hold onto me?"

"Aye. The brute savages got a fight out of me. But I got me some spunk left."

Stone, with some help from the wounded man, got him up in a sitting position. In the moonlight, for the first time, Stone caught sight of the man's head. He was bald—right down to the bone. Dirt and dried grass had clotted the blood and somewhat replaced the hide and hair taken by the Comanche. With all the two men could muster between them, the wounded man was finally in the wagon, lying on Stone's bedroll.

"Try to get some sleep," Stone said while he gave the man some water. "I'll do my best to quickly get you to a doctor."

"Aye," the man acknowledged, nodding weakly. "It is my good fortune. The Good Lord has sent me a man of the cloth to rescue me. That is more than the heathen I've been deserves."

"Oh, yes, well…" Stone muttered, remembering for the first time since he'd been awakened that he now lived the part of a preacher.

"Quiet now," Stone said. "Rest is important."

Stone pulled himself up onto the wagon seat. He rested his wooden leg across one of the bags of jerk meat. Just when he was ready to start back the trail, the dog suddenly got tense. He raised his nose and looked up the trail that he and his master had come from. Stone didn't take time to look that way.

"Eey ahh!" he yelled as he shook the reins, slapping them across the backs of his horses. They started back the trail, lit only by the moon and stars.

CHAPTER 6

Hours later, in the early morning sun, Stone pushed his team across a section of the trail that was exceptionally rough, Stone felt something tugging on the back of his coat. He reached back and touched his passenger's hand, clenched tightly to his coat. Stone slowed the team, then found a fair sized oak tree and pulled up to its shady side. He slowly, painfully, dismounted.

"Bless you, Preacher. I got to have me some water. Need to rest me bones from the shaking of this old wagon. Never knew me old body could hurt so much."

Stone didn't doubt that. That the man still breathed paid tribute to his strength and determination.

"Me dog? What about Dinger?"

"Dinger, you say? He's right here. He's not going to leave you."

"Saved me life, that hound did. Them savages came at me every way but Sunday. Got all me sheep, every last one. Got me, too. Staked me out on them baked rocks folks call earth in these parts. Stole me britches and buckskin shirt—cussed thieves. Dinger, he saved me. He was right there when me came to me senses. He chewed through the rawhide they had me tied down with. Them savages, they left me strung out to die, so me say."

"Be a puttin' a nix to that," the man slowly continued. "Soon be gettin' healed up. Then Dinger and me be a huntin' them down. We'll kill us that whole bunch, if'n we can. Thought they were me friends. Had 'em in me camp, many a day. Fed 'em me coffee, me beans, too. No more friends with Foss Haffer. Never trust them savages, Laddy. Take it from old Foss."

"Foss Haffer, you say? Justin Stone. Parson Justin Stone. What are you doing out here?"

"Fled the old country. That be what you call the down-under, Australia she be. Long been a man on the run there. Ten years back, me made land off a ship in Galveston Bay. Then me headed out west here to where no one would be the bother to me. Bought me some sheep. Them wooleys didn't take to the hot of it out here too much, though." Foss remained quiet for a moment.

"Always traded fair with them Comanche, until this. Had to be that Mex they was after. Me reckoned he was bringin' trouble when he showed up in me camp. Figured he be on the run. Didn't know it'd be from the Comanche. They followed him right to me. Don't know what he did, but they must a figured me was a comrade with him. Swear me never saw the bloke before early eve tonight."

Foss was silent for a moment. Stone gave him another ladle of water.

"Them heathens don't know who they crossed. When me gets healed up, they'll be feelin' the wrath of this old Aussie."

Stone looked around. He spied a patch of grass about a hundred paces to their south.

"I'm going to lead the horses to that grass over yonder. I'll not unhitch them. We can't stop for long. You feeling up to getting out of this wagon? Can you help me get you back in, later?"

"If you'd be so kind to give me another ladle of water, me'd be fine staying right put. Looks to me that grass be under the cool of those trees. Best to soak in all the coolness one can. Be fixin' to be mighty hot come high sun today. Old Foss best not disturb me bum leg anymore than has been done. Me side, she burns as flaming fire, too," he said, pointing to where Stone had removed the arrow. "Just some water, that's all me need. If you'd be so kind."

Stone gave Foss another ladle of water, then poured some into a concave slab of granite for Dinger. He watched the dog cautiously lap the hole dry. Stone filled it again. When he stepped back, Dinger rapidly lapped up all the water. His tail twitched slightly.

They left about an hour later, then they stopped again for several hours in the heat of the day. It was then that a traveler came by, heading for San Antonio.

"Mercy," exclaimed the man when he looked at Foss. He went over to his wagon and opened the under-seat box. He returned with a bottle of home-brew whiskey.

"Might help ease his pain," he said, handing it to Stone. Then he hurried on.

Stone gave Foss a healthy dose of the firewater, himself a good swallow also. That seemed to help Foss' pain some—his too.

When they'd been back on the road for hours, with stars bursting out into the darkening sky, Stone again felt Foss's tug at his coat. He pulled over to the side of the road.

"Be burnin' up, Preacher. Be on fire. Fear it be the fires of hell comin' ta get me," Foss said weakly.

Stone got him some water, then got another ladle and splashed it on Foss' face. He then gave him another nip from the bottle.

"Chew on this," Stone said, giving Foss a strip of jerky. He then also tossed down a piece for Dinger. Dinger grabbed it, then jumped up in the wagon and whined. He then laid his head against Foss' good leg.

"Aye, Dinger, me friend. Finer friend, man or beast, me never did have. If this be me time to go on, you take up with this preacher man. You do for him the way you've always done for me.

"You hear that, Preacher? Me don't make it, you take Dinger with you. He'll keep you out of trouble. He has for me, many a time. He tried to warn me yesterday, but me didn't listen. Me didn't listen. Me didn't…"

Stone let Foss sleep until the moon was high enough to light the road, then he slowly moved on. Dinger stayed lying beside his master. Stone was tired. The team was tired. However, Foss was dying.

It was faint at first, but while Stone drove on cautiously in the dark, the smell of smoke grew stronger. Then, rounding a bend in the trail, he saw fire—fires, really. There seemed to be dozens of them, all well off in the distance. This had to be a company of troops, the one scheduled to leave a few days after Stone did. Suddenly, a sentry stepped out in front of him and called him to a halt.

"Got a man badly wounded here. Comanche," Stone said. "Where's your surgeon?"

"Is that you, Parson? I saw you around the camp in San Antonio. You lit out before we did. We cut out early, too. Got permission to come out here and wait for a few days before we forge on. Figure you'd a caught up with the boys ahead by now."

"That was my plan," Stone said. "Your surgeon—this man needs your surgeon."

The young man walked over and looked at Foss laying in the wagon.

"Oh Lordy! Ain't never seen the likes. Over to the south, that last fire. That's where I last saw Doc Mauer."

Stone nudged his tired team into motion and headed for the fire the sentry had pointed to. There was instant action once the young, German-immigrant surgeon saw Foss. Frans Mauer had the tail board of a wagon set up to use for an examining table and ordered all available lanterns be brought to light the area.

"Be a mite in fear, Preacher," Foss said to Stone. "Never did me do what was right. Was a downright scoundrel in me young days. If me don't make this—is there anyway an old heathen the likes of me can avoid what he be deservin'? Heard told many a tale of hell. Know that well be what me be deservin'. Me was just wonderin', if you talked to the Good Lord for me…"

"Me?" Stone asked. "Me talk to God for you? Ahhh—well, why don't you talk to him yourself? I suspect he'll listen to you as much as me."

"If you say so, Preacher. Me just thought you bein' such a holy man, and such, well, thought you might have more sway, that's all. You done me right, Parson Stone. Most blokes would have looked at me and kept on goin' and let me die out there all alone."

"Easy now, Foss," Stone said. "Looks as if the doctor is ready to start fixing you up. I'll talk to you in the morning."

Foss nodded weakly. "In the mornin', Parson Stone."

Not wanting to watch the doctor, Stone turned to his horses. He started to unharness them when suddenly a hand reached up and grabbed the harness from him.

"You go on 'bout your business, Mista Preacha. Be my place to tend to these nags. Go on, now. Be my wish to serve a man of God the likes of you."

"Who are you?" Stone asked.

"Be Potlicker, Sir."

"Potlicker?"

"Growed up in the kitchen with me mammy. When I be a little toad, I licked all the pots clean. Masta just called me Potlicker. Never had me no otha name."

"What are you doing here?" Stone asked. "Are you a soldier?"

"Shoot no. Belong to Masta Dumont, *Captain* Dumont he now be called."

"Is he the Company Commander?"

"He surely be. That makes me the high, top darkie here 'bouts."

"But you're still a slave?" Stone asked.

"That's what I be. 'Course, I hear if'n the Yankees win this here war, then I be a free man. That be so, I gonna be a banker, or store owner, or such. Be real important then, so I will."

Stone nodded, without comment. He reached under his wagon seat and found his tin cup. He slowly started walking toward the dwindling cook fire.

"Thank you," he said as he turned after he'd gone several steps. "I thank you for your help."

"You jus' tell the Good Lord for me that I done ya right."

Stone nodded.

If I ever talked to God the way these folks want me to, why, God might just fall out of Heaven. That's if there is a God or a Heaven.

Returning from the fire after getting coffee, Stone lay on the ground while the coffee cooled. He looked up at the stars for a minute, then he closed his eyes. He was tormented by the groans coming from Foss. Pushing himself up on one elbow, he saw a young man approaching him.

"Private Hicks, Sir," the young soldier said when he reached Stone. "I have orders to lead you to Captain Dumont's tent. The Captain said if you felt up to it, Sir."

Stone nodded in agreement. It was only right that he respond to the Captain. He rolled over, pushed himself up with his cane, then picked up his coffee cup. He quickly downed its contents, then set it on his wagon seat.

"Lead on, Son."

As Stone approached the tent entryway, he saw Captain Dumont sitting at a table, playing cards with his two lieutenants and the first sergeant. A half-empty bottle sat near the center of the table.

"Parson—come on in, Parson. We'll continue later, men. I have business with our guest now." The tent emptied, with each man acknowledging Stone as they left.

"Tell me, Parson, where'd you find this man you brought in?" Dumont asked.

"He crawled into my camp last night. Figure it was several hours past midnight. We've been riding this way all but about two or three hours since. Comanche, he said."

Captain Dumont nodded his understanding.

"I saw you in San Antonio. What brings you out into these parts, with the war and all?"

"I'm actually going out to New Mexico Territory. The Methodist Churches out there have been abandoned for now, so I'm to assist with the needs of our parishioners and keep an eye on the buildings and such until it's safe to send in full time pastors again."

"Regardless of how it turns out?"

"Peace is all I'm interested in. I've no dog in either side of this hunt."

Captain Dumont again nodded his satisfaction.

"You've had a long day. You must be tired and sore," he said, looking at Stone's wooden leg. "I don't suppose you're a drinking man, Parson, but how about one tonight to relax with?"

"Well—I," Stone hesitated.

"Of course, no one need to know," Dumont said while reaching into a wooden trunk. He brought out a tin cup. He passed that, along with the bottle to Stone.

"We're not too fancy out here."

Stone took the bottle, held it for a few seconds, then poured himself several ounces of the dark liquid. He lifted the cup in honor and thanks to the Captain, then took a healthy sip.

"You had anything to eat?" Captain Dumont asked.

Stone shook his head. "Hadn't thought much about food, all day, I guess."

"Corporal," the captain yelled to the young officer on guard at his tent entry.

"Sir," he answered.

"Tell Potlicker to fix the parson a steak. Tell him I said so."

"Yes, sir," the Corporal said as he saluted, then he turned and quickly left.

"How many sheep did this fellow lose to the Indians?" Dumont asked.

"He didn't say. We didn't talk much."

Dumont nodded.

"When we get up there, maybe we'll check things out. I may send some men after the sheep. It would do them good to get into a real fight with the Comanche. They need all the fighting experience they can get. Of course, them thieves will be miles away by then.

"Tell me, Parson," the captain continued, "tell me what you know about the rumor of a large cache of gold out where you say you are going. Out in Santa Fe, I hear. Who's supposed to have it? Is someone really going to give it all to the Yankees?"

"All due respect, Captain, I'd have no way of knowing about that. I've never been to Santa Fe. If I was interested in gold in Santa Fe, I'd be there, not out in this forsaken part of Texas."

Captain Dumont nodded.

Changing the subject, Stone quickly spoke.

"Needing money for expenses, when I got to St. Louis I bought a wagon and hired on with a freight train to haul supplies to San Antonio—lead for your army, so it was."

"I think there's gold in Santa Fe," Captain Dumont said, his eyes closed and his head pointed skyward. "It's my personal goal to find it—for the Confederacy of course—then move on to Colorado. Those Mormons in Utah hate the Union. They'll join up with us in a minute once we come rolling into Colorado from the south. They'll come in from the west. There's thousands of them. Let them have the towns and farms. I want the mines. I've got power now—it's meaningless. I want to be rich."

The captain talked on for some time. Stone sipped his whiskey, and listened. People such as this made his job, his spy job, easy. After some time, Potlicker showed up with a plate piled with beans and a thick slab of steak filling nearly half the plate. Stone ate slowly while the captain rambled on.

"We've got spies in Santa Fe, also. They think it's some old Mexican mine fellow who has this gold hidden. He has a sick wife. Maybe we can use that to get him to talk once we get there. Nobody has seen him for some time now. He's probably gone to one of his mines down on the Mexican border. I hear he has millions. Oh, to be that rich."

"Does he live in royalty?" Stone asked, noting what Captain Dumont had said about the gold owner being a miner. That could explain some things. However, how did any rumor of this get into Rebel hands?

"Big hacienda, couple of servants, Indian slaves I'd say. That's all I know."

"Slaves?" Stone asked. "If he has slaves, why would he be giving money to the Union?"

Captain Dumont leaned forward and looked at Stone.

"I hadn't thought of that. How'd you come up with that? I never knew a preacher who was all that smart before. You got a good mind, Stone. If you wasn't a preacher, I'd say we hire you as a spy. That would never work, though, you're too conspicuous. You best stick to preaching, Stone. However, if you stumble onto anything, I'd be obliged if you let me know."

"I owe you," Stone said. "You've been most hospitable. However, if I may be excused, Captain, I desire to get some rest. I had little last night and—"

"Of course, Parson. I've enjoyed your company. We'll talk again."

Stone started to leave the tent, taking a good part of his steak for Dinger, when Captain Dumont called him back.

"Parson, I know what Sibley ordered about civilians traveling with us, but I think with this new Injun threat, and such, I think it best if you travel with us, at least for a spell."

"I'd be much obliged, Captain."

Stone went over to where the young doctor was working on Foss. No one was saying much. Stone quickly left and went to his wagon. He tossed the steak over to Dinger, then rolled out his bedroll under the wagon. He lay there, but was unable to sleep. He was exhausted, yet he had too much on his mind to sleep.

Did the Confederacy know too much about the gold in Santa Fe? Was it all a hoax? Had they planted the story and letter to throw off the Union? Would Foss live? Was Buck in Franklin?

Screams from Foss directed his attention back there. He knew what Foss was going through. A moment later he heard the frightful zish, zish ,zish of the saw cutting through bone. Stone shuttered. He closed his eyes, yet he couldn't close out the memory of that Mexican doctor years ago crudely sawing off his shattered leg.

The stump of his left leg began twitching. He reached down to steady it. Failing to do so, he pushed himself from under the wagon, then sat upright. He grabbed the side of the wagon and pulled himself upright. He reached into the front of the wagon and groped around with his right hand. He found it. Carefully, he wrapped his fingers tightly around the neck of the bottle of home-brew. He looked around to see if anyone was looking, then raised it to his mouth and slowly let its potent contents trickle down his throat.

CHAPTER 7

Chink...chink...chink... Though coming from well outside the camp area, the rhythmic pounding of pick axes on bedrock awakened Stone the next morning. The sun had already been up for a good half-an-hour. The smell of coffee boiling in tall, blackened pots and sowbelly sizzling in greasy iron skillets overcame the stale, human and animal odors that settle over any military camp dwelling in one place for several days, especially in sweltering heat. Stone rubbed his face, then he rolled his thumbs around his thumping temples. He squinted across the camp. The low angle of the sun's rays pierced his bleary eyes like daggers.

That picks were chipping their way down through the rock meant only one thing: men were digging a two-by-six foot hole as deep as they could. Stone pushed himself up on one elbow, then looked for the grave site.

Instead, the first thing he saw was young doctor Mauer sitting off by himself, his back against a large, live oak tree, his head buried between his knees. Stone slowly pulled himself out from under his wagon, then to an upright position. After steadying himself for a moment, cane in one hand, cup in the other, he limped off toward the closest fire.

"Mornin' Parson," a man, teenage boy really, greeted him. "Fix you up some eggs to go with this here sowbelly we got fryin'?"

"Thanks, but not now. Coffee'd be just fine."

"Sure thing, Parson. 'Spect you figured out 'bout that fella you brung in last night. Sad way to start our march. Some of the fellas been sayin' this'll be a bad omen. Some say you should'a left that fella to die out there, far away from us. You should'a knowed he would die and you just should'a let him be. Heard one fella say you just should'a put a bullet in him to put him out of his misery. I stood up for you, Parson. Said that ain't no way to treat no man. Lettin' him die all alone, or shootin' him as one would some sick old dog."

Stone nodded. "What's your name, Son?"

Zachary Faulk. Kin folks call me Zach, well—little Zach, usually."

"Got a good family? Named for your pa, I 'spect."

"Yup. Missin' them already. Got two little brothers and three sisters. Sister Sarah, she's older'n me, the other two be little bumpkins. After we win this war, I'm goin' back home and help Pa put in the best crops he ever had. Figure if things go well, we'll be home by Christmas."

"Home by Christmas? Is that what they're telling you?" Stone asked.

"Some be sayin' that. Shucks, Parson, how long can it take to lay claim to the likes of New Mexico Territory? I hear tell many of them Yankee soldiers done run off lickety split for their homes back east. Ain't nothin' left but some Mex farmers and a few Apache. I've fought the Comanche—ain't afraid of no Apache.

"I don't see why we have to wait on General Sibley," Zach continued. "There's enough of us advance troops to do the job. John Baylor and 'bout three hundred fine boys been out there for two months, or more, now. With them, plus those on the trail up ahead of us, why shoot, by the time we get there, we can put our heels to anything out there without any help from the main companies still a fussin' and primpin' back in San Antonio.

"Turn us loose and we'll be in Colorado in a month, then on west to the ocean," Zach continued. "I surely do want to see that ocean. I wish I could take some of it home for Ma. Gonna lay claim for Texas everywhere we set foot. I'll be makin' my pa most awful proud."

"Did he want you to join up?" Stone asked.

"Naah. He reckoned I was too young. Ma fretted even more. She bawled every time I brought it up. Had to sneak away. I'll make 'em all look up to me for sure. They'll be plumb proud, so's they will."

Stone finished his coffee, re-filled his cup, then walked over to where Frans Mauer sat. A short few yards away lay a deadfall on which Stone then sat on the thick end of the log. His back faced the rising sun. Its rays felt good. Their heat penetrated the depth of his stiff back. The young surgeon never looked up. Dinger came aimlessly over to Stone and lay against his good, right leg. The old dog whined softly. Stone reached down and stroked the lonely dog's head.

Frans finally raised his head and looked at Dinger. He said nothing for several moments, then he spoke. More to the dog than to Stone.

"I did my best. If he hadn't lost so much blood. If those cussed Indians hadn't been so…" Frans picked up a dried stick, snapped it in two, then tossed away both pieces.

"Maybe someone better than I could have done more," he continued. "I couldn't."

"Don't be so hard on yourself," Stone said. "He won't be the last man you'll do your best for, and still lose the fight. Better get a grip on that right now, Doctor."

"I don't' know if I can go on. I'm not prepared for this."

"You mean you'd be such a coward as to turn back now and send these boys off into battle without a surgeon?" Stone asked. "You that kind of man?"

"No. Of course not," Frans said. "I just mean, well, if they had someone more experienced, someone better. If they—"

"Quit pitying yourself! Where they're going, these men will need a man to treat them, a man with confidence and grit. Stop hating the circumstances you're in and start hating death. Hate it to the point you'll always try to defeat it no matter how bad the odds are. That's what these men need. Most don't have any idea what awaits them. When the harsh reality of war comes, they deserve to have you thinking about them and their welfare, not yours, Doctor." Stone pushed himself up to his feet.

"Life ain't easy. I speak from experience." Picking up his cane and coffee cup, he walked back to the fire, Dinger by his side.

"Private Faulk. I'll be much obliged for that offer of breakfast now, if you can still rustle up some."

"Be my privilege, Parson. Looks as if the boys'll soon be 'bout done with that restin' place for Mr. Haffer. I know you hardly knew him, but I 'spect you'll be sayin' some good words over him. Want you to know I'll be leanin' on every word you say."

Stone jerked his head up. Of course! Foss wasn't a soldier to receive a military burial. With his now being a preacher, well sort of, he'd have to hold some kind of funeral.

"I need to go over to my wagon, Private Faulk. I must prepare for the funeral. Could you be so kind as to bring my breakfast to me when it's ready?"

"Be my pleasure, Parson. Whatever you be needin', I'd be mighty pleased to do it for you."

First a wedding—now a funeral.

Stone figured this should be easier. He'd been to more than one gravesite funeral, and Foss couldn't hear if he bungled what he said.

Stone reached into his bag, pulled out the book on special services, then slumped to the ground. Finding the section on funerals, he put on his spectacles, stroked his beard, then started reading.

───────────

Sitting in the shade on the ground under his wagon, Stone watched the men shovel the sand and rock filled soil into the shallow grave. They saved the larger rocks for the top, hoping to protect Foss' remains from coyotes and Indians—especially the cannibalistic Tonkas who still roamed this area. He was glad few of the men attended the short service. Not that he hadn't read it well, and it seemed to pass muster with those who attended. What young Zachary Faulk had heard about this being a bad omen had apparently flowed through the camp, and most men seemed to be avoiding him.

Stone lay his tired body down on the rugged, rock-strewn earth and looked up into the clear blue sky. Foss was dead. Where was Foss now? Was there anything after death? Preachers, real preachers, believed in a Heaven and a Hell. In the last month, he'd read enough of his Bible to know some of what it said. He was still skeptical of the whole thing, yet it seemed that believing in a life after this one gave some sense to life itself. Maybe he just hadn't gotten to the simple explanation of all that yet. He needed to read farther on in his Bible.

Part of him, a curious something deep inside, wished he could now go back to old Elias Crump. That old preacher had spent those two weeks trying to teach him to be a preacher—how to act like one, anyway. Of course, Stone was confused most of that time and had no idea of what Elias was telling him. Now that he had a tad of knowledge, and a little hands-on experience, he wished he could find some real preacher to study under, just a little.

He now had a passel of questions. One that kept coming back was that if God was so good and so powerful, why didn't he make the world a good place? Stone looked down at his leg and suddenly his anger rose.

Where were you, God?

Stone closed his eyes. He figured this troop would be here for another four or five days before moving out. He'd think more about all this God stuff later. Now, he needed rest. If those buzzing flies and other bugs would leave him alone, he'd get some sleep here in the wagon's shade.

Dinger curled up against his good leg. Amidst the old dog's panting from the heat were meek whimpers, cries for his fallen master.

"It's alright, old boy. You and me, we're a team now. That's what Foss wanted. Guess I can use your company. I can't really talk to anyone, not a real person. Neither one of us has anyone else out here, so we'll do fine together. Go ahead and cry, though. Sometimes ya just gotta let it out.

———

Buck Rafter sat on an adobe wall, watching the sun set behind the treelike, saguaro cacti off to the west. He'd been in Tucson several weeks now, with orders to keep watch for any Yankee activity coming in from the west. So far, the only thing coming out of that way was an occasional breeze. The locals here, most anyway, were quite content to let the young rebels hoist up their flag and claim this area. Buck had learned, though, that deep inside, many here who called this valley-of-heat their home really wanted neither Union nor Confederacy, but for things to go back to Mexican control— their homeland.

Buck was in command of the dozen young men, east Texans all, and was starting to have some difficulty keeping them busy, thus out of mischief. In the calm of the evening, from out of the east he heard the soft footsteps of an approaching horse. He turned and watched a lone rider, slightly slumped over and looking unsteady. He acted as if exhaustion was winning the battle of staying in the saddle or falling out of it.

The rider stopped. In the dimming light, Buck saw that it was a lone dispatch rider, most likely sent out by Colonel, or Governor as he now called himself, Baylor back in Mesilla. This wasn't good. Where were the others? At least three would have been sent out.

Buck slid off the wall, then he strode quickly toward the rider. Apparently seeing him coming his way, the rider nudged his horse toward him. As they met, Buck spoke first.

"Looking for me? I'm Corporal Rafter."

"Yes, Sir," the young man said as he straightened slightly in the saddle, and gave an anemic salute. "Private Harrison, Sir."

"The others," Buck asked. "Where are the others who were with you?"

"The spring at Apache pass. We didn't see them. Soon as we dipped our canteens in that water the area was filled with them. Must have been twenty, or thirty." The rider paused for a moment, then he slowly started talking again. "Two others. Didn't have a chance. Got me. My leg."

It was then that in the dim light Buck noticed that the man's right trouser leg was blood soaked. A short arrow shaft protruded from the meat of the thigh muscle.

"Help ... Help me," the young rider said as he started slipping off the saddle. Buck caught him, then helped him to stretch out on the ground. He looked around and spotted a group of young boys who'd been drawn to see who this rider was.

"Get a doctor, medicinar!" Buck yelled to them. "Get help. Ayudar, pronto!" The boys took off running.

"In my bag," Private Harrison said. "Pay. Your unit's pay. Letter for you. That's all."

Buck took the pouch with the pay and slipped it inside his shirt. He then opened the letter. In the dim light, it was hard to read. He turned away from the rising moon, letting its meager light fall on the written page.

He slowly got to the main sentence: You are hereby promoted to the rank of Sergeant. Buck folded the letter. He'd rather it had been orders to return to La Mesilla, or maybe that he'd be leading a push north. Were they ever going to start their invasion northward? Would he be part of it, or would he be stuck out here in this forsaken outpost forever? Actually, he really wanted to spend some time around Las Cruces before leaving again.

Looking up the street, Buck saw the doctor approaching quickly. "Doc's on his way, Private. "You'll be gettin' fixed up now. Be stuck in this forsaken place for a spell, though, I 'spect. Hope you like beans and peppers."

———

Three weeks later, Parson Stone rolled his wagon through the open sally port at Fort Lancaster. He'd held back some at camp this morning, wanting to come in an hour or so behind the troops. He appreciated Captain Dumont's hospitality in allowing him to travel with them, but suspected it might bring a reprimand, or at least require an explanation, if Dumont's superiors found out.

Stone quickly sized up this fort. It wasn't much. The fleeing Union soldiers had wasted little time in destroying such a pitiful fortress. He shook the reins, nudging his team toward a spot left open by the troops. The horses tugged the other way, toward the water trough.

"Easy now. Gotta get you two out of this harness before you can get to the water. It'll only be a few minutes," Stone told the team, trying to comfort them. Dinger took off running.

"Hey Parson! Hold up. I'll help you with that," Zach Faulk yelled to him while Stone eased down from the wagon seat. He waited until Zach reached him before removing any of the rigging.

"Potlicker and the other darkies are all doin' for their owners and such. Got my spot all laid claim to. Half shelter up, bed rolled out and all. Captain says we'll be here 'bout a week. I sure be wantin' to get on to New Mexico, but takin' a break makes sense, I reckon. Some of the horses are mighty tuckered out. I hear tell the worst part of the trip is up ahead. Hard to figure it to be worse than what we just come through, but that's what I hear."

Zach talked on while they removed the harness and strung it across the wagon. Stone took two lengths of flexible, half-inch rope and in minutes had a hackamore all twisted and tied on each horse. He handed the leads to Zach.

"I'd be beholding to you if you'd take them down to the water. I intend to rest a mite right here if you'll do that for me."

"Be honored, Parson. Watched you make them halters. You do it a bunch different than Pa taught me. Your way is quick, works just as good, too. Where'd you learn that?"

"Ah…" Stone stumbled. He'd used a hitch he'd learned down in Mexico. That was a slip. He wouldn't have done such an out-of-place gaff fifteen years ago.

"That's just something quick. I use it when I'm tired, or lazy, I guess. I'll do it up right later. I'm sure the way your pa taught you is much better." Stone hoped no one else would notice.

Stone watched while Zach led the wagon horses to the water trough. Only a few of the troopers still watered their stock. Most were settled in on other things. Stone turned around, leaned his arms on his wagon, then rested his head on them. He had to get his mind focused on his mission.

Never had any cover required so much time to learn, and none before had been as hard to keep straight. Then, too, he was out of practice. The drive and excitement weren't there now as they were back in his youth.

Now, he just wanted to find Buck, get things made up right with him, then settle down somewhere, and live a quiet life. Well, maybe he'd do a little checking out some of these God things.

"Just play the part of a preacher," Lincoln had said. *"You'll get brought home for chicken and dumplings, and people will tell you anything you want to know."*

It sounded easy enough at first, but so far he'd been spending too much time with his mind on the preacher end and not enough on the spy end of his mission. The truth be told, he really wasn't that interested in any gold in Santa Fe and if the Confederates won this war, so be it. After his being left behind by his government in Mexico, he had a tough time being as pro-Union as he should be to do this job with the attitude needed.

Later, Stone awoke to the rustling of dried grass and the nickering of one of his horses. The sun was down. The moonless sky was dark. Stone sat up quickly. Flames and glowing coals of numerous campfires now dotted the small fort's grounds. Stone looked around, searching for the source of the rustling noise.

"Over here, Parson," a voice in but a loud whisper said. "Be me, Pot-licker. Didn't mean to frighten you none. Figured ya'lls horses be needin' some hay to fill they's bellies. Bein's only the fightin' men's horses to be getting' this hay, I waited 'til it got good 'n dark. Then I rustled up some for these two here. Figure you be part of us anyway."

"Don't get in any trouble for me," Stone said. "I'll gladly pay for what-ever my horses eat."

"Pay up you will, Parson. Being's tomorrow be the Lord's day, I'm sure you'll be a preachin' the sinners home in the mornin'. 'Course most of them sinners be off suckin' on some old bottle, or the likes, all night. You preach it good and loud and maybe some will hear the call. What time ya'll gonna start?"

"I—ahhh…"

First a wedding, then a funeral, now I have to preach a sermon?

Well, it may be better to practice out here with these men than have to do it in a church in front of a bunch of women folk who know all about God and the Bible.

"What time do you think?" Stone asked.

"I'd say 'bout an hour before high noon. Me and some of the boys'll be singin' and such over by the old jail. You just join us when you feel the call."

"Yeah, I'll join you when I'm ready."

———

"May the Lord go with you and protect you, amen."

Stone took is handkerchief and wiped the perspiration from his fore-head. He'd read this sermon silently six times since daylight, and had gotten through it now without stumbling. He feared that someone would ask him to explain something he'd said—or rather read. He turned and slowly headed for his wagon. His hip was thumping from standing on it too long while he'd spoken.

"Mighty fine preachin', Parson," Potlicker said. "You truly do have a way with words. You say it so's even this poor darkie boy can make out what you say. Yessa, it sure be clear you got the call. Bless you, Parson Stone."

Stone had stopped while Potlicker spoke to him. He looked the young black man in the eye, then slowly nodded.

"Thank you. Ahh—I'm awfully tired now. I'll see you later on."

———

Nearly three weeks later, Stone lay awake one night, staring up at the stars in the black sky. He'd traveled on with Dumont's men when they'd left Fort Lancaster until they came to Fort Davis, a week later. Stone wasn't surprised when Captain Dumont called him in and informed him it would be necessary for him to travel alone from here to Fort Bliss.

"Stay close. Just stay a spell behind—few miles, really," Dumont had said. "You're safer being where we've already been than out in front where we haven't gone yet. Besides, we'll be needing your water and jerk meat once we get out in this desert. So, fill up those barrels. I'll leave word that you have my permission. Do it before the next company arrives. I've been out through what's up the road ahead. Most of these men haven't. They're not prepared.

"Pick up any stragglers, if you can," Captain Dumont had requested. "I'd say a bunch of these horses won't make it. Those owners will end up afoot, something many aren't used to."

Now, out here alone on the third night, Stone lay there listening to a distant coyote call out to its mate. He knew the troops were less than a mile ahead. A few more days, a week maybe, and they'd be at Fort Bliss, just outside Franklin and very near the New Mexico border.

Even more than his body, Stone's mind tossed in numerous directions. Sleep wouldn't come. Would Buck be at Fort Bliss? How would he handle that, given that he couldn't, at this time, tell Buck who he was? Then Stone thought about himself. Could he pull off this preacher cover until Christmas? Would someone identify him? Back on the train, Judge surely tried. Who is this Judge fellow anyway?

Stone lay there exhausted, yet unable to sleep. Was this whole thing worth it? Or, should he just head south, go back into Mexico and spend the rest of his life there?

Suddenly, Dinger raised his head. He lifted his nose high in the air. A muffled, throaty growl came from his teeth-bared mouth.

Stone pulled himself up. He grabbed the lariat he'd been laying on. He pulled his hobbled horses in tight to the wagon, then threw a hatch in their halters, tying them tightly to the right, rear wagon wheel.

As best he could, Stone crouched down beside Dinger. His fingers wrapped around his small revolver. Then he stuffed that inside his belt, hiding it under his coat.

Indians? Around here, Stone figured this was mostly Mescalaro Apache territory. He'd been told they never liked to attack at night. So, was it some wild animal, maybe? Stone felt Dinger tense even more.

"Easy, boy," he whispered to Dinger. "I'm backing up over to that mesquite bush to watch from there."

Stone moved half backwards, half sideways as stealthily as he could. He waited. He kept close watch on Dinger, yet scoured the skyline in all directions. Suddenly, Dinger lunged toward the front of the wagon, snarling and snipping at something.

"Oh, Lawdy! Lawdy! Save me from this beast. Be sorry for what I be doin'. Save me, Lawdy."

Stone moved in a semicircle to where he could see the scuffle.

"Who are you?" he called out.

"Save me, massa. Get this beast off me, I be beggin'!"

Stone moved in closer, revolver in hand.

"Dinger. Back off Dinger." The dog let loose his hold on the man's forearm, but stayed only inches away, still snarling.

"Who are you, I asked?"

"Oh, save me, massa. Be H B. I's a free black man. Got's me papers right here. Be so sorry I tried to take from you. Oh, forgive me. I beg of you."

"H B you say? On your knees. Hands against the wagon side. You run, I'll shoot you."

"Ain't gonna run, massa. Don't shoot me, please. I begs you."

"Dinger, back off. You, H B, now get up slowly and come over this way, so I can get a good look at you. You alone?"

"Be all alone. Ain't got no one, no more. Got no kin. Masta, he fled from Texas. Headin' for Colorado, he say. Gonna fetch gold and get rich. Gave me papers makin' me a free man. 'Course, I can't read 'em myself, but that be what he say they read. H B ain't nobody's slave no more."

Stone peered at H B as he slowly rose to his feet, then shuffled toward Stone.

"That's close enough," Stone said when H B was two steps away. "What are you doing out here?"

"Oh, Lawdy, forgive me. I come here a fixin' to fetch me some grub. Ain't et in days now. I knows it be wrong, and you can beat me if'n you must, but I just needed me somethin' for my belly."

"You got a gun, or knife?" Stone asked.

"Ain't never shot no gun. Got me a knife, though. Masta gave it to me. He tell me to go fetch somethin' to eat. Can't get close enough to kill nothin'. Gives me the shivers thinkin' 'bout stickin' a knife in some little critter anyway."

"How have you been living?"

"It shames me to say. Been stealin' from the troops, and any such who goes by. Been over to Fort Davis three times and been most lucky. Got me a whole sack a vittles last time, then got away without gettin' caught.

"But deep in my innards, I surely know it ain't right. I just don't know what a simple old darkie such as me is to do. Got no masta to do for so's I can earn my keep. Hear tell of a town way up yonder in New Mexico that be full of freemen such as I now be. Goodly number of run-a-ways there, too. Be wantin' ta go there in a bad way. Don't know how."

"Take your knife and stick it into the side of the wagon where I can see it," Stone said.

Stone watched while the man did as told. In the faint sliver of moonlight, Stone saw the form of H B, a form of little but skin and bones.

"How long since your master took off and left you?" Stone asked.

"'Bout two months, leastways that. 'Spect he be up in that Colorado place by now. Begged him to take me with him, but he say slaves wasn't no proper thing up there. He say he gonna fetch gold and get rich."

Stone, revolver extending from his right hand, stepped toward H B. He shoved the gun right into H B's belly for a few seconds. He felt the quiver of fear back through the gun barrel, then he lowered it.

"Go sit on the wagon tongue. I've got some jerk meat here. I'll get you some. Some water, too. Don't run."

"Bless you. Oh, bless you. Ain't gonna run. No sir, got no strength to run. All my life I ain't never stole a thing 'til I had to. Just got so hungry… I don't wanna ever steal no more. H B'll work for you—be your boy. That be what I be, your boy."

Stone said nothing while he reached into one of the burlap sacks and took out a large strip of dried meat. He handed it to H B, then got him a cup of water. H B chewed his meat in silence for some time.

Stone threw down a piece of meat for Dinger who wagged his tail in appreciation. When H B finished eating, he started talking again.

"Take me with you, massa. One can see you got a game leg and could use H B to do for you. Won't eat much, I promise. Swear before the Good Lawd himself that I never be stealin' from ya'll again. What it be you do anyway?"

"Preacher." Stone said after several seconds of silence.

"Oh, Lawdy, Lawdy. Forgive me. Oh, forgive me," cried H B, falling to his knees. "I done tried to steal from the Lawd himself. Ya'll be a man of God and I come like the thief in the night. Lawdy, don't strike me dead."

"Calm down," Stone said sternly. "Get some more water from that back barrel if you want, more jerky from that back sack, too, then find a place and get some sleep."

Stone untied his horses from the wagon, tossed the halter ropes across his bed, then took H B's knife and tossed it to the ground beside where Dinger had settled back down.

"We'll talk in the morning. What does H B stand for anyway?"

"House Boy. That be what I growed up as. No one ever gave me no other name. Just always be called House Boy. Masta started callin' me H B when I got growed up and wasn't a youngun' no more."

———

Sergeant Buck Rafter walked through the dusty streets of Tucson. He'd received a dispatch today that he'd hoped would be his orders to report to Governor Baylor's office, soon. Instead, the letter told him to expect to remain in this remote outpost for the next several weeks, maybe longer. He pondered what this meant. Sibley must still be dragging his feet, he concluded..

Buck stopped and looked around the plaza. Really, this hadn't been so bad. At least he'd been safe here. Most of his men were having a grand time with the local girls who seemed taken by these perceived important young men from Texas. Buck partook in none of this revelry. He'd met a young girl during his short time in La Mesilla—across the river in Las Cruces— and his heart was smitten. As much as he wanted to lead a scouting party up the river, he hoped he had at least a few days off duty to hang around there before he had to leave again, once he ever got there. He even had thoughts of settling down. When those thoughts came, so did thoughts of his mother. "Miss you Ma," he whispered softly. "Even more than Pa, I miss you. Ain't right you're gone. Ain't right I'm all alone. Ain't much of anything right…"

———

Two days after passing Van Horn's Wells, Stone picked up his first straggling soldier. The young man sat by his horse, trying to revive the spent animal.

"It's no use, Son. That animal's too far gone," Stone said. "If you want, I'll take care of him for you."

52

"Can't let you do that, Parson. I was there when Patches was born. I raised him, then broke him all by myself. He'll be alright after a little rest, I just know he will."

"No—no, he won't," Stone said. "I've got water for you, but I can't let you give any to that horse. He's just too far gone."

"Preacher be right," H B said. He'd been riding with Stone for several days now.

"Ain't right for you, or the preacher, to have to put him out of his pain, but it's got to be done. Ain't right to let no animal suffer as such."

The young man stroked his gasping horse's head one last time, then got up and walked away. H B took his knife, put it to the horses' throat, then he froze.

Stone pushed him away, drew his revolver and shot the horse down behind the ear. The young soldier fell to his knees. Stone heard him sob for several moments.

"I just couldn't do it, Preacher," H B said. "Thought I could do it so's you didn't have to, but I just couldn't do it."

"It's alright, H B. Let's get this fellow in the wagon, then push on to catch up to the troops. They should be ready for some water by the time we reach them."

Several nights later, Stone camped within sight of the distant lights of San Elizario, the most eastern village on the Mission Trail east of Franklin. His water barrels and jerky sacks were now nearly empty—he'd given their contents away, or sold it all for a pittance, knowing few of these boys had any money and all were hungry and thirsty. H B started talking to Stone.

"Lookin' as if we be comin' to the fort tomorrow."

"Late in the day, I'd say," Stone replied.

"Got to tell you, that be a frightful thought to H B. Be fearin' what might happen with so many folks there abouts with me bein' a darkie, free as I be. Got me papers and all, but—"

"You're going to have to get through there somehow if you're going on up into northern New Mexico," Stone said. "It's either take your chances with all the people in town and the fort, or strike off alone, head out through the desert and risk the Apaches."

"Wish I be a man a God as you be, Preacher. Then I'd be fearin' nothin' and would be knowin' for sure the Good Lawd be with me. I got to tell you, Mr. Parson Stone, I be mighty feared somethin' bad 'bout to happen to H B."

"Stick with me. No one will harm you that way. Get some sleep now."

"Got this fearin' thing way down in my belly," H B said.

"Fear won't help anything," Stone said. "Go to sleep, now."

In the morning when Stone awoke, H B was nowhere to be found.

CHAPTER 8

"Mr. Hart. Mr. Simeon Hart. You are Mr. Hart, aren't you?"

The man Stone called out to stood in the arched doorway, staring out into the bright afternoon sun, looking to see who was approaching him. He then stepped forward onto the clay-tiled floor of the portico and pointed toward the man on the wagon that had pulled into the yard of his flour mill.

"You're that preacher fellow that I've heard came in with that last column of the troops. You're right. I am Simeon Hart. Tell me, Preacher, how may I help you?"

By this time Hart was briskly walking towards Stone's wagon. Stone set the brake, then eased himself down from the seat. He shook Hart's hand when the businessman reached him and extended his in greeting.

"Welcome to Franklin, Reverend uh—"

"Stone. Justin Stone. Folks call me Parson Stone."

"Well, Parson Stone, what brings you to these parts, times being what they are and all?"

"Our churches, the Methodist Churches that is, the pastors have gone home for their safety. They sent me out here to keep an eye on the buildings, and to help our people anyway I can. Personally, I'd say they put me out to pasture—way out to pasture. I know that in my situation I haven't been very productive. I think this solved two problems. What to do with the churches here, and, what to do with old Parson Stone."

"I'm honored you came to see me," Simeon Hart said. "You have some cause, some financial need, I surmise?"

"Not what you might think, Mr. Hart. Of course I wanted to meet you, with you being such an influential figure in this area. Yes, my purpose here is business. I have this wagon and team, as you see. I'm told you are buying such?"

"I am indeed. Yes, you came to the right place," Hart said while walking around the wagon. Then he inspected the team and harness.

"You want to sell it all?" he asked.

"Everything but my personal gear. I'll keep this seat pad and, of course, Dinger." Hearing his name, the scruffy dog wagged his tail.

"Well, beings that I do need more wagons, and the fact that the money is going to a good cause, I'll double what I normally would offer. Six hundred dollars, Parson Stone, for this wagon and all the harness. No one else in town will give you nearly that much."

Stone nodded. "I'm told you trade in all types of horses. I'll trade you two for one. This team of workers for your best buggy-horse."

"A buggy-horse? Well, I surely have just what you need. Two for one, you say?" Hart walked around the worn out team Stone had used to pull his wagon all the way from St. Louis.

"Of course, we have a deal," Hart said. "They're tired, but I think a month's rest, some of our good grass and grain, too, will bring them back fit for another day."

Stone nodded and shook the hand Hart again offered to seal the deal.

"May I store my few things here at your mill until I get a buggy?"

"You mean you don't have a buggy? You want to buy one here? Rare as hen's teeth here-a-bouts these days. I'm afraid there's no one here making such any longer."

"Oh? Back in San Antonio I was told I'd find a fine buggy maker named Rumbaugh here," Stone said.

"Rumbaugh? Who told you about him?" Hart asked.

"One of the freighters I hauled with from Missouri."

Hart looked out across the town, toward the river and beyond. He remained silent for a moment, so did Stone.

"I shouldn't do a blasted thing to help that old Yankee. But, since it's for you—". Hart nodded toward Mexico, to the town of El Paso del Norte, right across the Rio Grande.

"He's over there. He's on the west side of town. Flies a confounded Union flag over his place. If you don't mind dealing with such, you'll find him there. He is a fine buggy maker. The fool will starve over there, though. Ah, but that's his choice. Where do you come down on secession, Parson Stone?"

"I've no side in this fight at all, Mr. Hart. Since my calling to preach, I've never so much as voted. My dedication is with the life beyond much more than here. I do hate the thought of an all out war with much bloodshed. If I could stop that, I would. I know I can't, so I'll mind my own business, the Lord's business, really." Stone was surprised these words so easily came out of his mouth—almost as if he really meant them.

Hart remained silent for a moment. He seemed to still be thinking about the old German buggy maker.

"Say you're going up into New Mexico? When are you leaving?" he finally asked.

"Soon. Once I get a buggy, I'll head up to Las Cruces. I'm told we had a little church on that side of the river. I guess over in La Mesilla folks lean toward the Catholic way."

"Be mostly Mex's over there. I don't pay much attention to any of their religious ways. They give me a good day's work for their pay. I hire all I can."

Hart looked at Stone for a moment, then spoke again. "You'll then be going up the river. Will you be coming back this way?"

"I'll be going from Las Cruces to Santa Fe and back often, I believe. I'm not starting anything new, just holding onto what little we have left."

"I'll tell you what I'll do for you," Simeon Hart said. "Tomorrow, I'll have one of my hands take you over to see old Rumbaugh. It's a long walk and, well, with your leg and all, I'll do that for you. You'll be my guest here tonight."

"I don't want to be a burden to you."

"No Burden I have guests all the time, Parson. And, tonight you will be my welcome guest at a dinner meeting. We're starting a new castle for the KGC. It's an oversight castle to coordinate the affairs of all the men who belong to castles back in their home areas. You familiar with the Knights of the Golden Circle, Parson?"

"I spent several weeks in San Antonio and came across Texas with men who belong to one castle or another. Are you saying you want me to attend this meeting? What would the KGC want with me?"

"You are my guest. I'm simply inviting you to listen to our speaker. He's a man who's just been up north, Washington, really. There will be others of influence here who you should get to know, Parson. You have no fear of knowledge, do you?"

"I shall enjoy being your guest tonight, Mr. Hart. Forgive me if I seemed a mite disinterested. I'm still quite exhausted from my trip. I apologize if I acted ungrateful. You're being most kind to me."

"Understood. Sundown then. We'll have supper before the speech." Hart turned back to his mill and pointed.

"Pedro! Come." A short, dark-skinned man quickly came to Hart's side.

"Take this team and wagon to the corral," Hart told Pedro. "Later, you can take the tack and oil it well. See to it this dog is well tended, lots of water and some fresh meat. Put him in the tack room tonight. Then, take the Parson to my house, to the guest room, where he will be staying the night. Then, tomorrow you will take him over to old Rumbaugh's shop."

"Señor. To Rumbaugh's? But you say—"

"I know what I've said. Just do what I tell you."

"Sí, Señor Hart. Pedro do as you say."

Stone rose from a short nap and looked out the window of the second story room he'd been led to by Pedro. He could see the river, and well beyond. Off to the west, just out of his sight, he knew the sun was nearing the horizon. He poured fresh water from the pitcher into the bowl on the dry sink. He washed his face. He then daubed it dry with the towel hanging on a hook on the wall.

Then, for the first time since leaving Washington, he looked at himself in the mirror on the wall. For several minutes he studied how he'd aged. His hard life, much of it his own choosing, had him looking well beyond his fifty years. This was good for his cover—bad for his ego.

No man wants to face up to the fact that his best might well be what he reminisces about—not what he dreams about. After several moments, Stone turned, then walked out of his room and down the stairs, where he was greeted by Simeon Hart.

"I trust you are rested some, Parson. Dinner will be served when our main guests arrive. Our speaker, and several others, are coming from La Mesilla. They should be here momentarily. Come, let me introduce you to some of those already here."

Hart led Stone into a huge dining room. The walls were lined with vibrant paintings, fine guns, and exotic trophy heads. Stone immediately recognized Captain Dumont and several of the other officers he'd seen around San Antonio and here at Fort Bliss. When he had been introduced to the last of the men in the room, Stone then heard footsteps on the hard tile floor out in the hallway, the steps of several men coming toward the dining room. Hart rushed to the side of one of the men.

"Gentlemen," he spoke loudly. "Gentlemen, your attention, please. Most of you know this man well, but for any who don't, allow me to present to you Colonel John Baylor, the honorable Military Governor of this new Confederate Territory of Arizona. Here stands the man greatly responsible for the organization of the coming expedition, and a man of great vision for the manifest destiny of the newly-formed, Confederate States of America. Might I also add, especially for the great state of Texas."

Hart shook the Colonel's hand, then Baylor started around the room greeting each man individually. Stone's eyes flashed across the room to the other men who'd come with Baylor. The one still in the archway had his back turned to the crowd, obviously talking to someone in the hallway. Then, Hart introduced the second of the three men, Robert P. Kelly, editor of the La Mesilla Times, a paper Stone already knew to be pro-secession.

Hart next stepped to the man with his back turned to them and placed his hand on the man's shoulder. The man, feeling Hart's hand, turned to partially face the crowd. As he did, he was still conversing with the man who'd been in front of him. "...viajar el camino hacia el norte..." Stone heard him say. Stone's mind raced through its memory. Those few words of Spanish...

"Let me introduce our featured speaker this fine evening," Simeon Hart said loudly. "Gentlemen, this is..."

Judge!

Stone felt the color drain from his face. Instantly, after hearing only a few words of Spanish spoken by Judge, Stone's mind hit the right spot in its distant memory. He and Judge had been on the same path before—sort of. Stone had only known him by his long ago picture, and his voice speaking broken Spanish. They'd never really met, but had crossed paths. Fifteen years ago he'd embedded this man's voice in his mind. Before him now stood Captain Brock Kanter, son of well known plantation owner and politician, Milton Kanter of New Orleans. This was the man, this man now calling himself Judge, who Stone, as Colonel Tyrone Rafter, had been sent into Mexico to rescue.

Stone and Judge now had several things in common: both were considered to be dead, both were considered heroes, both were using an alias, and now both were mixed up in this complex war. Stone knew his game, what was Judge's?

He knew now for sure that Kanter was the man wearing the blue, U S Army officer's trousers he'd seen walking away from him that day when he'd been left to die a slow death in the Mexican sand. He also knew now for sure that Kanter, now calling himself Judge, was responsible for all he'd gone through in Mexico, and for the loss of his family. Stone took several slow, deep breaths to help keep control of himself.

True, they'd never met, but surely before he went to Mexico, Captain Kanter had seen a picture of the then well known Colonel Tyrone Rafter. Stone knew he now appeared much older, was full-bearded, and looked vastly different than he would have as a polished, young army officer in any picture that Judge, as Captain Kanter, might have seen years ago. Still, given time and the desire, Judge might make the connection.

Judge hadn't yet looked his way. Stone quickly scoured the room. He looked for another exit, finding none but the windows. He'd been lax having not looked out them when he first entered the room to see what lay outside them.

Another blunder. You're acting as old and rusty as you look. You're a spy first. You're not really a preacher—you're a spy.

There would be no way of avoiding a conversation with this man who'd desperately tried to figure him out on the train. Suddenly, Judge's eyes met Stone's.

"Well, my old train companion. Parson Stone, I believe it is?" Judge said while moving toward Stone.

"You know the parson?" a surprised Simeon Hart asked.

"Back a spell, we spent several days together on a train. That was out of Washington, if my memory serves me right," Judge said, stopping several steps away for Stone.

"Maybe, or was it Philadelphia?" Stone replied, moving slowly, yet boldly toward Judge. He wanted to better see the man's eyes and to show that he wasn't intimidated by him.

"I was returning from visiting my sister in Philadelphia before coming west. I don't exactly remember where you got on. It may have been Washington."

Judge studied Stone, his eyes showing great inquisitiveness. Stone knew he was still safe. Judge hadn't yet placed his identity.

"You made it to Texas, safely, I see," Judge said. "Now, you're going to New Mexico, as I recall."

"Mr. Hart so kindly bought my wagon. Tomorrow, I plan to buy a buggy, then, I'll continue on. I must see what shape our churches are in."

"Yes, yes, that's what you told me on the train," Judge said.

"Gentlemen, the food is served," Simeon Hart announced. "Judge, to the head of the table."

"Later, Parson Stone. We'll talk later," Judge said, still staring intently at Stone.

"And so my fellow Confederates, I leave you with a challenge similar to that of our founder, the honorable George Bickley, when he challenged us while moving the home Castle of the KGC to San Antonio from Cincinnati in that land of Yankee tyranny. We need railroads and telegraph lines running from the ice and snow of Canada to the blistering beaches of Sonora. My only change to the challenge is that they not only be running on Confederate soil, but, that all of it be *Texas* soil.

"It was the inspired words of God Almighty, I tell you, when Andrew Jackson urged Texas to claim California, and all the land in between. In California, we have 16,000 loyalists, with many of them flying the Golden Bear flag in our support. In Colorado we have over 7,500, with some of the brave flying the flag of the rattlesnake in defiance to the Union tyrants still in control there. I believe that all of the Mormon nation is just waiting on us to arrive so they can revenge the injustices imposed upon them by the pious lords of Yankee arrogance."

Judge stopped for a moment, took a drink of wine, then he continued. "We were cheated in the compromise of 1850 when we forfeited our two western counties, Santa Fe and Worth. We all know that true Texas soil runs along the Rio Bravo to its birthing spring in what is now called Colorado, then beyond. We were cheated when the Gadsden Purchase was reduced in size by the Free-Soilers. We were cheated when this greatly reduced purchase was added to New Mexico and not set up as a new territory, a territory where the superior white man could hold his rightful property, all of his property, and use it however he deems fit."

Judge again paused for a moment, looked across the crowd, then leaned forward and stretched out his arms. "We have a right, an obligation, to take these lands and all they hold for our use. The hand of God Almighty is upon us. United we shall overcome whatever stands in our way." He cleared his throat. "I thank you all for coming this evening. 'Until we meet again." He raised his wineglass in a toast.

Applause filled the room. Stone casually joined in the clapping, but refrained from the cheering and other vocal adulation bestowed upon the speechmaker. It had been a long speech, informative, but full of questionable content. Stone rose, pushed against his cane as he stretched his aching hip and lower back. He then slowly started for the door, keeping himself well away from Judge.

"Leaving so soon?" Simeon Hart called out to Stone when he spied him moving toward the doorway.

"A most informative and enjoyable evening, Mr. Hart. Your hospitality is graciously appreciated. However, I must retire now. You understand, I'm sure."

"I'm sure you suffer much discomfort, well, pain is probably a more appropriate word. If you rise early, breakfast is at sunrise. I trust your room is satisfactory. If I can be of any service…"

"The room is splendid. I haven't slept in a bed since leaving San Antonio, well over a month ago. I shall see you for breakfast. Again, I sincerely thank you."

———

"We were friends—must have been nearly ten years, could be more." Simeon Hart said, fixing his gaze toward the dusty, adobe-hut lined village across the river. "I just couldn't reason with him. When a man is guided by some set of inner principles instead of the base human drive of wanting all one can get, reason doesn't work. It wouldn't on Rumbaugh, anyway. He could see what was about to happen in these parts. Fat government contracts for all of us were just ahead. He had his principles, he said. Slavery was wrong, thus making money from anything to do with such was wrong in his mind.

"I'm no slave owner," Hart continued. "I pay my help as much as anyone here, more than most, really. I'll even go so far as to give him the fact that slavery is probably wrong. However, it's my true belief that making money by selling what one makes, or trades for, isn't wrong, no matter who you sell it to. Oh, I wouldn't sell guns to the Apaches, or anything such as that."

Hart paused for a moment, then continued. "I've lived by this code for years. Why am I so tormented by these things now? Why do I give any of this a second thought? It's Rumbaugh, and his pious, high-and-mighty ways. The fact that he's willing to give up everything for something he believes in scalds me to no end. I've shut him out. I forbid my family, or help, to have anything to do with him. Yet, he haunts me."

"I'm tormented because he's willing to make such a sacrifice for his beliefs. Something inside me tells my soul that he's a better man than I. Some nights I lay awake, unable to sleep until morning. Sometimes it seems hell itself visits me in the quiet of the darkness. I never even believed in hell—now I live at its gate."

Stone sat silently in the crisp, autumn, morning air. The sun's soft, warming rays slowly broke over the wall of the open courtyard. He was moved by the emotion of his breakfast host. A few short months ago, he wouldn't have understood Hart's torment, or Rumbaugh's stand. He'd never looked at the world around him with any sense of moral compass, no thought of any absolute right or wrong. All decisions were made on what he saw to be best for him at the time. Stone now wrapped his coat tighter around his chest, then sipped his mug of hot coffee.

"Pedro will take you to see Rumbaugh," Hart said, breaking the silence. "Take an extra horse so you can return with your buggy. I'll have that zebra-dun, that smoky one that you saw yesterday over at the tank drinking water, all cleaned and curried for you by the time you get back," Hart said. "He's a natural in harness. Don't know why, but I'm giving you the best I've got. Oh, I know that's what we bargained for, but ordinarily..." Hart paused for a moment, then looked back across the river.

"Let me know how he's doing, will you? Tell him... No—I must let it go."

Simeon Hart then rose. "I'll send Pedro for you, shortly. 'Until you return, Parson Stone," Hart thrust his hand toward Stone, who shook it heartily. With clasped hands, each peered hard into the other's eyes.

———

Stone said little to Pedro while the two crossed the Rio Grande—Rio Bravo to the local Texans—then rode through the streets of El Paso del Norte. Most of the way, Pedro, unaware that Stone understood border Spanish quite well, talked to himself, and the mule pulling the buckboard. In time, he got to comparing the mule to his boss, Simeon Hart. Stone, at one point, had to force a cough to keep from breaking out in laughter.

They pulled up to a wooden barn—the only wooden building in sight. Stone noted a forge and beside that was a smooth, round oak stump with a tire traveler laying on it. Beating a band of hot iron with a soft mallet was a man Stone knew would be Rumbaugh. Pedro led the mule up beside this man, then pulled it to a stop.

The deep, labored breaths of the workman produced vapor in the brisk, late autumn air. A gust of wind caused Stone to draw his coat tighter against his body.

Stone slowly descended from the buckboard. He stood leaning against the wheel, then, after a moment, he started toward Rumbaugh who stood observing both men.

"You must be that preacher fellow I heard tell's been asking about me over yonder."

"Parson Stone, I am. You must be the craftsman everyone calls Rumbaugh."

"Crazy Rumbaugh, you mean?" he asked as he shot a glance at Pedro. "That I just may be, but I'm right. Better for a man to be right and deemed crazy than wrong and rich. I'll face my maker with clean hands, Parson Stone."

Stone felt as if Rumbaugh stared deep into his soul. Rarely did anyone make Stone uneasy, but right now Rumbaugh, was doing just that. This was not a man to easily be fooled. He reminded Stone of someone…

Lincoln! That's who this man reminded him of. Stone could imagine similar words, and piercing inquiry, coming from the tongue and eyes of Abe Lincoln. Though much shorter, Rumbaugh even had Abe's rawboned frame and looks.

"Well, this is a first—me preachin' to a preacher. Tell me what it is you need, Parson Stone. I'll do my best to oblige you."

"I believe you will," Stone replied, now letting his eyes roam across the buggy-maker's yard.

"You can see that I need to be able to easily get up to the seat, and back down. Something to hang on to when I step down would help me. A place for my leg, this handmade one, would be good. At times it would ease my discomfort greatly if I could rest it on something out over the dashboard."

Stone glanced at Pedro, who'd moved away from the buckboard and over to where he had a better view of two señoras appearing to be on their way to the market. Quickly getting back to his needs for his buggy, Stone looked back at Rumbaugh.

"A covered compartment also, maybe under the seat. It must provide good protection for my books, and such."

Rumbaugh continued to stare at Stone, making him nervous. Stone leaned over on his cane, then he stretched his back, after which he took a step backwards. His attempt to distract Rumbaugh's inquisitive mind didn't work.

"Did Hart send you?" Rumbaugh asked, his eyes still locked on Stone.

"A freighter named Cole, a man I'd hauled with from St. Louis to San Antonio, he told me to see you once I got to Franklin. I sold my wagon to Hart. When I asked him about you, he reluctantly told me where you now are, and why. He misses your friendship greatly. I don't know if…"

"That's over. The blood of slaves is on his hands. I call no such man my friend."

Stone nodded. The fight wasn't his. He sensed that nothing he did at this time would end the feud. He drew Rumbaugh's thoughts back to the buggy.

"How soon?"

"Soon?" Runbaugh asked, wrinkling his forehead.

"The buggy, the carriage we're talking about. How soon can you have one for me?"

Rumbaugh stared at Stone for a few seconds, then motioned for him to follow when he turned and went inside the barn. Well organized rows of wheels, iron tires, axles and other parts filled two-thirds of the building. Off in the far southwest corner sat one complete buggy, and another one up on blocks, still under construction.

"Made this one here three years ago for Hank Sauter," Rumbaugh said, pointing to the complete buggy. "Older fella. Had the rheumatism bad in his legs. He could only walk a few steps at a time. It's what we called a coal-box type up in the Commonwealth. I put this here drop front on it. I saw one made in Philadelphia such as this, so I used the idea. That ought to work for you as well. Put this hand-pull on the side, thought it a good idea. Been putting such on all my buggies ever since. No fancy velvet cloth for the seat and top. Good old bull-hide. Be a mite heavy, but it will outlast ten of them fancy fabric tops, no matter what anyone tells you."

Rumbaugh gently rubbed his callused, hardened hands across the side of the polished, deep-plum colored seat back in the way one would stroke his prize horse, or even his child. Stone walked around the small, four-wheeled coach. The bright, cherry-red wheels and trim stripes stood out even in the poorly lit barn. One would be hard pressed to tell this buggy had ever been used.

Would it do for a preacher? Might it be a flaw in his cover? Back when he prided his ability to blend in unseen most anywhere, Stone never would have considered anything but basic black. Now, would it matter?

"I'll cut out a gully in the dashboard," Rumbaugh went on. "Mount a rest out there on a thin strip of spring for your bum leg. I've put gun-boxes under the seat often enough—'course you want yours for your books, you say.

"Be done by dark. You can send Pedro back to Hart. Simeon can get some good out of him at the mill. If he lusts after the maidens over here all day he'll be in trouble by sundown.

"Just make sure he leaves that extra horse. You didn't pay for that one, I hope. I'll set up old Hank's rigging for you. Throw it in with our trade."

Stone nodded. He wanted to ask how much this "trade" was going to cost him, but thought that would insult Rumbaugh. He instead just nodded again, then went to find Pedro.

————

A few fires flickered down the street, mostly in the outdoor hornos used to cook the family food. With the sun now setting, Rumbaugh made a final adjustment to the traces, then he handed Stone the reins.

"Watch out for that fresh paint on the new parts. I did it all up just as we talked. Bring it back in time so I can go over it for you. I try to keep up with my coaches. Got some around I crafted more than ten years ago."

Stone stared at the work Rumbaugh had done today. It truly was just what he'd hoped for.

"How much?" Stone asked as he reached into his coat pocket.

"It's my gift to God," Rumbaugh said, raising his hands indicating for Stone to leave his money in his coat.

"Ain't figured out what you're all about, Preacher Stone, but I know when the Good Lord puts his hand on me to be his helper here 'bouts. Besides, I ain't been in any house of God to give in the plate since I came over here. I'd say I'd be owin' this much, even more."

"I can't accept this," Stone said, shaking his head.

"Ain't no room to hassle none about it. You're God's servant, ain't you?"

NO! Stone wanted to cry out, but instead said, "Well—yes. But, your business is down considerably over here. You need money. I sold my wagon and…"

"Mister, you and me could argue, but I don't argue with the Good Lord. I've got his word that he'll meet my needs 'till I leave this earth. Be that in old age, or, by sunup tomorrow. I figure when my money runs short, my time will too."

Neither man said anything for a moment, then Rumbaugh spoke, again.

"It's getting dark quick-like. I'm fixin' to have me a mess of kraut and hogs feet, then a good night's sleep. You care to join me, you're most welcome. All this talk though, is over."

Stone looked out across the river at the few lights that now glowed on the other side. Why did he feel guilty? With all that had gone wrong in his life, why not take all he could now?

…It's my gift to God… Rumbaugh had said.

All the rantings of Elias Crump still haunted him. He didn't want to be beholding to Rumbaugh—much less to God.

"Go on now, Preacher Stone. God be with you in whatever you're doing. May his hand be upon you in these troubled times," Rumbaugh said, then he turned and started toward the barn.

"Thank you," Stone called out as Rumbaugh walked away. Stone turned and looked at his buggy—or was it God's buggy? Stone reached out for the handgrip to pull himself up onto the seat. He jerked his hand back before he touched it.

Lincoln would get a good laugh out of this.

Stone looked around. He was already in Mexico. He could walk away, slip back into his old haunts, then hide until he died, really died. No one would know, hardly anyone, anyway. He took several steps away from the buggy and stared across the river at the widening array of lights over there. Then, he looked off to the south, out into the vast expanse of mountains and desert.

Suddenly, the air was cut by the striking up of a chord of music coming from a cantina down the street. Tequila, that's what he needed to help make the right decision. He slipped off his cape and bell hat. He tossed them in the buggy. He ran his quaking fingers through his hair, then he grabbed the horse's halter and started toward the music.

CHAPTER 9

Stone awoke the next morning to the sound of voices at the mill. He slowly sat up and looked around. Hart's horse, the one loaned to him to bring his buggy back from Rumbaugh's, was in the corral. He vaguely remembered doing that last night. It must have been before he'd wrapped up in his blanket, then lay atop the large stack of dried hay where he now found himself.

In the faint warmth of the morning's early sunrays, he eased his cold, stiff body down off the hay, and balanced himself with his cane. The sun hurt his eyes. His head seemed hollow, yet swollen to the point of bursting at the same time. It thumped with each heartbeat.

When the memory of anything Rumbaugh had said about God came to mind, Stone quickly quenched all such thoughts—he tried to, anyway. Hart was right. Rumbaugh was crazy.

Stone blinked his eyes, then squeezed them tightly for several seconds. Opening them slightly, he then slowly walked around his buggy. Reaching out to the coach, he rubbed his hand gently over the smooth paint and supple leather. He'd never owned anything such as this before. Growing up, his family had been poor, only having the bare necessities. What little they had was always of inferior quality, or nearly worn out.

Looking back now, he realized that was one reason he enjoyed being in the military. The military offered a poor boy, one who could only see that same dire state for the entirety of his future, a way to be somebody different, to seem richer, maybe even better. At least there he seemed to be equal with one born into splendor. The military, especially on the battlefield, was a great equalizer.

Stone looked over into Hart's corral and observed the mottled, silver-gray horse that now belonged to him. Through the years, he'd learned some of the ways to determine a good horse. From all he could tell, especially from its eyes and backbone shape, this horse had solid breeding.

"Padre Stone," he heard someone call out to him. He turned toward the mill and saw Pedro. "Padre Stone, me come to you. Señor Hart, he worry 'bout you. Me take you to hees house, pronto. Sí, me bring carriage."

Stone waved to Pedro to let him know he'd heard him. Simeon Hart— what would he want to discuss this morning? Rumbaugh, of course. He'd want to know, probably without directly asking, how his old friend faired. Stone looked in the buggy and there found his hat and cape. He went to the water trough, then wet his face with the cold water. That cleared his thoughts a little, but not the pounding in his head. He reached in and scooped out another handful of cold water and again splashed it on his face. He walked over to the tack room and opened the door. Dinger lay there, seeming to be well fed and very content. The old dog thumped his tail on the dirt floor several times before he rose and came over to Stone, then he rubbed up against his good leg.

"Looks as if you got your belly full of good food. Have some new friends, too. Don't get too comfortable. We'll be hitting the trail soon. Then, it'll be none of this soft life for either one of us for a good while, I 'spect."

A short time later, Pedro led the horse up to Hart's house where Stone got down from the carriage. Looking toward the house, he saw Hart standing in the doorway.

"I've waited breakfast for you," Simeon Hart called out while motioning for Stone to join him. "I sent Pedro out looking for you. I became concerned when I found your room empty this morning."

"I meant you no trouble. It was late, well after dark, when I arrived here last night. I needed some time alone, to ponder some things. I slept down at the mill."

"Then you got all taken care of with a buggy? Rumbaugh treated you well then?"

"He treated me better than I deserve, I'd say."

"Come, breakfast awaits us. Today, the air is brisk, a mite chilly at this early hour. Still, I trust it meets your approval that we shall dine outside. The sun will warm us." Hart then silently led the way to his southerly facing courtyard.

After the two men were seated, Hart leaned slightly forward. He looked inquisitively at Stone, then asked, "Well, how are things over on that side of the river? Is that moralistic zealot ready to come back home?"

"If you refer to Mr. Rumbaugh, he's fine, really. It appears he's busy enough to survive. There's no hint of his coming back here."

Hart took a deep breath, then slumped his shoulders. He slid back in his chair.

"I had hoped..." Hart slowly shook his head, then he looked down at the clay tile floor.

A servant brought a large platter of steak, fried eggs and corn tortillas. He set it between the two men. Stone waited for his host to take the first helping. Hart seemed oblivious to the food. Finally, he nodded, then motioned to the food.

"Help yourself. You must be hungry." Both men ate in silence for some time. With his plate still half full of food, Hart lay his fork down, then looked out toward the village on the other side of the river. Stone took very little food, then toyed with what he'd put on his plate. When finally finished, he pushed himself back from the table. Hart turned to him.

"I thank you for letting me know how he is. I know you must be about your business, but if you ever come back this way..."

Stone nodded. "Yes, I must leave now, but, someday I'll be back. Maybe soon, surely in the spring. Whenever I return, I'll go see Rumbaugh, again. Of course, I'll come see you, also."

Hart nodded. "Then let's go to the mill. I'll have your horse in harness in no time. Then, you can take up your things and go on to Las Cruces. That dog of yours, he's become quite a fixture around the mill hands. They'll not want to let him go."

"Well, I can't leave him. He's a gift from a dying man. Dinger's been good comfort and protection out on the road. Under different circumstances, maybe—"

Hart raised his hand to shut Stone off.

"They'll understand. I wish you well, Parson Stone. Do come back and see me. Maybe the next time we'll have more time to talk."

Stone pushed open the church door. It wasn't locked. Actually, it had no lock. Small footprints crisscrossed the wisps of windblown sand that covered the clay tile floor near the door. Stone walked up to the old piano, touched one of the keys, then listened to the note echo off the bare, wooden walls and ceiling. He picked up the hymnbook resting on the piano. Leafing through it, he found a few of the titles that sounded a little familiar. Most of these were under the section marked: Christmas.

He looked over at the homemade podium—pulpit, he remembered it was called in a church. For a fleeting moment, his mind again told him it wasn't too late to turn south and go back into Mexico, just disappear once and for all.

He pushed himself up on the platform, walked over to the pulpit, then stood there looking out over the rows of empty, wooden pews. He thought of the sermon he'd been reading, getting ready to "preach" in these abandoned churches. He stood there buried in thoughts of presenting a sermon to people out on those seats. He leaned against the pulpit, thinking of what he'd have to do to pull off this part of his cover.

Acting as a preacher out and about the world was one thing, but pulling off the part in a church in front of people, some of whom knew more about God than he figured he ever would, or thought he cared to, that took the cover to another level. However, standing there behind a pulpit for the first time, he somehow knew it would all work out. A strange peace came over him.

Dinger, who'd come into the building with him and now sat at his feet, suddenly let out a soft, throaty gurgle. His ears pointed up, as did his nose. Stone sensed someone lurked outside the door. He slowly, and as quietly as his wooden leg would let him, eased down the left side of the building, then across the back to the door.

He reached over with his cane, hooked the knob, then he jerked the door open. There, barefoot, and bedraggled, stood three children who obviously had been trying to observe what was going on inside.

"Well, who have we here?" Stone asked. "Who might you be?"

"Didn't mean no harm, Mister. We was just a makin' sure it weren't no robber or such in the church, honest," the largest of the three said. "You a preacher, or such?"

"That I am. And I ask again, who are you?"

"J J Slater. This here be my brother Billy and little sis Liza. We hale from up this trail 'bout half hour's jaunt. Got us a farm up yonder. Pa says we got the best well around. We raise—shoot, guess that don't mean none to you. We gonna have a meetin' here come Sunday?"

"If I can get the word out, and the building cleaned, yes, we'll have a church service Sunday. How many people usually come?"

"Whole bunch," J J said. "Leastways twenty, or more. Ma will be most happy. She plays the piano. Pa don't come, though. He says church is for women and younguns. We come, of course. 'Spect when I get a little more size Pa will let me stay home and help him. Pa works most awful hard."

"I'm sure he does," Stone said. "Who usually cleans the church building?"

"That be the widow Hays and all her brood," J J said. "Folks usually bring her somethin' they fixed up to help her out, bein's she got six 'bout like us to tend to. We'll run tell her. Sure she'll have this place all trim and smart come Sunday. When is that anyway?"

"The day after tomorrow," Stone said. "Run along now. Tell widow Hays and your ma I'm here. I'll spend the night here in the church. Tomorrow, I'll try to come out to see your folks."

The three young ones took off running. Stone stepped outside, then pulled the door shut behind him. He'd seen a cantina down the street on his way into town, and now his stomach reminded him it had long been empty.

Minutes later, Stone sat off in a corner of the cantina, sipping coffee, waiting on his meal. Around the corner, in the saloon side of the building, men played cards, billiards, or just conversed noisily. Suddenly, a man stepped through the archway dividing the two areas, someone familiar to Stone. Governor John Baylor headed straight for Stone's table.

"I knew you were in town," Baylor said. "Checking out the church, I assume?"

"You have some spy network, Governor. I only rode in less than an hour ago. How could word get from here to you across the river in La Mesilla?"

"I was over yonder." Baylor nodded toward the other room. "Had a meeting with some men from here. I saw you drive up the street. Couldn't miss you. That's quite the rig you have. I've never known a preacher to have anything but the most conservative of anything around. Usually everything is basic black."

"Well, Governor, I'd say I'm not your normal preacher. I don't cotton to extravagance, but don't see where a little color corrupts one's life. I think God used a lot of color when he made this earth, don't you? I see nothing wrong with a buggy-maker using some also."

"You've convinced me," Baylor said. "You still going north?"

"I want to be in Santa Fe for Christmas. That's my plan. I hear they really do up the festivities up there. Of course, a lot could change by then. From what I hear, you might be there before me."

"We would if that turtle Sibley would ever get here. I've had scouts up to Santa Fe, halfway over to California, too. If we could move now, we could walk right into Colorado. At least that's what Captain Coopwood and his men tell me. Come Christmas, I'm afraid there might even be Union troops from California in here. I've got eyes over by Tucson. My man Rafter over there keeps me posted on anything he hears about the Californians coming."

Rafter! Buck is in Tucson.

"This Coopwood, he's the fellow from down San Elizario way that Simeon Hart told me about?" Stone asked.

"Yeah. He's got some mighty good men, nearly twenty."

"Rafter, the man who's over in Tucson, you said. I feel as if I should know that name."

"Buck Rafter. The kid's nothing special, good man, though, living in the shadow of his father," Baylor said. "Fifteen years ago the father was a revered spy who got killed in Mexico. Became bigger than life after that. Legend stuff. Some even say his ghost still rides this Rio Grande border, raisin' cain.

"Kid's got some of his father's ways," Baylor continued. "He'd do anything ordered. Fearless, but has a mean streak. Hear his step father made him that way."

Baylor leaned forward, looked around making sure no one else was listening, then he spoke softly, staring deep into Stone's eyes.

"You know anything about a cache of gold in Santa Fe? Have you heard anything?"

"Ah—gold?" Stone's mind couldn't focus on the gold. It was on his son. Buck had been here. He'd missed him again. "Gold, yeah, rumors. Back in San Antonio I heard rumors. I've no interest in—"

"A million dollars, maybe more. That's the story. Could be just that, though—a story. I'll tell you what, Parson Stone, you get to Santa Fe and learn anything, you let me know." Baylor again looked around to make sure no one could hear him.

"Here's what I'll do for you. You lead us to that gold, I'll give you, through your church of course, a full tithe on it. That's ten-percent of a million, or whatever is there. Think what all you could do with that. You could build new churches all over the state. Sure as we're sitting here, the Union wouldn't so much as give you thanks. I mean it. I've got the authority to see my word through, trust me."

"That's quite an offer, Governor," Stone said. "I don't know how I could turn that down."

"It's settled then. How about a drink to seal the deal? Waiter! My bottle from the other room. Two clean glasses, also."

Stone's mind whirled. *Buck is in Tucson, about three hundred miles to the west. Santa Fe, though, is nearly that far to the north. ...a tithe on up to a million dollars... I could turn the Santa Fe money over to Baylor instead of Lincoln, then slip back into Mexico. With that tithe I could live as a king for the rest of my life. It really doesn't matter to me who wins this war. What do I owe the Union, anyway? I am what I am because of them... Buck's with this side. It would be easier to connect up if we were on the same side...*

With the tinkling of glass on glass, the waiter set Baylor's half-empty bottle and two glasses on the table between the two men. Baylor picked up the bottle.

"May I?" Baylor asked, then he slid one of the glasses in front of Stone, and started to tip the bottle over it."

In a flash Stone's mind switched to the liquor now filling his glass. He swallowed the saliva his mouth produced in anticipation of receiving the biting fluid. Gaining his senses, Stone raised his hand to stop Baylor before he filled the second glass.

"I was distracted, I guess. I was thinking what your offer could do for our churches. I'll seal my end just as well with this cup of coffee, Governor. No offense, but you take this glass," he said, then slid the glass in front of him over to Baylor.

"No offense taken, Parson. I thought for a minute you were going to help me finish off this bottle."

Baylor lifted his glass, Stone his coffee cup.

"To our deal. Contact me at the governor's office, anytime. You'll find we're the kind of people you'll enjoy being associated with, Parson."

"May that prove to be true," Stone replied.

Baylor emptied his glass, then put the cork back in the bottle.

"I must get back to my other business, Parson. Are you preaching Sunday?"

"If the church gets cleaned, and the word gets out."

Baylor nodded, then rose and started for the saloon side. "Be safe until we meet again, Parson Stone. Remember, we're a team," he said as he walked away.

Moments later, the waiter set Stone's plate of steak and beans in front of him and refilled his coffee cup. Stone sat for several moments without touching either. Buck was in Tucson. If he went there first, could he still be in Santa Fe in time to meet his contact there? Yes, that shouldn't be a problem. However, what would it accomplish? He couldn't even tell Buck who he was.

For a moment, his mind turned dark. What if the Santa Fe gold turned out to be a hoax, a Confederate ruse, or what if he failed to accomplish his quest? Worse, what if Buck was killed, or something?

Still unsettled, he picked up his fork and knife, then slowly cut into the thick steak.

Stone paced back and forth across the small porch in the front of the building. He looked at his watch. Maybe no one was coming. No, that wasn't it. It was still nearly an hour before service time.

"What do you think, Dinger? Am I going to pull this off?" The dog wagged his tail, seeming to give his approval.

He'd gone out to see the Slaters yesterday. J J, Billy and Liza excitedly introduced him to their mother who warmly greeted him and fed him a filling dinner. Mr. Slater, Silas, as he introduced himself to Stone, was obviously disinterested, but cordial.

When Stone returned to town, the church had been cleaned. The polished wood pews glistened in the light, and the tile floor had been mopped, removing all dust and footprints.

Early this morning, he'd put on his clean suit of clothes. Seeing how dusty the other suit was, he thought about washing it in the river, but thought that might not be fitting for a preacher to do on a Sunday morning. He then sat in the front pew and read his sermon one more time. He'd been looking over several others in his book of sermons he'd been given, just in case he had to preach more than once somewhere. He'd then come out to the entryway porch where he now paced back and forth.

About half an hour before service time, he saw a column of dust approaching. In a few minutes, he could see the wagon that stirred up the fine sand into dust that the breeze then lifted skyward. Several more minutes and the wagon pulled under a cottonwood tree at the edge of the churchyard. A woman climbed down from the seat, then helped several small children to the ground. When she led the column of children toward the church door, Stone observed that she was attractive, yet weary-eyed.

The children all seemed shy, with some not even looking up at Stone. Like lambs to water, they followed their mother up to the church.

"The Hays family, is it?" Stone asked when they reached the porch.

"For sure we are, Parson. I'm Tillie and this is Billy Joe Jr., and this is Mary, here's Sarah and over there are Robert, Tom and little John." Tillie pointed to each of the children, and Stone nodded a greeting to each, yet, some only looked at their feet. Though all were scrubbed clean with their simple clothes neat and mended, that Tillie Hays struggled in raising her family showed.

"I'm Parson Stone, Mrs. Hays," Stone said when he shook Tillie's extended hand.

"I did my best on the church, Parson Stone. I trust it's clean enough. I came early in case there's something needin' done yet, we can—"

"Everything is fine. You did a splendid job. When I came the other day, there were months of dust in here, now it sparkles."

"Oh, thank you," Tillie said, a smile beaming across her face. "We all have our jobs, even little John. It don't take too long with so many hands."

So many hands... So many hands...

That repeated itself over and over in Stone's mind. He'd learned, from talking with Mrs. Slater, that Tillie Hays' husband had been killed by Apaches. She'd come upon his mutilated body, herself. That had been three years ago now, three months after little John had arrived.

Soon, several other wagons and buggies arrived, including the Slater family— minus Silas. Stone stayed busy greeting people.

His main purpose in going to see Mrs. Slater yesterday was to make sure she would pick out the hymns, and lead them. Stone convinced her he couldn't sing a note, and if they were going to sing, she would have to lead it.

"Why, Parson Stone, I'll be most glad to lead the singing," she had said. "You just do your best to follow along. If you don't mind, my younguns and I just might have a song ourselves."

"I would most appreciate that," Stone had told her, figuring that would take some time, and the regulars would enjoy it.

Standing under the small porch roof outside the church door, using its shade and cool air to subdue his nervousness, Stone now looked at his watch. It was time to begin.

As he started to turn, from way down the street, he saw dust rising. Someone else was coming. They appeared to be rapidly approaching. Inside, Mrs. Slater started playing the piano. Stone turned, then entered the door. Whoever was coming would have to wait until after the service to be greeted.

He sat on the front pew. He sang along the best he could. He made note of the songs, assuming they were common, well-known ones often sung by church people in this area. After the Slater children sang, he walked up on the small platform and stepped behind the pulpit.

Seldom in his life had he been more nervous, more afraid of making a blunder. He'd been more comfortable wiggling out of being caught outright in a lie than he was now standing in front of a group of people who knew a whole lot more about what he was planning to say than he did. He took a deep breath, then straightened up and looked out at the people.

"It's good to see each of you," he said, smiling at each one, starting at those in the front. Finally, his eyes reached the back row.

Governor Baylor!

What was the governor doing here? Stone didn't know if he should acknowledge the presence of the governor, or not. With Baylor arriving late, and his taking a seat in the far back when there were many empty ones up front, Stone assumed the governor wanted his privacy. He nodded silently to the governor, who returned a like greeting.

Stone had two of the men pass their hats around while Mrs. Slater played a song on the old, very out of tune, piano. While they were doing that, Stone took out his spectacles, then stroked his beard several times. When the men were finished, he started reading his sermon.

When Stone reached the summary, Governor Baylor quietly rose and left. When the service was over, and most of the people were out in the yard visiting, one of the men who'd taken up the offering came to him.

"Parson Stone, what do we do with the offering?"

"The offering? Ah—what do you suggest?"

"Well, usually it ain't much, but that fella in the back—ain't never seen him here 'bouts before—he put in a whole stack of these twenty-dollar gold pieces. I ain't never seen the likes of this in all my days."

Stone looked at the stack of gold coins, five to be exact. Suddenly, he knew what to do with all this money.

"Give it to the widow Hays," Stone said.

"All of it? There's a powerful lot of money here, Parson. Don't you figure you should have some of it, maybe the church fund also?"

"Give it all to Tillie Hays."

"Whatever you say, Parson. Figure you know what the Lord wants done with his money. Widow Hays can most surely use it."

Stone stood confused by what he'd just done.

I've got no idea what God wants done with that money. How could I? Just something in my gut tells me there's no greater need than Tillie Hays. I surely don't want to put it in some church fund.

"Hurry, Parson Stone. The chicken will be ready by the time we get home."

Chicken? Yes, he had promised to have Sunday dinner with the Jackson's, one of the families here in town. He donned his hat, stepped outside, then pulled the church door closed behind him.

———

Early the next day, Stone crossed over to La Mesilla. He thought he might run into Governor Baylor and get some comments on his appearance yesterday. The money Stone understood. That was to obligate him to the Governor, to seal their deal, so to speak.

In his normal observing way, Stone saw how the impoverished locals, mostly Mexican farmers and merchants, were trying their best to avoid the Texas soldiers. The boys from east Texas were bored and their boredom was leading them to mischief. He'd heard from several people at church yesterday that they'd be glad when the war was over. They wished the north would win and re-open Fort Fillmore for protection from the depredating Apaches, as well as these frolicking, young Texans.

Stone was about to leave town and start his way north when suddenly he heard a man scream. It stopped him in his tracks. Dinger growled.

"I be a free man, so's I be. Don't go a doin' that to me. No! I ain't no run-a-way. Got me papers right here. Masta set me free. No—no!"

Stone hobbled quickly toward the man fighting for his life. A man whose voice he recognized. Then, there came the crack of a gunshot.

CHAPTER 10

Reaching the crowd, Stone pushed his way to the front. Dinger beat him there, fiercely growling at those standing over the fallen H B.

"Let me kill that mutt before he bites someone," yelled a young soldier as he pointed his revolver at Dinger, then cocked the hammer.

"I wouldn't do that," Stone warned, stepping between Dinger and the gun.

"You some holy man, or something?" the young soldier asked as he slowly lowered his gun. "I'll shoot this mangy cur anytime I want to." At that, the young soldier stepped to his right, then again pointed his gun at Dinger, who paced behind Stone.

Stone whipped his cane down across the man's hand, sending the gun flying and shattering several bones in the man's hand.

"Eeeeehh!" he cried, slumping to the ground. "You... I should kill you right here and feed you to the buzzards along with this here darkie. Oh..." He held his shattered hand.

"If you look in this man's pocket, you'll find his emancipation paper. He's as free as any of us," Stone said. He looked around at the other half dozen men involved.

"What's your purpose for this?" Stone asked.

"He was walking up the street ahead of us. He should have stepped aside to let us by. Darkies got to learn their place," the man still on his knees said. "Why don't you take your Yankee ways and get out of here, Mr. Preacher man. I don't need to hear no sermon from the likes of your kind."

Stone bent over and took H B's paper from his pocket. He unfolded it and started reading it out loud.

Suddenly, one of the other young men standing close by, grabbed the paper, stuck one corner into the bowl of his pipe, then threw the burning paper on H B's body.

"Ain't nothin' sayin' he's a free man no more, Preacher. He looks the same as any other dead, run-a-way darkie, now, don't he? You best get out of here, old man. The Knights be a runnin' this here town, now on. Ain't no such thing the likes of free darkies around here. Never will be. Don't 'spect we'll have any more trouble with them for a while, now, anyways. How about you, Preacher? You with us, or are you fixin' to get yourself in a mess a trouble you can't get out of?"

"I can take care of myself against fools," Stone said, looking down at the young man still on his knees. With the tip of his cane, he pointed to each one of the young men.

"Don't ever threaten me, again. You don't know who, or what, you're up against."

None of the young soldiers said anything.

"Come on, Dinger. We have better places to be, and better people to be with."

Stone turned, then started away from the crowd. He took several steps, then stopped when a man stepped into his path. It was Judge.

"That sure is some way you handle that cane, Parson Stone. Sorta like that book on the train. You're right, those boys don't know who, or what, they are up against. Neither do I. The way you handle yourself in times of trouble tells me it's no stranger to you. You didn't learn how to handle yourself like this in church.

"I don't dwell on my past, much," Judge went on. "I've buried most of that, bedrock deep, so I have. But, my gut tells me that there was a day when we've either been at odds, trying to kill each other, or we've been in the same fix, fighting side by side."

"I apologize for losing my temper," Stone said. "I should have been more gentle, more—well, more the way one would expect from a man in my position. I'd met H B out in the desert. He was a comfort to me, a big help really. I can't agree with what happened here. It's not a slave thing at all. Just a common decency thing, I'd say."

"Maybe I see your point," Judge said. "However, there are other points to see, also. You best leave town, quickly, Parson Stone. I'll take care of anything that comes out of this. Be careful if you come back."

"I'm obliged for your help, and warning. If you'll see that H B gets a right burial," Stone reached into his vest and pulling out a ten dollar gold piece. He handed it to Judge.

"I shall be well north of here by sundown," Stone said.

"No need for you to pay for that. I'll see to it that—"

"I do need to pay for this. I owe that to H B. He was a good man, just born the wrong color. At least that's how folks here see it. See that he's buried with dignity," Stone said. "The Methodist cemetery over in Las Cruces. I'll hold a service over him when I come back this way."

Stone, with Dinger at his side, then moved as rapidly as he could hobble up the street to his buggy. He quickly climbed up and slumped into the soft seat. He turned and looked back toward the plaza. It now seemed eerily quiet.

"Let's go, horse. Let's get out of here," Stone said as he gave the reins a shake and the buggy lurched forward. "I guess I should give you a name. You ever have a name before? Right now the only name that comes to mind, with the mood I'm in, and that fits your looks, is Stormy. Those different shades of gray stripes mixed in with your base silver looks as if one bad storm is brewing. So, Stormy it is. Fortunately, we're leaving this storm behind.

"What do you think, Dinger?" Stone said as he looked down at the dog that ran by his buggy's right front wheel. "I didn't do well back there, did I? Might have gotten us both killed. I didn't do my cover any good, either. I'd sure relish shaking that Judge character off our tail."

Stone shook the reins again.

"Go on, Stormy. Let's find us a quiet place up the river. Someplace all alone, where I can think."

Stone's stomach felt as tight as sun-dried rawhide and his hands shook like aspen leaves in the autumn wind. Near the edge of town, at the corner of a street where he needed to make a right turn, mariachi music flowed out through the bat-wing doors of a tattered saloon. He reined Stormy to a stop.

His thoughts were filled with the old comfort senses he knew would be found inside. His mind smelled the smoke of cigars, the too-long-worn clothes of the mind-numbed men, the cheap, enticing perfume of the women, the kegs of tepid beer, the bottles of cheap whiskey, and the tobacco juice spit all over the floor. His mouth, his throat, his stomach all ached, craved, cried out to be filled with the fire of large gulps of crude whiskey.

With a trembling hand, he moved his wooden leg off the side of the buggy to the step. Then, he leaned back in the seat and closed his eyes. The staccato bleat of the horns and the twang of the base strings suddenly went silent. The crass voices of men arguing over a card game came through the doorway, followed by the earthy laughter of a woman, then came the vulgar curse of a man. Stone slowly lifted his leg back into the buggy. After straightening up in the seat, he shook the reins and Stormy moved forward.

"Go on, Stormy. Get me out of here. I don't know where I belong, but this isn't the place to start looking."

Well after dark that night, Stone tossed another small log on his meager fire. He picked up a rock and aimlessly threw it as hard as he could. He wanted to tell someone, everyone, how rotten his world was. He started with God.

"Hey, God. If you don't care about what happens to us here, such as with H B today, why should I want to have anything to do with you? Right now, I'm mad at you, God. I don't think you're what you claim. You're not reliable. If you worked for me…" He cut off his one-way conversation mid-sentence, then continued. "Another thing, God, if you're so great, why couldn't you have worked it out so Buck was here, and we could have talked without me giving up my cover. If you're really so wonderful, why didn't you do that?"

Stone then thought about the awful war that lay ahead, how it would take many young lives, maybe Buck's.

"Yeah, God. What about this war? Men on both sides claim you're with them. Why don't you just come out and say whose side you're on? Why the big secret?"

Dinger came over to Stone and laid his head on Stone's thigh. Stone stroked his fur.

"What about you, Dinger? What do you think about God? Then, what would you know? He surely doesn't care about you if he doesn't even care about people. I thought I was beginning to understand him, even know what he wanted. Huh—I sure was up on my high horse, wasn't I?"

––––––––––

After a fitful night, the next morning Stone rose early—early and still angry. He knew he should be moving on, but had no desire. Finally, about mid-day, he picked up his Bible and started reading. The Psalms—he remembered old Elias Crump had told him that when he got into tough times to read the Psalms.

The next morning Stone awoke in a little better mood. After reading the cries and pleadings of the Psalmists yesterday, he didn't feel quite so mad at God—not quite so alone. Still, he felt rejected and abandoned, but knew he wasn't the only one who ever felt that way. Not that this helped him understand God any better.

He sat in the early morning sun, sipping coffee while he patiently hopped the dried bug on his fish hook across the slow flowing water as if it were a dragonfly. Dinger roamed up along the river, just barely in sight. The old dog gnawed on a half-grown jackrabbit he'd caught shortly before dawn. Stormy stood hobbled about fifty yards to the east in a patch of lush grass that hadn't yet been stunted by frost.

Suddenly, Stormy jerked his head up, snorted and twitched his ears. Stone quickly pulled in his line, grabbed his cane, then he pushed himself up to his feet. Dinger was now at Stone's side, growling softly, his nose pointing toward the east, away from the river. Stone looked at his buggy, some twenty paces away.

"Easy now," he said softly, yet loud enough for Stormy to hear. "Let's me and you ease over to Stormy, old boy," he said to Dinger. "If this is Apaches, they might let me go if they figure I'm unarmed. They'd more than likely take Stormy, though."

Stone reached his nervous horse, picked up the hackamore he'd hung on a low tree branch, then gently slipped it over Stormy's head.

"Come on now, Stormy. Hobble along as best you can. Let's go over to the buggy. Whatever it is out there, it's in no hurry to make itself known. Maybe…"

"You up there," came the sudden call. "Keep your hands where we can see them. We're coming in."

A flash of relief surged through Stone. It wasn't Apaches. Robbers, maybe? He stood with his hands in front of him, holding the soft rope lead of the halter. Three men slowly walked into Stone's camp, leading their horses.

"What in tarnation ya'll doin' out here all alone, old man. What's with the black duds? You a preacher, or such?" the tallest of the three, and the group's apparent leader asked.

"That I am. Parson Justin Stone, folks call me. The Methodist Bishops sent me out here to keep an eye on our churches, beings all the regular preachers who were out here have left for safer lands."

"Who's supposed to keep an eye on you, Parson Stone?" the tall man asked.

"God," Stone said, surprising himself.

"I've seen sod busters, Mexicans, a few savage Apaches and far too many darned Yankees out here. Ain't never seen hide nor hair of God anywhere in these forsaken parts, Preacher. Figure God got better sense than to waste his time out here."

"Coffee's hot," Stone said. "Hope there's enough for all of you. I wasn't expecting company."

"Got lots of coffee up at our camp, a piece upriver. Why don't you hitch-up that buggy and join us? The Captain will be wanting to talk to you."

"The Captain? Might that be Captain Coopwood?" Stone asked.

"You know the Captain?"

"Simeon Hart talked a lot about him. Governor Baylor did also. The Governor told me you fellows were up this way. Figured I'd run into you before long."

"Well—here, we'll help you, Parson. I didn't know—pardon my ways. I just, well, it's sort of my job to be suspicious. I'm Sergeant Walsh, Axtel Walsh. These other two, they's privates Moore and Monk. Monk's the taller one. Jump to it, boys. Help the good parson, now."

————

Stone drove his buggy into the remains of old Fort Thorn. Sergeant Walsh introduced him to Captain Coopwood.

"You say you know Hart?" Coopwood asked over coffee.

"After he bought my wagon, and we traded horses—my draft team for Stormy here," Stone nodded toward his horse, "I spent a couple of nights as his house guest."

"When was that?" the Captain asked.

"Oh, last week. He had a KGC meeting there one night. Man named Judge spoke."

"You met Judge?" Coopwood asked.

"Met him a few months back. Just saw him the other day in La Mesilla, too." Seeming satisfied Stone presented no threat, Coopwood relaxed.

"You must be hungry, Parson. It's nearly high noon. This isn't much of a place, but, please join me in my humble quarters." Coopwood talked most of the afternoon with Stone. He said little about the information this troop of confederate scouts had gathered. Stone observed all that he could, but asked few questions. He saw quickly that these men were bored. Too much free time was their biggest enemy. He kept hoping to hear something about Buck, but nothing was said.

"I wish we could offer you better accommodations, Parson," Coopwood said that evening as they ate their supper of fresh venison steak and beans.

"This is very tasty. I've had little meat for weeks, now," Stone replied.

"Some of the boys brought this back from the Cookes Peak area. That fort over there, Fort Cummings the Yanks called it, that's a much better facility than this. It's just in the wrong place," Coopwood said.

When the stars began their nightly glowing and flickering, Stone curled up in his blanket near one of the fires the men built near the corner of a now roofless, adobe building. The walls confined some of the heat and reflected it over the sleeping men.

The next morning, after a quick breakfast of more venison and some grease-fried biscuits, Stone harnessed Stormy to his buggy.

"You're welcome to stay a spell, Parson," Coopwood said. "I've enjoyed your company."

"Likewise, Captain. Your hospitality is much appreciated. 'Spect we'll be seeing one another out here again."

Stone whistled and Dinger came running.

"If you ever want to free yourself of that dog…"

"No deal, Captain. Dinger gives me great comfort out on the trail. Good protection, too, I might add."

"No doubt, Parson. Be careful," Coopwood said. "Apaches are everywhere. I wouldn't trust them Yankees up where you're going much more than them."

"I'll be careful, Captain. You do the same."

About the time the sun reached its apex, Stone stopped to rest Stormy and to stretch his stiff body. For hours now, he'd felt he was being followed. At this point, he doubted it was Apaches. One rarely sensed their presence until it was too late. He suspected either Coopwood had sent someone to follow him, or, some Union scout had found him a curiosity.

"Yeah, someone's back there," he said to Dinger who paced back and forth, his nose lifted, trying to get a good scent.

"Just relax. They'll either leave us or join us."

Stone knew he could pull a defensive maneuver on whoever was on his tail and confront them, but that wouldn't be what a bumbling, old preacher would do. After a good rest in the warm, early-afternoon sun, he climbed up on his buggy and continued up the river trail. He was breaking dried sticks off a fallen cottonwood limb for his evening fire when two riders rode slowly up to him.

"Howdy," Stone said. "I'm just fixin' to set up camp here for the night. You fellows care to join me?"

One of the men leaned over and spit a stream of tobacco juice near Dinger who lowered his tail and growled. The other man kept his eyes on Stone. After a few seconds, he spoke.

"Right nice place to camp. Too bad you won't be stayin'. We don't want no trouble, wouldn't want to do the likes of you no harm. You just get back up in that fancy buggy of yours. We're all goin' on up river."

CHAPTER 11

Stone eyed up both men. They weren't Texans. They held what appeared to be Union carbines, and they sat on McClellan saddles with the letters U S stamped into the tapaderos. They could be deserters, but he thought not. Stone saw no reason not to do whatever they told him to.

"Well, if you fellows got a better plan for camp, I'm not the type to argue."

"Just get that buggy rollin'. Ain't much daylight left," said the one who'd done all the talking, so far. The other man sat silently in his saddle, but Stone knew he was aware of everything around him.

"Might as well be friendly like, beings we're traveling together. I'm Parson—"

"We know who you are, Preacher. Got no idea what you are, though. Been wantin' to talk to you since you was down in Franklin. The Captain will have a passel of questions for you. Save your voice."

The sun was long gone and a sliver of moon was high in the star-filled sky when Stone halted Stormy at the perimeter of the well-hidden camp he'd been led to. They'd turned off the main trail and had followed a dry streambed up a canyon full of large, sycamore trees that towered into the now inky-black sky.

Stone sat in his buggy, waiting for instructions, or permission, to do something. Semi-prisoner, was what he figured his status to be. The two men who'd brought him here went into a large, officer's tent. Other men scurried around, seemingly oblivious to him. Quite a few minutes went by. Finally, a man came over to Stone.

"Let me help you, Mr. Preacher-man. Seems everyone's either afraid of you, or, a mite too lazy to help you. Come on down off that seat. I'll strip that harness off your horse and picket him with the others. He'll be just fine. You must surely be hungry. Got us some kind of stew in that pot hanging over by that second fire. You go help yourself. You got a bowl and spoon, I 'spect."

"We ain't such an unfriendly bunch, honest we ain't," the man continued. "It's just that we've all been out on patrol every-which-way for days and we surely be all tuckered out and a mite on edge. Then, of course, you sorta get to looking at everybody twice in our business, if you know what I mean.

"Name's Parker," he continued. "That's all anybody ever calls me. Just Parker. Some says I shoulda been born a woman 'cause I talk too much. Just my way, I 'spect."

"Stone. Parson Justin Stone. Pleased to make your acquaintance, Parker."

"Be my pleasure, Parson Stone. You load up that belly of yours, then I can see you surely do need some rest. Got an extra half-shelter around here someplace, if you'd desire that."

"No need for that. I'll sleep under my buggy. It is getting a mite cold at night, though. If there's an extra blanket someplace? If that wouldn't put you out."

"I'll rustle one up for you, Parson. Don't worry about a thing, here now. All will be just fine come morning."

Stone slept for a while, then woke when the guard changed. The men coming off first-watch stirred the fire, then refilled the coffeepot. Stone lay wrapped up in his blankets, contemplating his situation. Dinger lay curled up by his side.

If he had been watched in Franklin, he'd have some explaining to do, but that should be easy enough. What bothered him was that he never knew it. He didn't recognize either of these men who'd brought him in. He figured they'd have been on other horses, and quite possibly would have worn very different clothes, but still, he should have picked up their tailing him days ago, if they'd really been doing that. Maybe they had another contact in Franklin. That would make more sense, but still, he remained very uneasy about the whole thing.

He had about two months, maybe a little less, to keep this cover up. Then what? That would mostly depend on Buck. He lay there thinking about his son for some time. Thinking of Buck always brought thoughts of Laura. Thoughts of having lost Laura always made Stone feel as if he'd been ripped open and much of his very life yanked out of his soul.

Eventually, Stone drifted back off to sleep. He awoke in the morning as the men shuffled around the camp, reviving fires and starting to heat up coffee and blackened, iron skillets. He rolled over, then slowly pushed up his cold, stiff, pain-racked body. He stood leaning against his buggy for a moment, observing the camp's activities. No one paid him any attention.

After a few moments, a red headed, rugged looking man stepped through the flap of the officer's tent. Almost at once, he stared Stone's way. Stone heard him call Parker's name, and the young man hurried to him, saluting as he reached the officer. Stone couldn't hear the conversation from the officer to Parker, but after only a few seconds, Parker again saluted, then turned and started towards him. Stone watched the young man skirt around fires, and other men, as he headed his way.

"Morning, Parker," Stone said to him as he neared. "Fine morning, for this late in the fall and this high in the mountains."

"Surely be, Preacher," Parker said. "You sleep good? I surely did. I was tired as an old dog after all our scoutin' about for days. Be hangin' around camp today. One of the boys brought in a young deer last night. We'll feast on that for a day or so. Almost be like home—sorta, anyway."

"Almost like home?" Stone replied.

"Not really, but I try not to think much about home, and such," Parker said. "Makes me homesick to think of Ma back there by herself."

"Where's home?" Stone asked.

"Up on that big river in Ohio. Pa died of the fever nigh on five years now. Ma lives with her family. Gonna get me a piece of land, or such, when this is all over. Make Ma proud. What about you, Preacher? You gonna stay with us a spell?"

"Well, I wouldn't know. Do you have a message for me?"

"Message? Oh, yeah. The Captain wants to see you. He said to come to his tent for breakfast."

"Captain? Might that be Captain Paddy Graydon?" Stone asked.

"It surely is. I'm most proud to serve in his unit. Ain't nothin' Captain Graydon be fearful of. He'd climb a tree and drag down one of them mean mountain lions with one hand, if we needed meat for the pot."

"You don't say," Stone said, as he started walking toward the captain's tent. Walking at his side, Parker continued his accolades for his commanding officer.

Reaching the center of the camp, they parted. Parker headed for the nearest fire, Stone continued on slowly toward the captain's tent. From the corner of his eye, Stone saw Paddy Graydon standing in the entryway of his tent, staring intently at him. Giving Graydon plenty of time to size him up, he never made eye contact until he was within a few steps of the tent and Graydon extended his hand to him. Stone stopped, leaned on his cane, looked at the Captain eye-to-eye, then took hold of the extended hand and gave it a firm shake.

'Parson Stone, I'm told," Captain Graydon greeted Stone, still studying him intently. "I'm Paddy Graydon, captain of this outfit. Come in. These mornings here in the mountains this time of year are too brisk for me to eat outside. The food gets cold too quickly. I can't stand cold biscuits."

Stone entered the tent, then sat on one of the fold-up, canvas chairs setting beside a small table. He stretched out his wooden leg off to the side where Captain Graydon wouldn't trip over it. He heard something at the tent door. It was Dinger.

"Out of here," Stone told his nosey dog. "Go on now. I'll feed you later."

"I've never known a preacher who traveled with a dog, before," Graydon said.

"Reckon I'm not your normal preacher," Stone replied. "The normal ones have all left here. Only an old fool such as I would accept this assignment."

"This assignment, just what is that, Parson Stone?"

"Keeping an eye on our buildings and helping our people anyway I can. Even in war times there're weddings and other needs. Funerals, I expect there might be far too many funerals."

"You came here from Texas, I'm told," Graydon continued his inquisition.

Stone nodded. "Someone needed to see what was going on in Texas with the Confederate takeover. Something such as this can be devastating to a group such as ours. All the hard work of so many people can be wiped out if some out-of-control government has no respect for the church."

"How did you find things?" Graydon asked.

"Fine, really," Stone said. "There seems to be more than enough confusion to keep everyone in a tizzy just trying to figure out what to do next without anyone looking for something to take over, or, to cause unneeded trouble."

Graydon seemed to weigh Stone's answers. He waited for several moments before speaking again.

"Franklin and Fort Bliss, you seemed to spend quite some time there."

"Not really. I had a freight wagon and team to sell. I needed to buy a buggy, also. I left for Las Cruces as soon as my business was completed."

"Simeon Hart. I'm told you took up well with Mr. Hart."

"Mr. Hart was very gracious to me. He bought my wagon and team, for much more than they were worth, I might add. He helped me get over to El Paso del Norte where I bought my buggy. He and Mr. Rumbaugh, the buggy maker and old friend of his, are at odds over this conflict, yet Hart helped me buy my buggy from Rumbaugh. Mr. Hart graciously put me up in his house as his guest."

"And guest at his radical political meeting. What do you think of the Knights of the Golden Circle, Parson Stone?"

That's it! Graydon had an insider at that KGC meeting.

"It would have been rude of me not to attend that meeting, given I was a house guest of Mr. Hart's. I left immediately after the speaker finished. I have no ties to anything the likes of the KGC."

Paddy Graydon seemed to digest Stone's reply. Parker brought in a tin platter covered with thick strips of fried sowbelly with some tough looking biscuits on one side.

"A plate and fork for the parson, Parker. Think, man, think," Captain Graydon said. "How's he supposed to eat?" Parker left, but quickly returned with a plate and fork.

"Sorry, Parson," he said.

"Thank you, Parker," Stone replied.

"I can't be the host Simeon Hart was, but I do offer you our best, Parson," Paddy Graydon said.

"It's much appreciated, Captain. Tell you the truth, all that opulence goes against my simple nature."

Paddy Graydon said nothing while he ate. When finished, he pushed back his plate, then pointed to the food still on the platter. "Finish up, Parson, then take what's left for that dog of yours."

"He'll get lazy if he spends much time around your camp, Captain."

"Where are you going, Parson?" Graydon asked.

"I've often heard how beautiful Santa Fe is for the Christmas celebration. I hope to be there this year to experience that for myself. This gives me plenty of time to stop off where needed along the way."

Captain Graydon seemed to drift out of his interrogator mode.

"Colonel Canby will want to talk to you. We're going there now."

"Colonel Canby?" Stone asked. "Where do we find him?"

"Fort Craig. Two days ride, upriver. We'll leave in an hour."

"It's kind of you to invite me to travel with you. I have been concerned somewhat with all the stories I've heard about the Apaches. I've heard frightful things."

Captain Graydon looked at Stone, then nodded.

"We'll be glad to protect you, Parson Stone. We wouldn't have it any other way."

———

A cold, northern wind blew across the open plains when Stone drove his buggy through the sally port of Fort Craig. Off to the west, the deep-purple colored mountains of the Black Range poked ominously into the brilliant, blue sky. Their white tipped peaks, products of a late-fall snowstorm, glistened like huge diamonds.

On the other side of the fort, the Rio Grande flowed swiftly southward only a few hundred yards to the east. Jutting several hundred feet up out of the plain on the opposite side of the river stood Black Mesa, a flat topped, volcanic plateau that appeared to be out of place.

Stone sized up this fortress. The location was excellent. No enemy could get within a mile in any direction without being exposed. Much of the exterior wall was chest high, mounded dirt, though there was some rock construction around this main entryway. A moat type ditch lined most of the perimeter, not for water, but to inhibit attackers from scaling the make-shift walls.

All in all, the fort seemed well protected against an infantry, or cavalry, attack. Artillery shells might be different, though. The pole in the center of the fort proudly carried the red, white and blue of the Union flag, even if it was an outdated, thirty-three star one.

A bugler suddenly announced the troop's arrival and bleated out the call to assembly. Stone pulled his buggy off to one side, over near the quartermaster's office, then watched the fort come alive and to attention. There appeared to be a base of well trained, attack- ready men. Then, too, there were the masses of local volunteers and others who failed to even form a straight line. Colonel Canby had his hands full. When the men were released, Parker came over to Stone.

"Captain told me to care for your horse, and such. He wants you to meet him in the officer's quarters, pronto. You don't worry about a thing, Parson. I'll take special care of this fine horse."

"Thank you, Parker." Stone started off slowly, leaning heavily on his cane for the first few steps. Then, nearing the stone building of the officers' mess and office, he heard voices coming through a window, open slightly for fresh air. Stone stopped and listened.

"Sure he's a preacher. No one could fake that. I just say watch him. Who knows what all he heard, or saw, in Texas. Talk to him. He might have seen something important and not even know it. He spent at least one night in Hart's house."

"Alright, Captain," Colonel Canby said, "your points are well taken. Just don't make more of this than it is. He's a preacher. You can't expect him to have observed things in the way you would have yourself. I'll not make him a prisoner. Go on now. I'll talk to him. You and I will talk at breakfast."

Stone moved forward, toward the door. He and Graydon reached the door, at opposite sides, at the same time.

"Captain, I surely do thank you for your escort these last days. If you, or anyone else, will be going north in a few days—"

"My mission, for now, is watching the enemy to the south, Parson. You'll have to talk to Colonel Canby." With that, Captain Graydon quickly stepped past Stone and walked off into the courtyard. Stone turned and stepped to the still open doorway. As he reached up to knock on the latch-post, a voice came from inside.

"Come in, come in. You must be this Parson Stone I've heard so much about. Come, sit yourself down. I'm Colonel Canby. I trust Captain Graydon treated you well. Sometimes—"

"He was a splendid host. I'm much obliged that he allowed me to travel with his men. I promise not to be a burden while here. I'll be on my way, shortly."

"A burden? Away with such a thought. Talk to me, Parson. Tell me what you're doing out here. Where you're going, and such. Tell me about yourself."

Stone cleared his throat.

"Well, I'm out here…" Stone spent the next few minutes telling his standard story. When finished, the Colonel asked him some questions.

"I know you paid little attention to what the rebels, ah, the Confederates, are planning, but did you ever hear any talk of them coming into New Mexico up the Pecos River?"

"Up the Pecos? Well, as a matter of fact, I do remember hearing some talk about that. Yes, it was out at Apache Wells. Some of the men were quite upset one day. It seems they were all ready to march up the Pecos right then, but had gotten word that plan had been canceled. They were given orders to move on to Fort Bliss and prepare to come up through here. That's why I've got to stay ahead of them. I must warn our people, all people really, of how these hungry and cold, young men will steal anything not nailed down, and much of what is. Most are good men, but others— when I think of what went on in La Mesilla…"

Colonel Canby slouched back in his large, horsehair stuffed chair. Stone knew he'd sized the Colonel up correctly and had said the right things to put him at ease. It was late when they finally stopped talking.

"In the morning, Parson. I'd be honored if you'd join me for breakfast. We have a short staff meeting. That might be of little interest to you, but I want you to meet my junior officers. Captain Graydon will be there. He'll have a report for us."

"I'd be delighted, and honored, Colonel. I shall see you in the morning, then."

––––––––––

Stone left the fort two days later. Colonel Canby sent him off with an escort to Socorro.

Riding into town, he observed how the Catholic Church dominated the central town area. He circled the business area, getting a feel for the commerce and lifestyle of the people who lived there. He watered Stormy at the communal trough, then found a cantina and went inside.

After eating, he inquired about the Methodist Church from the proprietor who spoke some English. Heading off to the north end of town as directed, Stone found the small building with a meager steeple and cross on top. To his surprise, when he opened the door, he found a group of four women inside.

"Oh," he said as he took a step inside before seeing anyone. "I wasn't expecting anyone. I thought I'd have to clean things up, but, it looks as if you ladies, or someone, has been keeping thing quite tidy."

"You're a preacher," one of the women exclaimed. "God has answered our prayers."

"Well, I'll only be here a short time. I'm Parson Justin Stone. Who might you be?"

The four ladies introduced themselves, with the one who seemed to be in charge of their study group calling herself Sis Martha Gomez. Stone went on with his usual explanation of what he was doing out in these parts. He then talked about Sunday.

"I'll be here for service on Sunday. I trust you can get the word out? I'll be staying here. I see a good stove and an ample supply of wood. This will be just fine. I'm very pleased at how you've been taking care of this building."

"It's God's house," Martha said. "You might stay here, but you're coming home with me for supper tonight. Won't have it any other way. My husband, that's Hector, why, he'll be mighty pleased to see you here. The others can fight over who feeds you tomorrow, but tonight you're coming to my house."

Stone wasn't about to turn down that invitation. It was two days until Sunday. At least he'd be well fed for the time being. In his mind, made plans to leave right after he spoke on Sunday. He felt that if he spent too much time here with these friendly people, he jeopardized his cover.

The church was full come service time. Stone had arranged for some of the ladies to take care of having some music ready. After that, he had a small offering basket passed around, then he started reading his message. Actually, by this time he really knew it by heart and didn't have to read it. He got through about two-thirds of it when he came to a place where it talked about Jesus being our replacement for our sins. Though Stone had been through this part dozens of times, it had never meant anything personally to him before. This time it did.

He didn't know what was going on inside of him, but it was as if the words he was saying were being burned deep into his soul. He had to stop for a moment. He swallowed, then seemed to get his voice back. A moment later, reaching the place about Jesus being brutally beaten and crudely nailed on a cross to take our place, Stone again couldn't go on.

Leave me alone, God. This can't be for me. I've done way too much for this to be for me. I'm sorry if I've offended you. It wasn't my idea. Leave me alone!

He faked a cough, swallowed hard, but still couldn't go on. He looked out at the people sitting on the homemade benches and saw tears in nearly every eye. Finally, he was able to speak again.

"Jesus took our place. All the judgment we deserve, he took upon himself…"

When he'd finally finished, most of the people gathered together in the back. Then one woman came up to him.

"For you, Señor. To keep hour hands warm when you travel so far to spread God's word." She handed him a pair of hand-knitted, woolen gloves. Stone started to refuse, then saw the joy in the woman's eyes when she handed them to him. How did she know his hands were the first things to get cold? Already, in the brisk fall mornings, he'd wished for just such gloves.

"Thank you. You don't know how much I need these. You're so kind."

"He told me. He told me one would soon come and again give us his word. He said this one would need what I could make with the small bag of wool from my one sheep. Jesucristo told me to make these for you, Señor"

Stone stood speechless. Suddenly, one of the men approached him and handed him a scrap of simple brown paper with some small coins in its fold.

"It is to honor God that we bring you this offering in His name. It is for Almighty God that we give this to you, His faithful servant."

"I can't take…" He couldn't say anymore. He looked at the small handful of coins, mostly Spanish reals, centavos and bits, with a few pennies and dimes mixed in. Stone felt weak. He stepped back, then slumped into a chair against the wall. He looked at the old man who'd placed the coins in his hand.

"Thank you—gracious," he said, then he looked out to the others. He then placed his face in his hands and stared at the floor. Stone didn't need these poor people's money. However, he somehow sensed that these people needed to give of what they had. It made no sense. Not much did these days. What would he do with such a sacrificial donation?

He'd given his sermon in English—he figured a few of these people couldn't even understand much, if anything, of what he'd said. Still, they gave—it seemed they also received.

He looked up just in time to see the last person exit the church. He folded these meager coins into the scrap of brown paper, then put it in his pouch. These people thought they were giving to God. That thought scared him as much as anything had in his entire life. He thought of old Elias Crump's admonitions.

———————

The sun was high when Stone reached the edge of town. Suddenly, a young boy jumped out in front of his buggy, frantically waving his arms for him to stop. Stone pulled on Stormy's reins.

"Whoa!" Stormy stopped just as he reached the boy.

"Boy, what are you trying to do? You could have gotten hurt."

"Por favor, you come, Señor. Chico, he hurt bad. You come, help." The boy pointed over to a cottonwood tree. Stone saw a small boy lying under it. He jerked the reins that way and drove right up to the fallen boy on the ground. Stone got down and quickly saw that the little boy held onto his left arm.

"Hees arm, Señor," the older boy said as he came running. "Be broken, most surely."

Stone nodded. The little boy looked up at him with pleading, tear-filled eyes.

"Get in the buggy," he said to the older boy. "I'll hand Chico up to you. Then, I'll take you home."

Stone followed the older boy's leading and ended up at a nearly washed away, twelve-foot square, adobe hovel.

"Mamá!" the older boy called out as Stone stopped the buggy. In seconds, a frail, weary-looking woman, wearing a frayed old rebozo across her shoulders burst through the doorway and ran to the buggy. Behind her straggled two small, barefoot girls.

"Dí tree, Mamá. Chico, he fall from dí tree. So sorry, Mamá."

The woman quickly took the small boy and carried him through the door of the mud house. Chico clung to his mother with his one good arm. She took him over to a wooden bench that sat against the wall. As the boy sat there with silent tears wetting his face, she cautiously looked at Chico's arm. Stone walked to her side.

"Allow me, please." He gently ran his fingers down across Chico's broken arm.

"The bones seem to still be in line. If you put a splint on it, I think it will heal just fine. Of course, to be sure, you should take him to a doctor."

"No doctor, Señor. No dinero for doctor."

Stone looked around at the poverty this family lived in.

"Perhaps your husband—"

"He is dead, Señor. Is only me, and my children. Roberto, he is a help, but he is still so young. The others—you see."

Stone nodded. This lady surely had her hands full. He took several steps toward his buggy, then stopped at the doorway. He reached into his coat pocket and took out his pouch. He removed the folded paper containing the handful of small coins.

"Señora. For you." He handed them to her. Her eyes opened wide. She looked up at him.

"Oh, Señor. Jesucristo has sent you. I shall say a prayer for you each day, forever."

Stone again nodded, having no words to reply. He again started toward his buggy, taking several more steps, then stopped again. He reached back into his pouch, withdrew a twenty dollar gold piece, then motioned for Roberto to come to him.

"Give this to your mother," he told the boy, then placed the coin in his little hand.

Roberto looked at the coin. His eyes and mouth opened widely.

"Mamá! Look, see! Now we can get milk for dí little ones, forever, Mamá!"

Stone climbed up on his buggy seat. He looked back at the woman and her four small children.

"Bless you, Señor," she said. "No one has ever done such for us before. Jesucristo bless you."

Stone shook the reins and Stormy started back out of town. He rode for about two miles, then stopped. For a long time, he sat there thinking of what had just happened, what he'd done.

———

Four days later, Stone rode into Albuquerque. He'd made some quick stops along the way, warning the local people that the Confederate Army was coming, and it may well act as a swarm of locust, stripping empty all the storehouses and also commandeering any other provision its men found.

Now, it was dark. After finishing his supper, he'd asked the owner of the cantina where the Methodist Church was located. The man looked at him for a moment, then he gave Stone the directions he'd requested.

In the moonlight, Stone rode off to the edge of town where he found the church. He unharnessed Stormy, then he tied him with a long rope to the right-rear buggy wheel. The hungry horse immediately started munching on some of the dried grass within its reach.

Dinger ran off after a jackrabbit he'd routed from a tuft of bear grass growing against the church wall. Exhausted, Stone took his bedroll, walked to the church door, pushed it open, then he stepped inside. He stood for a second in the dark, letting his eyes adjust to the lack of light, then he closed the door.

Suddenly, he felt a gun barrel poke against his ribs.

"Figured this is where you'd come. I've been waiting on you. I know who you really are, Parson Stone."

CHAPTER 12

Stone took a slow, deep breath. Was it over? Had his rusty clumsiness betrayed him?

Think! Use your head.

"Well, we meet again," Parson Stone said. "Can't say this is really a surprise. I'm not going to run off. Let's sit and talk."

"You're supposed to be dead, Colonel," Judge said, as he cautiously sat where he could clearly see Stone, as clear as possible in the darkness.

"So are you," Stone replied. "I knew better—but never told anyone. Why are you back up here? You double cross your Mexican friends?"

Judge didn't respond for a moment, then spoke. "My business why I left Mexico. Toss that cane of yours over to your left, now. I've seen what you can do with that thing," Judge said. "I probably should be more concerned about what I haven't seen than what I have. What else do you have up your sleeve, Colonel?

"Up my sleeve? Such as that hidden card rig up yours back on the train?" Even in the faint light, Stone saw Judge's head jerk when he said that. When both men were seated, Judge stared at Stone through the meager light for a moment, then he spoke.

"Well, Colonel, talk to me."

"It's Parson Stone. Never, never call me Colonel. It's Parson Stone. If you blow my cover, President Davis will have your head."

"President Davis? Come now. You were in Washington."

"So were you," Stone said

"Yes, but I had my reasons," Judge said.

"So did I."

"Try and convince me you're not still the Union's secret weapon," Judge said. "What are you really trying to do for them?"

"The Union. Me support the Union? Think, man. After what they did to me? When you were believed lost down in Mexico, they sent me, and seven of the best men they had, to find you and get you out. When I disappeared, who did they send to help me? No one. Not one person. They let me rot in that jail. They just declared me dead. Dead! They said I was dead. They told that to my wife, my little son, too. Soon, my friend, they shall see the life that still runs through my blood."

Judge said nothing for a moment. Stone knew he had him thinking.

"Texas. What were you doing in San Antonio?" Judge asked.

"I had a message for General Sibley that couldn't be trusted to written communiqué. It had to be delivered orally, by someone believable."

"Message?"

"Stay out of Santa Fe until after Christmas, and I get the gold," Stone said.

Judge peered through the darkness into the face of Stone.

"So that's why Sibley is moving so slowly? Can't you speed up your contact?"

"No one, not even the Union, knows who it really is. That's why I was in Washington—one of the reasons," Stone said.

"There were other reasons? Judge asked. "What else?"

"I had to waylay the Union's own 'Parson Stone.' That poor fellow is now on an extended trip around the horn on his way to California. An old friend of mine is the ship's captain. He'll keep him out of reach until January, at least. By the time he gets in touch with Washington, we'll have the gold.

"I just assumed his identity—his fake identity," Stone went on. "He has nothing to backup any claim that he is anyone but who he really is, Henry J Wilson, that's his real name. I have all his documents that were to make him, but now make me, Parson Justin Stone."

There was silence for several moments. "Anyone else out here know any of this?" Judge then asked.

"Not a soul. It must be kept that way. You cannot talk of any of this to anyone. No one."

Judge peered at Stone, then very slowly nodded his head.

I've pulled it off! But I lied… I'm a spy. I have to lie, right? But is that right? Did I make God mad at me? What else could I have done?

"There's a KGC meeting out on a ranch west of Socorro in four days. I'm leaving in the morning," Judge said.

"I have the time. I'd appreciate going with you. I can see there's nothing here for me to do. The less things I do, the better, really. Fewer chances of making a mistake, or being identified. I don't want to get to Santa Fe much before Christmas, either. Going out into the country for a few days seems to be just what I should do."

"You had me fooled, on the preacher part that is. I thought you really were one. However, there was always just something…"

Stone nodded. "In the morning then."

"Where are you staying?" Judge asked.

"Here. I'll take care of Stormy, that's my horse, and let Dinger, my dog, in with me. I'm used to this. My cover, you know."

Judge nodded. "Early then. I'll see you about sunup."

96

Judge picked up Stone's cane, handed it to him, yet held tightly to the other end for a moment while he peered through the darkened room at Stone's shadowed face. He then let loose his grip.

"In the morning," he said.

Stone nodded. "Rest well, Judge, rest well. Remember, not even a hint of this to anyone."

Stone rose, pushed on his cane, walked out the door behind Judge, then watched him walk up the street towards the lights of the town. Letting Judge out of his sight was a risk, one he had to take tonight. Come morning, he'd be a constant shadow to Judge.

He knows too much. He wants that gold for himself.

Stone felt as if fire were flowing through his veins. The violent pumping of his heart seemed to echo off the barren wood walls of the rustic church. The old spy had awakened out of dormancy and had taken over his mind and body. Stone knew what had to be done. The risk not to was far too great. Before they reached that ranch out in the country, he'd have to kill Judge.

Buck Rafter left Governor Baylor's office where he'd received his new orders, then stepped out onto the town-square of La Mesilla. A replacement had been sent west to take over his watch-dog duties in Tucson, and he was being sent north, well above Captain Coopwood's men.

"I need you up north," Baylor had said. "Socorro to Santa Fe, really. This is not like Tucson where you operated openly among friendly locals. Up there, most of those small-village Mexicans won't have a good attitude toward you, beings you're from Texas. Try to put up a good front—be on your best behavior. Pretend you're anything but Confederate spies. Scrap your uniforms, and all else like that. Leave everything behind but your eyes, ears and minds. In addition to finding out all you can about the Yankees' activities and such, line up any caches of supplies and possible sympathizers you can learn about.

"Keep in touch," Baylor had continued. "I'll have someone at Fort Thorn—might move there myself—so send anything important down to there. Make sure your dispatch riders watch out for the other side's spies, especially around Fort Craig. Those Yankee boys will be looking for you."

Buck was excited. Part of him wanted to leave immediately. The other part—well, that part was very glad he had a week's leave before starting north. He looked eastwardly, toward the town on the other side of the river. He'd had a bath and shave earlier. He'd even put on new, store bought clothes.

"Hey Sergeant Rafter," yelled a man called Lacy, one of Buck's men and part of a group of four who were approaching him on the pathway.

"We're headin' up to his little cantina we saw the last time we were here. Gonna load up on tequila, then put the heels to some locals. Come on, there ain't nothin' better to do."

"Nah. You go on. I ah—I've got something else planned," Buck said.

"Too bad. Tomorrow then," Lacy said. "Hey, tomorrow we're all going over to the El Paso side of the river. We'll really paint old Mexico red. Ya gotta come."

"Yeah, maybe I'll see you tomorrow," Buck said.

The group moved on by. Buck quickly walked over to the livery, now occupied by the Confederate Army. He brushed and curried his horse's sorrel coat until it shone. He then put on the hand-woven blanket he'd purchased from a peddler who'd come up from down in old Mexico. Finally, he hoisted on his macheer saddle. After he'd drawn up both fish-cord cinches tightly, he slid his left foot into the tapadero-shrouded stirrup, then swung his right leg over the horse's back. He rode down a trail that went east, toward the river, and Las Cruces on the other side.

Buck soon sloshed his horse through the shallow water, then he let it dry off in the breeze while it pranced slowly into Las Cruces. He slid out of the saddle, then tied the reins to the rail in front of Cantina de la Palma. He removed his hat and soothed back his hair. He stepped up to the doorway, paused, then walked inside and stood for a moment while his eyes adjusted to the diminished light. He anxiously searched every corner of the place.

After a few seconds, he started for a table near the back when the cocina door swung open and through it strolled a young woman. She instantly flashed Buck a big smile.

"Señor Buck. You come back!" She excitedly motioned for him to sit closer to the entrance to the cocina. She quickly took the two plates of food she carried to two vaqueros playing cards over in a darkened corner, then she rushed over to Buck.

"Oh, Señor Buck, I've missed you so much. I've counted every day 'till you come back. Today is, how you say it? Seventy-two days, sí. I so wished you would come soon. So often while I lay dreaming in my bed at night, I wondered where you were, if you were safe, or, if you ever thought of me. I prayed you would come back some day, and we could talk and take a walk together and if you…"

"Hold on now, Lucinda. I told you I'd be back. Here I am." Buck said, looking around and becoming embarrassed that others were watching him. "I ah, I surely hoped you were still here in your aunt's cantina. I didn't want to have to look all over here, or in El Paso, for you. I would have, though, if I had to."

"Aunt Delora, she is hard to please. It is just her way. Still, I think I will be here for much time. If not, I will work for my other aunt, Carmen. She is Delora's older sister, as I have told you. Aunt Carmen has mucho busy cantina over in El Paso. That is why Delora, why she came here. She wants to have big place, as her sister has, but sí, I believe it will never be so. Still, I am glad to be here. I learn to speak American. This new country you say we now are, they speak same American as old country?"

"Sure. We're the same people. It's hard to explain what's going on, or why, really. You ever been out west of here? Out to those big, tree-like cactus? The ones taller than this building?"

"So tall? Now that I shall love to see."

"I'll take you there sometime. I mean—maybe, someday." Buck was cautious. He didn't want to make any promises he couldn't keep. He still remembered that his father had promised to come home from his excursion into Mexico. Yet, there was something about Lucinda that made him want to take her everywhere he went. He reminded himself that he only had a week's leave, then he'd be back off with the army again.

"Someday," Lucinda's dark eyes sparkled. "Someday I go with you, sí? Someday you and me—"

"Tomorrow, some friends want me to go with them over to El Paso for a few days," Buck said, purposely cutting Lucinda off. He wasn't ready for any big commitment. Besides, he had a war to help win before he could think of the things Lucinda thought of now.

"Can you go with me? I'd feel much better with you, I mean, well, you know your way around, and—"

"I shall ask Aunt Delora. I think it will be fine. I haven't asked for time away since last you were here. I waited for you to come back. You are going to stay and eat, aren't you? Maybe later—"

"Yeah. Maybe later we'll ah—how about a walk?"

"It's cold out. I'll think of something," Lucinda said.

"Yeah—something."

Lucinda leaned over and gave Buck a quick kiss on the cheek, then started for the cocina door. Buck heard several snickers from across the room. He felt the blood rush to his face. He was embarrassed for sure—but he felt so good he really didn't care.

The glowing, half-moon reflected abundant white light from its lofty position when Buck rode back to his camp outside La Mesilla. Two of his men were waiting for him under a large cottonwood tree.

"Howdy Sergeant Rafter. We was beginnin' to worry 'bout you. Thought maybe the Yanks got you, or somethin'"

"What did you worry for, Lacy? You should know by now that I can take care of myself. Where are the others? There were four of you when I left."

"Well, me and Kirk here got out when the knives and guns came out of nowhere. All we wanted was a good drunk and to show these greasers how we Texans are more men than the likes of them. I tell you, you never saw the likes of it. Chairs came a flyin', bottles smashin' and all else. I tell you there wasn't but six of them when we started, but by the time we jumped through that window, there were over a dozen.

"They musta been just waitin' for us to start something," Lacy continued. "Ain't hardly fair. It'd be hard to say what kinda shape Sly and Billy be in, or where they even ended up. We thought maybe you'd—"

"No!" Buck cut Lacy off. He'd had a great evening with Lucinda and had no interest in tracking down two of his wayward men.

"Well, dern it, Sergeant Rafter. Me and Kirk was fixin' to go with you."

"We still going to El Paso tomorrow?" Buck asked Lacy.

"By ourselves? What if Sly and Billy don't show up by then? I still think—"

"I'm going to El Paso tomorrow. I'm leaving early in the morning. You can come along if you want, Sly and Billy, too, if they show up."

"I'll go," Kirk said. "'Bout got skinned alive here today. Can't be no worse in Mexico."

"'Spect I'll be goin', too," Lacy said. "Sure would feel a bunch better if'n Sly and Billy would show up."

"Sun-up then," Buck said. "We're first going across the river to Las Cruces."

"What fer we gotta go and do that?" Kirk asked.

"I'm taking a friend with us. She was born over there. She knows her way around. None of us do."

"She? So that's what you got your head fixed on these days. You're sweet on some little greaser gal," Lacy said.

Buck shot him a hard look, then turned toward his horse and started to strip the saddle.

"Early in the morning then," Buck said.

"I'll have to think on it, now," Lacy said. "I kinda figure taking a woman might be bad luck."

———————

"Alright you two. I expect you to act decent. Miss Lucinda is a real lady. You understand?"

"How do you fancy this?" Lacy said. "We invite our sergeant to go with us to El Paso for a good time, next thing you now he's taking some gal with us and telling us we gotta behave as if our mothers are watching us. Knowed I shoulda gone looking for Billy and Sly instead."

"Ain't too late for you to turn tail and run," Buck said.

"Nah—just might be best to be going over there with someone who knows their way around, as you said."

Lucinda had biscuits baking and bacon frying when Buck knocked on the back door of the cocina.

"Only two?" She asked when Buck introduced Kirk and Lacy.

"The other two seem to have gotten tied up, or something," Buck said.

"You got any sisters, or cousins you can fix me and Lacy up with?" Kirk asked.

Buck shot him a harsh look.

"Well, don't look at me that way, Sergeant Buck. You might be my boss when we're out on duty, but you ain't my mother. It ain't right you got the only girl."

"Bad luck to take a woman, you said," Buck replied. "Now you want one for yourself."

"Got one, you might as well have a dozen, the way I figure."

"Eat up," Buck said. "We're burning daylight."

"You'd never know, would you Kirk, that you and me invited Sergeant Rafter here to go along with us," Lacy said. "You'd think he planned this whole thing. He's acting more as if he got stripes on his shoulders, stars even."

"If you're going with me, eat up. Otherwise, you can cut out now," Buck said as Lucinda brought more bacon from the wood, cook stove.

The sky glowed a fire like orange when they crossed the river to the Mexican side and rode into El Paso that evening.

"Where's your Aunt Carmen's cantina?" Buck asked Lucinda. "That's the best place to start."

"This way," Lucinda said, nodding to the right. "Follow me." She nudged her horse up a dusty street that seemed void of life.

"Back when a child, we ran and played all over this village." Lucinda said to Buck, who rode by her side. "We knew everyone. It was a safe place. The whole village was our home. We could trust most all. Only a few were not to be our friends. Now..." She paused, then spoke again. "It's even worse since..."

"Since all us east Texans have shown up?" Buck finished the sentence Lucinda had started. "I know what you were thinking." Buck looked around. He saw several groups of Confederate soldiers off in the shadows of the back streets and yards. All appeared to be in various stages of drunkenness. He could see that this wouldn't be a place where small children could now safely roam carefree.

"This will all change. Once General Sibley gets here, and we take New Mexico and Colorado and—"

"You will come back, won't you, Buck? You will come back for me when this is all over? We will see those big cactus, maybe even the ocean?"

"Sure. Maybe someday we'll do all that. Gotta first win this war. Ain't nothing going to happen unless we win this war."

"There," Lucinda pointed up the street. "That is the cantina. Come, quickly. Many of my family will be there. I want them all to meet you—and you them. I am much happy we have come here today."

Buck and Lucinda spent the evening talking with some of Lucinda's relatives and old friends. Kirk and Lacy quickly got into a card game with several other Confederate soldiers who'd come over here from Fort Bliss. It was well after midnight when Buck gave in to his droopy eyelids. Lucinda's aunt Carmen had offered Buck and his two friends the use of a loft above her stable. Buck went over to the table where the others still played cards.

"I'm turning in, fellas. See you in the morning."

"Night's just gettin' good, Sergeant. Why quit so soon?" Lacy asked. "Come with us. We get done here, we're gonna go harass some old Yankee these boys know about. He moved over here when we took over across the river. He even flies the Yankee flag, so they say. We're fixin' to fight the next battle of this war with this old timer. You oughta come along with us. 'Spect it'll be daylight 'til we get going his way."

Buck shook his head. "I'm turning in."

"Look, Sergeant, see that pretty little señorita over there?" Lacy nodded toward a young girl who smiled back at him. "I'm fixin' to go and really give her something to smile about. Think she'll believe I'm a general?"

"You've been drinking too much," Buck said. "Just look at those two hombres with her. Probably her brothers. Most likely got a knife for each hand and one to spare. Don't you remember yesterday? Billy and Sly?"

"You're no fun, Sergeant Rafter. Go on. Go roost with the chickens," Lacy said, all the while smiling at the girl across the room.

———

Early the next afternoon, Buck and Lucinda went looking for Kirk and Lacy, who'd not been seen since the middle of the night. Lucinda found one of her cousins who was an Agente de Policia. He told her of several Confederate soldiers being held in the cárcel, their jail. Lucinda led Buck to el zócalo, the town's central square.

The jailer opened the thick, iron-clad, timber door and let Buck look into the large cell that held the prisoners, all fourteen of them. Instantly, Kirk and Lacy were on their feet. They rushed toward Buck.

"Sergeant Rafter. Oh please. You gotta get us out of here. These people are crazy. We're in here with all these locals and there's bugs and look, look at that crazy fella in the corner over there. He's got him a snake in that gunnysack," Lacy said, pointing to a mangy looking man sitting on the dirt floor. "I swear I'm never gonna drink again. I won't be any more trouble to you, forever."

"Me neither," Kirk agreed. "Get us out of here, and I promise I'll never come back here again. I'd rather fight a she-bear grizzly than spend another hour here."

"I'll see what I can do," Buck said. "What did you do anyway?"

Lacy looked at Kirk, then back at Buck.

"Just raisin' cain, that's all," Lacy said. "Lawman said we was too loud and too drunk. Some old woman complained 'cause we was up on her roof."

"Them fellas from Fort Bliss had enough jingle in their pockets to pay off that lawman, but we was busted, broke."

"You go and bother that old Yankee?" Buck asked.

Lacy again looked at Kirk. Kirk spoke up. "He's a Yankee. He ran over here to hide. He deserved whatever he got."

Buck didn't say any more. Lucinda had been talking to the jailer. Buck saw her take out some gold, American coins and hand them to him. The jailer smiled and nodded, then turned toward Buck. He opened the inner, iron-bar door, allowing Kirk and Lacy to slip through. Swinging his cachiporra, he beat back the other men who also tried to squeeze out through the open door. Then, he slammed closed both the inner and the heavy outer doors.

"Señores. You must flee across dí river, pronto. Stop for nothing," the jailer said to his former prisoners.

"See you in La Mesilla in a few days," Buck said. "Lucinda and I are going to spend some more time over here. Try and round up those other two."

"We owe you, Sergeant—you too, Lucinda," Lacy said. "We'll make it up to you. Pay you back the money, and more."

When they were gone, Lucinda took Buck by the arm.

"Come. We go see the old man they talked of. If your friends harmed him, you must make right. He is Karl Rumbaugh, a friend of my family, a good man."

Buck knew Lucinda was upset and at least partially blamed him for whatever had happened.

A short time later, they reached Rumbaugh's place but saw nothing. Buck called out to Mr. Rumbaugh. When he received no answer, he went to the barn door, then pushed it open.

"Noooo—Oh, no," he cried out as Lucinda ran to his side.

CHAPTER 13

The sun was high overhead on the third day of Stone's and Judge's trip to the remote ranch meeting. At first Judge had incessantly inquired more about Stone's mission, but Stone rebuffed all conversations on that subject.

"You know too much already. Keep all this to yourself and everything will be fine. Mess this up, and you'll wish you were back in Mexico," Stone finally told him. After that, they'd talked very little, except when they stopped to make camp or to heat coffee. Now, in the warmth of the afternoon on the third day, Judge started talking again.

"I can't figure you out. If this preacher thing is just a cover, why do you have your nose in that old Bible every time I look at you?"

"I have to keep up my cover," Stone said. "Right now, I'm trying to find something."

I'm trying to see what God will do to me when I kill you.

Buck stood staring into Rumbaugh's shop.

"What is it you see?" Lucinda asked, pushing up beside Buck to see what he stared at inside the building.

"Get back," Buck said as he grabbed for her arm to keep her away. She pushed his hand away, stepped forward, then looked in at the stiffened body of a man dangling from a rope tethered to a roof-beam.

"Why? Your friends, why they do such a thing?"

"Let's get out of here," Buck said, backing up and pulling Lucinda with him. He turned to flee, but instead faced a man wearing a uniform with much colorful adornment, also a badge.

"Something wrong, Señor? You must know, I have many friends here. One of them, he tell me he hear mucho noise here when it be yet dark here in dí morning. Also, he say no one see dí old buggy man all day. I say to myself, I say, 'self, you should go look in on dees old gringo'. So, I come here. Look what I see. You and dees señorita. Dí barn. What is in dí barn that has you shaking the way of one who has seen a bruja, or ghost? A man who has done nothing wrong has no cause to flee, such as you were about to. Tell me, Señor Gringo, what is in dí barn for me to see? From what do you wish to run away from?"

"I didn't have anything to do with this," Buck said. "I just—"

"What, Señor? For what then did you come here?"

"I'd heard some friends might be here, that's all," Buck said.

"Ahhh. You friends, they do something here? You have names for me, por favor? Tell me who was here. Names, Señor. If they check out, you will be a free man, so with you, Señorita. Until then, you will be my guests."

Buck glanced around. This officer was alone, but more would surely soon come.

It's my father all over again. I'll never get out of Mexico alive.

"Is not good, Buck," Lucinda whispered to him. "I can no help. Thees policia, he is an enemy of my family. A very bad man. His father is one who killed my father. He does not know me—not yet. When he does, it will be very bad for us. You must do something, now."

"Come," Buck said to the officer. "Let's go in and see if there's any sign that my friends have been here." He turned, then quickly entered the barn, Lucinda at his heals. Caught off guard, the officer followed them inside. Buck went straight to the hanging body of Rumbaugh, looked at him, then he turned to the officer.

"No man deserves to hang such as this. Do you have a knife?" Buck asked.

Keeping his right hand on his cap and ball, single shot pistol, the officer reached with his left hand down to his boot where he unsheathed a shiny, six-inch-bladed knife. He cautiously reached up to try to cut the rope above the knot at the neck.

In that instant, with the officer's attention focused on trying to cut the rope with one hand, Buck grabbed the officer's right arm and twisted it away from his gun, up behind his back. With his other hand, Buck drew the man's pistol. With one swift move, Buck whipped the hard-metal gun barrel across the man's head. The officer slumped to the floor, his knife sliding across the floor.

"Get me a rope!" Buck yelled to Lucinda. She quickly grabbed one that was coiled and hung by the door. Buck tied the officer to the stair-post.

"Quickly now. We must go," Lucinda cried. Buck started to follow her to the door, then he stopped. He picked up the knife, cut Rumbaugh down, stretched him out straight on his back, and crossed his arms over his chest. The officer started to awaken.

"Now Buck! You know not what they will do to us."

"Get the horses," Buck yelled. Lucinda ran to her horse, slung herself up on the saddle, grabbed the other horse's reins, then with a yell and kick, she lurched the horses to the barn door just as Buck burst through it. In one continuous move his left foot stabbed through the stirrup and his right leg swung over the saddle. The horse never stopped, but kept pace with the one Lucinda rode.

"Across the river," Buck yelled. "Get us across the river!"

"To go through town is no good. I know another crossing upstream. When I was a little girl—"

"Just do it! I don't want to die here."

Lucinda turned her horse south, away from the river. After a mile or so, she turned toward the west. Buck followed her closely. After only a few minutes, she turned yet again, this time northward. After a mile or so, she suddenly pulled her horse to a stop.

"The river, it is over this bluff," Lucinda said. "We can cross there, if no one is watching."

"I'll check it first," Buck said, sliding off the saddle to the ground. "Hold these reins."

Buck moved forward, slowly, crouching low when he reached the bluff's edge. He scoured the area for several minutes, then he backed up and returned to Lucinda and his horse.

"I can't see anything. Let's make a run for it."

At full gallop, in tandem they burst over the edge of the bluff. Dust flew in the gusty wind as they raced their horses for the flat, shallow stretch of river. Then, from the direction of the city, a gunshot pierced the air, then another.

"Faster, Buck! Faster." Lucinda cried.

"Get low," he yelled to her. "Lay down in the saddle."

Suddenly, the dust changed to water as they splashed into the river. A bullet whizzed by so close to Buck's face that he sensed a puff of turbulent air.

"Eh—hah!" he yelled to his horse, spurring it hard. He heard another shot.

"Buck!" Lucinda yelled while flinging over the head of her tumbling horse, splashing headfirst into the water. Buck heard the wounded horse neigh loudly in pain. He spun his horse in mid-stream, then started back for Lucinda.

––––––––––

Parson Stone and Judge climbed higher up the mountain trail to the west of the Plains of San Agustín. Stone knew they had to be nearing the meeting place.

Stone, in his real life as Tyrone Rafter, had always done whatever his mission necessitated. Nothing got in his way. He had no fear of any consequences. What had been so simple before had now become very complex. He now continually looked around the trail while they slowly climbed up into the foothills.

"Any mines around here?" he asked Judge.

"About a mile to our west," Judge nodded in that direction. "I've seen it marked on an old mining map."

Then it was time. This was the place. Stone closed his eyes. He actually shuddered—from the cold wind, he told himself. He looked at the trail ahead. There stood a grove of ponderosa pines only twenty yards off the trail.

"That grove of trees. Let's stop for coffee," Stone said, heading Stormy that way.

Could he find the mine, or some other good place to hide the body? Surely there was a trail wide enough he could take his buggy and Judge's body to the mineshaft. The miners somehow had gotten supplies in, and ore out.

Nearing the trees, Stone reached down into his leather bag. He reached under the books and found the Baby Dragoon. He wrapped his fingers around it. While Judge was off alone, he'd changed the caps early this morning. However, he hadn't fired it for months. Had the powder drawn moisture? Would it fire the first shot? And, if it wouldn't...

He looked at his left hand holding the reins. Could he tighten his fingers around a man's neck until the life was gone? They'd done it before—but could they now?

Zzzzp! The first arrow found its target, slicing into Judge's shoulder. Stone instinctively ducked just as an arrow whizzed over his head. Stormy instantly turned away from the attack and took off to the north of the trail. A gunshot came from that way. Stone pulled on the right rein, turning Stormy back to the east.

Judge's horse had panicked and thrown him when he tried to get it to spin around. Judge now lay on the ground, an arrow still sticking out of his left shoulder. He reached up to Stone and called for help. Instinctively, Stone pulled Stormy that way.

A moment ago he was ready to kill Judge, now, he risked his life to save him. There was no time to reason, or even think, only react. Judge rose to his feet when Stone pulled Stormy to a halt right beside him. Stone reached down and helped pull Judge to the seat beside him.

"Apaches!" Judge cried. "Back down the trail. It's the only way out."

Stone was already turning that way. Suddenly, from behind them a bullet thudded into Judge's neck, causing him to start falling out of the buggy. Stone tried to grab on to him just when the buggy hit a rock, thrusting Stone off the other side of the seat. He landed about ten feet from Judge. Stormy kept on going down the trail, taking Stone's cane, and gun, with him. Stone started to crawl over toward Judge, but his wooden leg had jarred loose from his body in the fall. He hooked his real foot through the leg's leather harness, then he dragged it with him.

Reaching Judge, he felt for a pulse. He found none. Judge was dead. Stone feared that in a few moments he would be as well. He saw Judge's gun another ten feet up the trail. He started pulling himself toward it when he saw several of the Apaches brazenly walking toward him. They knew he was now no threat to them.

Dinger was by Stone's side, growling fiercely, trying to protect him. In a fit of anger, Stone grabbed his wooden leg, used it for a crutch to push himself upright, then he grabbed the leg by the foot and swung it around in a circle. He began to yell.

"Come and get me, you heathens. You want me, then come and get me." Suddenly, from the depth of his soul, Stone cried out to God.

"Save me, God! I've read about them miracles you did. You got any left, God?"

Soon, the crowd grew to nearly two-dozen Apache men, women and children who all stared at him from not more than thirty paces away. They were speaking loudly to each other with some pointing at his detached leg. Then, a woman stepped forward.

Stone stopped swinging his leg when he looked at her. Her long blond hair was braided, and her face was deeply tanned from the sun, though still somewhat lighter than the others. Her sky-blue eyes fixed on Stone's, then she opened her mouth and spoke.

"Them want to see you put leg back on. You do that, you live."

———

Buck hung off the side of his horse, a la Comanche warrior, as he lunged toward Lucinda.

"Grab a hold of me!" he yelled as he neared her. He kept his horse between himself and from where the gunshots were coming. Lucinda reached up and grabbed Buck's extended arm, then slipped off.

"Buck!"

"Tighter—grab on tighter." Buck spun his horse around, flinging himself to the other side of the horse. He again rushed toward Lucinda. Another bullet whizzed by his head. He reached down and got his fingers in a tight hold around Lucinda's right wrist. She grabbed his arm with her left hand and dug in her fingers.

Being a small girl of not much over one hundred pounds, Buck should have easily picked her up with one arm. But, her full, multi-tiered, broomstick skirt, made with many yards of now water-soaked, cotton material, seemed to double her weight. Each bounce of the saddle felt as if someone was puling Buck's arm in two.

Suddenly, the splashing stopped and they were once again kicking up dust. With one last burst of energy, Buck pulled himself upright, pulling Lucinda with him. She swung her leg over the saddle behind him, and they headed for a grove of cottonwood trees that would give them some cover. A bullet kicked up dust in front of their horse, causing it to lurch to the left, nearly spilling its riders.

They reached the trees, then headed for a trail that led around a ledge, then up to the top of a small mesa. By this time the shooting had stopped. Buck slowed the horse to a walk. It heaved and shook while it sucked air. He slid off the saddle and grabbed the reins. He ran beside the horse, leading it down off the mesa.

"Keep an eye out behind us," he yelled to Lucinda who slid forward into the saddle belly. "I don't know if they will come across the river after us or not. Where's the nearest road, or farm, or something?"

"Straight ahead," Lucinda said. "There is a farm. It borders the road to La Mesilla. I know the people. We will be safe there."

Safe? Buck wouldn't feel safe until he was back in La Mesilla, or Las Cruces. He pushed himself on, as hard as he could. At times he tugged on the reins of the laboring horse when it wanted to slow the pace. He was near exhaustion when they broke through a grove of mesquite trees and saw the homestead only a few hundred yards ahead.

"Oh, Buck, we made it," Lucinda said as she slid from the saddle to Buck's side. She threw her arms around him and drew his head down to her. She kissed him with a passion Buck had never before known. Buck slumped to the sand, heaving nearly as badly as the horse. His mind raced with thoughts induced by Lucinda's kiss, but his body was spent. He reached up to Lucinda for help getting up. He pointed to the adobe block farmhouse.

"Let's go," he said, "You've got to get into something dry. You'll catch pneumonia, or something. Pulling on the reins, he started plodding in that direction.

Several of the young Apache men retrieved Stone's buggy. Stormy pawed and snorted while he tugged against his reins. Stone figured it was the smell of blood and the unfamiliar odors of the Apaches upsetting him. Dinger pranced nervously back and forth in front of Stone. He growled and barked whenever any of the men moved their way.

Stone strapped his leg back on, then slowly walked to the buggy and climbed up on the seat. He was very surprised to find that nothing had been disturbed or removed. He'd expected them to have pilfered his bag and found his gun. Even Judge's leather bag was still intact.

Stone noticed most of the men kept their distance from him. Suddenly, something crossed his mind.

Maybe they think I have unusual power. Maybe they're afraid of me.

However, reality overrode those thoughts, and he concluded they probably wanted him for something—then they'd kill him.

Stone looked over at the half-dozen young men who were working over Judge's lifeless body. Stone shuddered, then looked away. The blond headed woman approached him again.

"You come. No run. Run you die. You come with us."

Stone nodded. He fell in line near the rear of the column of scantily clad men and what was most likely their families. They circled south around the plains. Then they climbed up into the mountains where the trail narrowed and became troublesome for the buggy. They reached the snow line and drifts soon became ankle deep.

Without warning, they dropped down into a canyon. Stone picked up the smell of smoke. They must be coming to a rancheriá, an Apache camp. Stone knew well that Apaches rarely took adult, male captives. Might he become the object of some ritual torture?

Then, there it was. A handful of dried-brush and elk skin wickiups surrounded by a dozen or so women and a few children playing by the fires. Over by one of the fires were another four men. One of them was very tall and had an unusually large head.

Mangas Coloradas? That's got to be him. Maybe he'll want to oversee my torture himself.

Stone had heard several tales of this well-known Membriño chief. He sensed a sulfur smell mingling in the air amidst the smoke. They were at one of the many mineral laden, hot, artesian springs that bubbled out of the rocky crags in this area. The Apaches used this steamy water for warmth and healing.

This wasn't a village. Nothing with these people was permanent. They had no such word for "home" in their language. However, by the looks of the area, they used it frequently for a camp.

The leader of the group who'd captured Stone now motioned for him to get down from his buggy. He then motioned for Stone to unharness Stormy and hand him over to the boy who seemed to be tending their horses. Then, this Apache man joined some of the other men at one of the fires.

"This might be it for us, old boy," Stone said to Stormy while he stripped the harness from him. "You might be useful to them for a while, but I see my chances as being slim to none. You be ready, in case I get some kind of break."

You're dreaming, Stone then told himself. There would be no way he could sneak off, jump on a horse and flee. He knew full well he couldn't ride a horse in the best of conditions.

Turning Stormy over to this young boy, Stone climbed back up on his buggy seat, and awaited further instructions. Fear brought back thoughts of his captivity and eventual escape from Mexico many years ago. That kindled a slight glimmer of hope.

As the sun lowered, Stone wrapped himself tightly in his blanket. Dinger jumped up beside him. Time passed by, it started to become dark, and the temperature plummeted.

The numerous fires looked inviting. However, Stone was too intimidated to walk up to one and sit by its warmth. He feared that if the Apaches didn't kill him tonight, he'd most likely freeze to death by morning.

Hunger pangs shot through his stomach. Mixed in with the wood smoke, the sulfur, the human and animal smells, Stone detected the aroma of meat cooking over a fire. He tried to shut that out of his mind. He closed his eyes and leaned his head back. He slid his hand down into his valise, felt around for his Bible, then pulled it out. It was too dark to read, but strangely, he found some comfort in just holding it.

Are you here, God? Can I count on you as your book says? Not that I deserve anything.

Then Stone's mind slipped into the morbid truth of his situation.

God, if I died here now, if I don't make it tonight, what will happen to me? I've read about Heaven, then I've read about Hell, too. But, well, what about me? Where will I go? I'm not sure, God. I never once gave the likes of this any thought, not until these last few weeks. These thoughts now are even more chilling that this cold. How do I know, God?

Stone put his Bible back into the leather satchel. Then in the dark, he slid out his little revolver. He slipped it into his coat pocket. Little good against this whole band, he knew, but it might hold them off for a few more minutes.

The men continued their parley around one fire. Stone knew they controlled his fate. He searched for the blond headed woman, but couldn't see her.

His body was now shivering uncontrollably. He wrapped his lone blanket tighter, but it didn't help.

Suddenly, the elk-skin flap over the opening of one of the wickiups pushed open. A slender woman then emerged carrying a young boy about three-years-old. Stone saw the happy look on the boy's face, he saw the bright colored clothes he wore, then he saw the soft deerskin boot he had on the foot of his one leg.

That's it! They want me to make this boy a leg such as mine—then they'll kill me.

The woman and boy went to the fire of the men in council. Then, the blond headed woman appeared out of a wickiup. She and the woman with the boy walked toward Stone. When they reached him, the captive woman took the boy, held him out to Stone and spoke.

"You make leg for Kenta. You fix Kenta. Them say you live."

Them say you live, she'd said. Would they really let him go? Stone knew the chances were small, yet he had no choice. At least he'd live long enough to make this leg.

"I'll make the boy a leg. You and the others must help. There are things I will need. First, tell me your name."

"Name?"

"Yes, what was your name before you were taken from your family."

"Name?" she repeated. She looked at Stone with a blank look. Then it was slowly replaced with a smile.

"Esther. My name was Esther."

"Esther. That's a pretty name. I'm Parson Stone. Tell them the Great Father has sent me."

"Them know. Them know. You fix Kenta's leg. We help. Come now. Come to fire—eat."

———

Stone awoke the next morning. He'd been given one of the wickiups to sleep in. It gave some protection against the elements. He again was served some boiled meat. What it was he knew not, nor did he care. He'd told Esther the things he needed: soft yet tough leather thongs, the sheepskin from his buggy, some stiff rawhide, and a good piece of hardwood.

Esther soon showed up with everything he asked for except the wood.

"Them go find wagon them burned. Bring back wood so you say," Esther said. "Be back when sun is up." Esther pointed straight up.

Stone nodded. He'd tried to explain to Esther that what he needed was wood from a piece of mining equipment or a wagon, anything with a piece of good oak or hickory large enough for a leg for little Kenta. Apparently, she'd understood him.

What was her story? How long had she been captive? Stone decided not to try and talk about anything until he'd made Kenta's leg. Maybe they could talk then—if he was still alive.

Stone soaked the rawhide in water. He cut a piece off his seat cushion and started fashioning the harness needed to hold the leg on. Kenta sat on an elk skin and played with Dinger most of the time.

As Esther had predicted, shortly after noon the men came into camp dragging a six-foot piece of the wagon tongue, burned off at one end. Stone tried to let the men know this would work, and he was pleased. He had no saw or rasp, only a small knife. He took his measurements, then started the ardent task of whittling through this stone-hard wood. By nightfall, he was less than halfway through on one end. Some of the men seemed to be getting nervous.

"Them want know when Kenta have leg," Esther asked.

"Tomorrow," Stone said. Once he had it cut to the right length, he planned to burn around the middle, scrape away the charred wood, then continue that process. He wanted the shaft of the leg to be a spindle of less than an inch to reduce the weight. The top where it would be attached to Kenta's hip and the bottom where it would serve as a foot would be left the full size of the tongue.

All day long the next day, Stone had many curious eyes watching his every move. None offered to help. The sun was going down when he made the final knots in the lace, and he motioned for Kenta's mother to bring her son, so he could fit the leg. It took quite some time to make the adjustments in the straps and padding.

Finally, Kenta stood on his new leg. His mother held his hand, then started to pull him forward. He stumbled and fell. She picked him up. Then, they started forward again. This time he took two steps, then fell again. On a third attempt he walked, with the help of his mother, across the ground into the arms of an older lady who Stone figured to be his grandmother, or aunt.

The men started talking among themselves, all at once, seeming to be happy. Mangas Coloradas raised his hand and there was silence. He motioned for Stone to return to the wickiup where he'd spent the last two nights. Stone knew this was it. Now they'd decide his fate.

I did all I could do, God. Now it's up to you, I'd say. You and them.

Stone slept little that night. Outside the Apaches had a celebration dance. The thumping of drums and the continuous chanting was the most unsettling thing he'd ever heard. Even Dinger was restless.

Come morning, there was a lot of activity in the camp. Stone stayed in the wickiup. No one brought him anything. After some time, he realized things were quiet outside. He waited for a few moments longer, trying to see through the sticks and skins, then he decided it was time to crawl out and see what was going on.

He saw no one. Using his cane and the side of the wickiup, he stood up and looked around. They'd left his buggy, still untouched, and over by a cedar tree was Stormy. It was then that Stone saw that he wasn't really alone. Beside Stormy stood Esther and another woman. Esther then came over to him.

"You go now. Them have fear to harm you. Think Great Spirit send you. Not even take you horse. Never do I see this before."

"Come with me. This is your chance. I'll take you back to your people, wherever they are."

"Come with you?" Esther's face lit up. "Me come with you?"

"Yes. You don't belong here. You're not one of them. You—"

"No. Belong here. Go. You go now." With that, her smile left, and she turned and walked back to the other woman, swung up on a blanket-laden horse, then started away. She turned back once and stared at Stone for a few seconds, then again, she followed the other woman.

"Goodbye, Esther," Stone said, even though he knew she couldn't hear him. He suddenly thought of the nurse in that Mexican hospital. She'd also vanished out of his life after saving him. Now Esther. He then thought of Laura. He closed his eyes and stood there in silence for several minutes.

"I'm alive, Dinger. I should be shouting for joy. However, what does living hold for me? Will I be sorry it didn't end here?"

Stone walked over to Stormy, untied him and led him to the buggy. As he hitched up the harness, he started thinking about God. Had God heard his pleading and saved him? Was this the miracle he'd cried out for? If God had saved him, then he'd be obligated to him. How would God want to collect on his debt? Owing some man was bad enough—but being obligated to God? That thought caused Stone great concern.

He slowly rode back to where he and Judge had been attacked. He wanted to bury the remains of Judge, but found that nearly all of what the Apaches didn't destroy, the coyotes and buzzards had. He gathered up what bones he could find, then, lacking a shovel, he buried them under a pile of rocks. He knew it was strange, but he suddenly missed Judge. He felt sorry for him.

Deep thoughts entered his mind. If there was a life after death, where was Judge now? How would he ever explain this to anyone? Standing over the makeshift grave, he again thought of Laura. Suddenly, he was surrounded by a host of old companions: anger, despair, hatred, confusion, depression, they all took their turn working on his mind.

He took Judge's leather bag and rummaged through its contents. A clean suit of clothes, his hidden card rigging, three new decks of cards, and a nearly-full bottle of expensive Tennessee whiskey. He tossed the bag and its contents over on top of the rock grave—all but the bottle. That he put on the buggy seat. He then climbed up on the seat and whistled for Dinger.

"Go on, Stormy. Let's get as far from here as we can. May I never have to come this way ever again." He looped the reins around his wooden leg, then picked up the bottle and popped the cork. He put it to his lips and took a good swallow.

"Phew!" he said when the whiskey bit all the way down. "It's been a while." He tipped the bottle again.

Later that evening, Stone approached the trail along the Rio Grande. It was much warmer down here. There wasn't even a hint of snow or sleet. The sun had warmed his back while he'd gone easterly all afternoon. He reached for the bottle again. It was gone. He groggily remembered now that sometime back it was empty, and he'd tossed it.

His body now craved sleep. His eyes kept going shut, and his head bobbed. He pulled hard on the reins and drew Stormy to a stop under a cottonwood tree. He swung his leg over the side, trying to find the step. He leaned too far and tumbled out of the buggy, hitting his head on a rock. There he lay, lacking consciousness. The sun went down behind the mountains. With the temperature rapidly dropping and the wind picking up, Dinger tried to revive his master. Giving up, he lay beside him, his back against Stone's injured head.

CHAPTER 14

For several days, Buck had spent every possible minute with Lucinda. As the sun set the third day, he sat on a banco under the portico of the cantina watching the scattered puffs of white clouds in the western sky turn pink, then orange and finally purple. Lucinda came out and sat beside him. Neither said anything for some time. Lucinda then broke the silence.

"For what you be so quiet, Buck? Have I done a thing displeasing to you?"

"No, of course not. I'm just thinking. I can't stay any longer. Later tonight I must go back to my men. Unless one of them has been checking up on me over here, they don't even know if I'm alive. There's just nothing in me that wants to go up north. I know it's going to be cold up there and—"

Buck was silent for a moment, then looked at Lucinda. "It's not the cold. The truth is, I don't want to leave you."

"Ah, Buck. That is sweet of you to say. May it always be so."

"I ain't been dealt much of a hand in life, Lucinda. Until I met you, it seemed I was frettin' away what little I had. Got no pa. Ma's dead now, too. Never had no brothers or sisters or the like. A fella needs someone. When I was little and my pa didn't come home, I missed him so awful much, but I still had my ma. Now that she's gone..."

After a time of silence, Lucinda asked Buck a question.

"What will you do to those two who killed Señor Rumbaugh?"

"Killed Rumbaugh? Guess I can't be sure they actually did it. I'd bet supper for a week they were there, though. If they actually put the rope around his neck, unless they admit it, I'll probably never know."

"Sí. But they could have stopped it," Lucinda said.

"Yeah. 'Spect they could have. But then, I wasn't there."

"You can't turn them over to the Mexican authorities," Lucinda said. "They would not live to trial. If they did, what kind of trial would it be?"

"And I have no way to do anything here," Buck said. "The crime took place in Mexico."

"So they go free? No punishment for such a terrible deed?" Lucinda asked.

"That might be so," Buck said. "I'd be inclined to think their conscience would be punishing them. Some men don't seem to have much of that, though."

"Sí. Men can be such brutes. Not you, Buck. You're so kind and gentle and—"

"Lucinda!" her aunt suddenly yelled out through the open door. "Los customers. You talka you man in dí light of dí moon."

"Later, Buck. We talk later," Lucinda said as she jumped to her feet, then rushed back into the cantina.

Buck sat there thinking of what to do about the Rumbaugh incident. Should he tell Governor Baylor? With Rumbaugh being an avowed Yankee, who'd sought protection in Mexico, Buck doubted if anyone in the Confederacy would care what had happened to such a man.

Did being a Yankee make Rumbaugh any less of a man? Much of this Confederacy thing seemed to be about slaves—but more seemed to be about power.

What was in this war for him? Buck wasn't sure he wanted to die just so the plantation owners could keep their slaves and a handful of powerful men got to be even more powerful. He'd joined to get away from old Roe, his stepfather, and his fear of going to jail after beating Roe nearly to death.

Still, he enjoyed the challenge of being a scout, a spy, of outwitting the other side. He often wondered if he had what it took to face the enemy close at hand and to kill someone staring back at him. Something in him told him he'd soon have to find out.

Again, the thought of running away came to mind. But to where? He couldn't go back to east Texas. He was sure he was a wanted man there already, without adding desertion to his name. Mexico was out. He'd been to the rugged desert to the west and saw no way to survive there. Colorado, California and the other western states, by all accounts he heard, would soon be part of the Confederacy. There'd be no safety there. Then there was Lucinda. He couldn't leave her and he couldn't take her into danger on the run as a fugitive.

Tonight, he'd go back to La Mesilla, then tomorrow he'd start north. Maybe it wouldn't be so bad. Maybe in a few weeks he could come back and see Lucinda.

———

While Parson Stone lay unconscious several hundred yards off the trail, his mind wandered through a maze of dreams. First, he fought off a large bear until he had no more strength. Then the bear turned into an Apache warrior and he had to fight all over again. Breaking free and running for his life, he was captured by the Mexican Army, back down in old Mexico. He then escaped from them and ran toward someone calling his name.

Suddenly, he stood at Judge's grave, and a hand reached up for him out of that pile of rocks. The rocks started rolling away, and then Judge's scalpless skull popped up and called Stone's name. He ran from that, then suddenly he saw Laura standing precariously at the edge of a high mountain caprock. He ran to save her, when suddenly, a faceless man stepped into his path, and they wrestled. He broke free and ran toward Laura. Then suddenly, everything started shaking and Laura disappeared.

He kept shaking and shaking while he heard noises that grew louder and louder. Growls—no, they were voices.

Slowly, consciousness returned to his mind. He forced open one eye. The sunlight caused him to quickly close it. He then slightly opened both eyes, letting in a slit of the morning light.

"Parson. Parson Stone. Wake up. It's me, Captain Graydon. Are you alright?

Stone raised his right hand to acknowledge Captain Graydon's presence. Slowly, he worked his leg, his good one, around to his side, then pushed himself up to a sitting position.

How did I get here?

His head thumped as if the Apaches were beating one of their drums inside it. As Dinger stood beside him, nudging him with his nose, his mind spun back pieces of the previous days.

"I must have fallen," Stone said. "I don't remember."

"You had us worried. We were on our way to meet up with a new unit up north of here. Your dog came chasing after us when we were passing by on the trail over there. If he hadn't, we'd have ridden right on by. You're hidden from our sight down here."

Stone reached over and brushed his hand over Dinger's head. The old dog wagged his tail. Stone checked his wooden leg, then he reached up to the hand Captain Graydon had lowered down to assist him up to his feet.

"I'm much obliged to you, Captain. I don't really know how—"

That bottle. It was that cursed bottle.

"What I mean is, we were—"

No! You can't tell about the Apaches without telling about Judge and what you were doing out in the mountains.

"Well, I guess I just slipped and fell getting down to make camp last night."

"We'll take you to the surgeon at Fort Craig. I'll have your buggy driven and—"

"No. No thank you. I'm fine, really. Just a bump on the head. I've got to get to Santa Fe, Captain. What day is this now anyway?"

"Day? Day of the month, you mean?"

"Yes."

"December fifteenth." Captain Graydon said.

Stone nodded.

"Parker, get up a fire," Captain Graydon ordered. "Make coffee for the parson, some of that dried beef, also. We have to get the parson's blood flowing, his belly full, and his mind fully awake."

Stone worked his way over toward his buggy. His head swirled and pounded. With one hand on the harness to steady himself, he reached out with his other hand and rubbed Stormy under the jaw. Only ten days until Christmas and he had nearly a week's travel to get there. It was time, then. Time to go and learn to the truth about Lincoln's letter and the cache of gold.

Buck rode into his camp in the middle of the night. He'd said his goodbye to Lucinda about midnight, saddled his horse, then crossed the river. He now stripped his gear and hobbled his horse with the others, all seven of them. So, everyone was here. He felt a twinge of guilt that he hadn't cared more about his men. The first thing in the morning he had some things to settle with Lacy and Kirk—Sly and Billy too, for that matter.

He took off his spurs, then walked quietly into camp. He found his half-shelter still strung up. He then spread out his bedroll and stretched out his tired body on it. He jerked his blanket over him. In minutes, he was asleep.

He awoke to the smell of coffee. He sat up, stretched his cold, stiff muscles, then he rose and looked around. The camp was eerily quiet—no one said anything. He figured everyone awaited some sign from him. Just how upset was he?

"Ya'll primed and flush to head north?" Buck finally asked, still not looking directly at anyone.

"Sure, Sergeant Rafter," Lacy said. "Say when."

Buck casually took out his revolver, then removed the cylinder. He removed the caps, then pushed out the balls and powder charges with a small brass bullet remover from his pocket.

He should have done this immediately after sloshing through the river when rescuing Lucinda. He took his time and carefully reloaded with fresh powder, replaced the balls, then he dropped in new caps.

No one said anything. Buck snapped the cylinder into the frame. He spun it and started to put it away. Then, he suddenly re-drew it and pointed it at Lacy, who sat on a log about ten feet in front of him. Buck snapped the hammer back and leveled the barrel square between Lacy's eyes.

"Hold it! Sergeant," Lacy cried as he slid from the log to the sand. "I know you're upset. Figure you got some cause to be so. Just keep your thumb on that hammer and let's me and you talk."

"Talk then," Buck said. "Why'd you kill that old man?"

"Wasn't me, not Kirk, neither. It was them boys from Fort Bliss. Honest. We didn't know what they had in mind. Tell him, Kirk."

"He's right, Sergeant. I swear it on my mother's grave. Besides, he was just an old Yankee. That's what we came all that way across that forsaken desert to do isn't it? Kill Yankees, right?"

"Soldiers, maybe, not harmless old men," Buck said.

"Ain't no harmless Yankees," Lacy said.

"He was a good friend of Simeon Hart," Buck said. "Governor Baylor knew him, too. If I don't kill you, they probably will."

"How was we to know?" Lacy said. "Besides, it wasn't us. I told you so. Just put that hog-leg back in your belt and let's get out of here. You need us, all of us. Ain't nothing we can do about that old man now. We didn't know that funnin' with that old Yankee would cause you any grief."

Buck raised the muzzle of his revolver slightly, then squeezed the trigger. The bark of the shot cut the cold morning air. The ball whizzed mere inches over Lacy's head. Lacy dropped face to the ground as did several others.

"Alright! I'm sorry. Is that what you want to hear? I'm sorry, Sergeant. Honest, Sergeant Buck, you gotta believe me. It wasn't us. We didn't know. Honest we didn't."

Buck swung the gun to Kirk, who sat nervously on the sand, leaning against his saddle. He looked down at his boots. Buck cocked the hammer, then let it back down. He repeated this four more times, then finally left the hammer down on the empty chamber. He then reached across his belly and slid the gun into its soft, cross-draw holster.

"Mount up," he said, as he looked hard at each of the men. "We're burnin' daylight."

Parson Stone guided his buggy into the town-square of Albuquerque. He'd been traveling for three days since Captain Graydon had found him down by the river. It had turned cold again. He had his coat drawn up tightly around his neck and had a blanket wrapped around his shoulders. He didn't want to spend the night in the dilapidated old church. He yearned for a hot meal, a hot bath and a real bed.

He spied a livery off to the west side of town, on a street leading toward the river. Pulling up to the open door, Stone stepped down off the buggy, then walked forward, stopping to talk to Stormy.

"We'll get you a good dose of grain, some molasses, too, if they have any. We'll have to leave soon, though. It's time we get to Santa Fe," he said while he rubbed the soft hair under Stormy's jaw. Stone then turned and stepped inside the barn.

"Mercy. Ain't seen the likes of you here 'bouts before," was the greeting by the stable hand. "You some kind of preacher, or such?"

"Didn't mean to startle you. Stone's my name. Parson Justin Stone. The Methodists sent me out here to keep a handle on their churches. Our people, too."

"Methodists you say?" the stable hand asked. "Ain't many of them here 'bouts. Got a church out at the edge of town, but I can't say as I ever knowed anyone who ever went there."

"Had 'em in Missouri, though. They did tend to get excited. Shoutin' Methodists, we called them back there. Tell you what, Preacher, this ain't no good time to be starting no new church," the stable hand continued. "Hear tell the cussed rebels be a comin' most any day now."

Stone raised his left hand as he shook his head.

"I'm not here to start anything. I'm on my way to Santa Fe. Just need to put up my horse for a night, or so. Give him the best. Molasses and corn, if you have any."

"'Spect I can rustle up a feedbag full of that for you. Beings you ain't here to do no hellfire preachin'. I'll oblige you with whatever y'all want. Four bits will get you the best I got."

Stone pulled out a half-dollar piece and handed it over.

"Where can I get a good meal and a room?" Stone asked.

"Widow Vega's got some rooms. Two blocks over yonder," he said as he motioned northward. "Best darned cook I know, too. You tell her Dusty Hood sent you over. She'll do you right."

"Much obliged, Mr. Hood. Can I leave my dog here?"

"Shoot yes. I'll bring in that fancy buggy I see out there, too. Won't be so cold on you in the morning. Ain't never knowed the likes of any preacher to have one such as that. Methodist, huh? Bit showy, I'd say."

"I'll see you in the morning, Mr. Hood," Stone said as he turned to leave.

"Yeah. Hey, Parson, I'd lay off the preachin' 'round here. Don't think many here-a-bouts would be hankerin' for any hellfire damnation talk. It'd just rile them up and do no good anyway."

Stone nodded, then walked through the door and headed toward the widow Vega's boarding house.

Three days later, in the waning afternoon sunlight, Stone arrived in Santa Fe. Having traveled all day on coffee only, he ate heartily of the plate full of tamales, frijoles and rice set before him in a cantina he'd spied entering town. When finished, he inquired about the location of the Methodist Church. He was pleasantly surprised to find it only a block from a livery—

neither one being far from this cantina. Finding the stable, but no one attending it, he turned Stormy into an empty stall and forked him some hay.

He closed the barn door and walked in the now near darkness over to the church. He pushed open the door and tried to see inside. He saw a candle on the windowsill beside the door. He struck a match, then put it to the candlewick. The meager, flickering flame illuminated the interior of the small building enough that Stone could see his way around. To his surprise, there was a small stove with a good stock of kindling and logs beside it. It was as if someone had anticipated his arrival.

"We're in luck, old boy," Stone said to Dinger. "I'll have this place warm in no time. Lay down there by the door and chew on that bone the nice lady down at that cantina threw out to you."

Half an hour later, Stone watched the flames in the stove flicker and jump while the sap-laden piñon wood popped and cracked. After he put in another large log, Stone closed the stove door, then he stretched out on his blanket.

Stone awoke to Dinger's growl. The first rays of the morning sun were piercing through the large, stained-glass window behind the pulpit, casting a multi-colored image on the western wall. Another growl from Dinger woke Stone more fully.

He suddenly realized he wasn't alone. He reached for his cane. He slowly pushed himself up to a sitting position. Then, he worked himself around to face the rear entry door. Standing in the aisle, not ten feet away, stood a man. Stone stared into this intruder's eyes. Neither spoke for a moment, then the stranger broke the silence.

"Buenos días, Señor. Permit me to present myself. I am Señor Juan Diego Don Francisco. And you, Señor, who might you be?"

CHAPTER 15

Stone stared at this man who had just introduced himself. Juan Diego Don Francisco, that was who he said he was. His palomino and crimson silk, bolero style jacket, his tight Californio pants, along with his flat-crowned, flat-brimmed, beaver hat were all decorated lavishly with polished, silver conchos. The deep-wine colored serape that draped over his shoulders was of a fine, soft fleece, most likely from the belly of the angora goat, Stone believed. Here stood a man of distinction, a Spanish or Mexican hidalgo.

Stone cleared his throat. He pushed himself up to a standing position, all the while studying this other man. Stone leaned on his cane, then finally spoke.

"Pardon the slowness of my response, Señor Francisco. I seemed to have been soundly asleep and was unprepared to greet anyone."

Juan Diego nodded, all the while Stone felt this man's eyes intently studying him.

"I'm Parson Justin Stone. The Methodists sent me out here to keep an eye on our buildings, also to help our people. I got in late last night. Are you one of our parishioners?"

Stone knew well that wouldn't be so. He was stalling for time and looking for some indication of just who this Juan Diego Don Francisco was. Stone hobbled forward, extending his hand to Juan Diego, who'd gracefully also moved toward him, then took Stone's hand firmly.

"My sincerest pleasure to make your acquaintance, Señor Parson Stone. How has your trip been? Where did it originate?"

"The trip has been hard, but good. I actually started in Washington DC, back east." Stone doubted he was talking to a secessionist, even if this wasn't his contact.

"Washington? Ah, the home of the bluecoat soldier. Symbolized by the great eagle of the sky. Someday I would esteem to visit that city."

Bluecoat soldier—Eagle of the sky—

"It can be cold back there this time of the year."" Stone said, staring intently into the other man's eyes. "It seems that even those eagles turn blue from the cold. Being one who has traveled with the freedom of the bird, I've been called that before: a blue eagle." Stone continued to stare deeply into the eyes of Juan Diego, who stared back with equal intensity. With a slight nod of Juan Diego's head, there broke a warming expression in his dark eyes, then a smile replaced the cold-serious expression on his face.

"Señor Stone, the blue-eagle I requested."

"We shouldn't be seen together here," Stone said as he nodded in agreement as to who he was. "Where can we meet?"

"I will send my sirviente, Orlando, for you later. You shall be my guest at my hacienda. It is customary for me to greet traveling businessmen, and others, in this manner. Your presence there, at least one time, will not be suspicious. Be prepared in one hour. Until then, Señor Stone, adios." Juan Diego turned and walked down the hard, wooden aisle as the large, silver rowels in his spurs jingled lightly.

Stone went to a side window and watched while Juan Diego rode his large, white stallion slowly up the street.

The contact had been made. Judging from this meeting, what Juan Diego had written to Lincoln would prove to be a reality. Now, a new problem presented itself: how to get such a large quantity of gold out of here with the Confederate army poised to arrive in mere days and with most certainly rebel spies and scouts already here.

"Come on, Dinger. Let's go over to that stable and straighten up with the owner. We just might be here for a while."

Stone walked into the stable to find the owner forking hay into Stormy's stall. The man looked up when he heard Stone approach.

"You and he go together, I'd say," the man said as he nodded toward Stormy. "Good horse. Fancy buggy out there, too. By the looks of you, you're either a preacher or a gambler. If you're a preacher, that rig and this horse don't fit, and if you're a gambler, them clothes be a mite stuffy. We get some mighty strange drifters in this town, but I declare, you just might be one of the most curious yet."

"Name's Stone. Parson Justin Stone. The horse and buggy were a gift, though I see nothing wrong with a preacher having the likes of it. I came to make arrangements with you, Mr., ah?"

"Ackley. Most folks call me Slim. 'Course with age and all, I ain't quite the way I used to be," he said as he patted his slightly bulging stomach. "Tell me, Preacher, what in the name of all that's good are you doing here, now? Ain't you heard, we're about to be invaded by them rebels?"

Stone went through his usual explanation of why he was here, then he got down to business.

"I may be here for some time. Might be in and out, but I expect to be here much of the next month, several weeks anyway. How about I put up ten dollars against my charges? When that runs out, or I move on, we'll straighten out then?"

"Sound fair to me. I've got some of the area's best corn and have some oats from Missouri and—"

"Give him your best treatment. Keep an eye on my buggy, tack also, please. I'll make that all right with you."

"Don't worry about a thing, Preacher. This is the first time any preacher handed me money. They always come around wantin' in my pockets, or wantin' free services, or such. You ever preach here, I might even come to hear you. Now that'd be a first."

"Well, Mr. Ackley, I just might be preaching something come Christmas. Gotta go now, but I might be back later today."

Stone left and walked back to the church. He thought about going over to the town square, but didn't want to attract any attention to himself, not until he'd met with Juan Diego.

Besides, that carriage would be showing up shortly, and he didn't want to make the driver wait. Stone pegged Juan Diego as one who put stock in punctuality and common courtesy. He was obviously a very successful man who commanded authority. Stone knew such men had to be handled with much care. They could often be strong headed and easily offended.

A short time later, after a short buggy ride, Stone admired the substantial, almost military-like, compound occupied by Juan Diego. As the enclosed carriage rolled through the portón he observed the stoutness of the adobe wall protecting the home and its supporting structures. Juan Diego stood under the massive front portico, awaiting the arrival of his guest.

"Welcome to my fair weather casa, Señor Stone. You are my guest of honor," Juan Diego said. "Come, let me introduce my family. Please understand that we are not usually here this time of the year. We traditionally reside in Santa Fe only during the heat of the summer. Down at the mines, that is south of Tubac down of the Santa Cruz river, the summer becomes unbearable hot for my wife. Her health, sí, her health is not so good, Señor. Now, here in this frigid cold, I fear my wife will never see the warmth of the mine country again. We will talk more of that later. Come now."

Stone followed Juan Diego across the saltillo tiled floor into a room facing an interior courtyard. The room had a kiva fireplace and at least a dozen wall niches, some held lit candles. Against the far wall of the room stood a large, hand-carved, four-poster bed. On it lay a frail form of a woman propped up on pillows. Her head was turned away from the doorway, facing someone sitting on the far side of the bed.

"Señor Stone, my wife, my true and faithful helper for nearly fifty years, Doña Ana Gardea Francisco."

Ana turned to face Stone, then smiled and raised her right hand to him. Stone took this limp, bony limb into his own hand, holding it gently.

"It is with pleasure that I meet you," Stone said. Ana nodded, then weakly turned her head and looked toward the person sitting on a chair at the far side of her bed.

"My daughter, Miranda Maria. My nurse and caretaker" Ana weakly said. "I am embarrassed to not be able to give you a proper reception, Señor Stone. I've had to turn all formalities, and even the basic functions of my life, over to Miranda Maria's care."

Stone let loose of Ana's hand when his eyes met those of Miranda Maria. With coal-black eyes, and a warmth that seemed to fill the room, she smiled at him. Not that she was a stunning, youthful beauty—she wasn't. She was a mature woman of grace and elegance, with an essence of goodness about her.

"It is my pleasure to meet you, Señor Stone," Miranda Maria said. "It is late in the morning, and I doubt if you have had a thing to eat."

"I—I had coffee, warmed up from last night. You must not—"

"Coffee? You must take better care of yourself. Mother will be fine for a while. I shall fix you breakfast. Father will excuse us, won't you, Father?"

Juan Diego nodded his affirmation.

"Come with me. Tell me about yourself," Miranda Maria said, rising and motioning for Stone to follow her."

"Por favor, my daughter is right," Juan Diego said to Stone. "Excuse me, but I wish to stay a spell here with my wife."

"I shall return to you later then, Señora Francisco," Stone said, then he followed Miranda Maria out of the room and down the hall toward the separate cocina area.

"Be so kind to sit at this table and talk to me," Miranda Maria said after they reached this cooking area. She took out a large, black skillet. "Father tells me you are the one Mr. Lincoln sent to us, that you are not a real preacher. Do you know him? Mr. Lincoln? Oh, to know such a great man."

"I'd—I'd rather not talk about any of those things. I don't know—"

"My father keeps no secrets from me. He was always that way with Mother. However, now as you see…"

"You are usually down at the mine in the winter, right?" Stone asked. "Have you been here this time of the year before?"

"Never. I have never been so cold, nor have I seen so much snow. I am told there is much more to come. I fear so much for my mother. I believe we must go south, no matter what the risk."

"To Tubac? That wouldn't work now. The Union has pulled all its troops from there and placed nearly all of them here along the Rio Grande. Many are down at Fort Craig. The area of your mine is now technically ruled by the Confederacy from their La Mesilla office. However, I'm told it is the Apaches—"

"Ah! Those evil devils. No one has told you, I am sure, but the Apache, they killed my husband three years ago. It was I who found his body, what they left of it. And, too, they took my son. I have not seen him since. We get word at the mine from traveling peasants, and others, who say he is now one of them. They see him on their raids and say he is as one of them. My sweet, gentle Jorge. I cannot imagine him riding with those heathens, killing, stealing and all the other vile things they do. I refuse to accept this as the end. Some day, he shall come back to me."

"I'm sorry to hear of this. How old is Jorge?"

"He is now sixteen. Three years and I have not seen or touched him. Mother has never given up hope, either. I believe that is one thing that keeps her hanging on. She wants to see Jorge back home with us."

Jorge is sixteen—Buck is eighteen. Maybe she's not that much younger than I am.

"Do you have any other children?" Stone asked.

"Sadly, none. Only Jorge." Both were silent for a moment.

"Tell me about you, Señor Stone. My woman's instincts tell me you have many fascinating things to tell about. Is there a Mrs. Stone?"

Stone weighed his words before replying. He'd seldom talked about Laura to anyone—never to a stranger. It was too personal. However, maybe he could tell just a little.

"There used to be. She's dead now."

"Then, you too, know the way it hurts to lose the one you love. Children? You have children?"

"Buck, my son. He—"

You're telling her too much. The old Colonel Tyrone Rafter wouldn't have told her anything.

"Buck, doesn't know I'm alive. He thinks I was killed fifteen years ago in Mexico. He's around here, somewhere. He's, well, he's with the Confederacy. Of course, that's just what I hear. I haven't seen him. I couldn't identify myself to him yet anyway. Before I leave this area, though, once my business with your father is completed that is, I must make contact with Buck.

"I shouldn't be telling you this," Stone said. "I've never talked about such personal things as this to anyone, well, I told Lincoln, but that's all. Everyone thinks I'm dead, really. Even Laura, my wife, did. She'd married another, a real brute he turned out to be, then she and Buck moved to Texas and…"

Stone had closed his eyes while he talked about Laura and Buck. He suddenly felt Miranda Maria's soft hand on his. He then noticed how forcefully he was gripping the edge of the table. Her touch felt so soothing. It sent a tingling warmth all through his body. He took a deep breath, relaxed his rigid grip on the table, and then leaned back in his chair.

"No more, Señor Stone. Tell me no more, not now. Someday, I believe you and I will talk much more. It will be good for your soul—as with mine, also. You eat now. You need your strength."

Stone nodded. He couldn't say anymore, not now, anyway. Why had he told this stranger some of his deepest held secrets? How could he be so careless? He'd broken nearly every rule he knew he needed to live by to survive as a spy. What if Miranda Maria let something slip to someone? What if—

"It's alright, Señor Stone. I know you hurt so bad inside. I know it is hard for a man to take care of what is inside of his heart. On the outside, he is big and tough, but on the inside, he is broken and weak. I know you, Señor Stone. God willing, I will help you. I will be your friend to talk to. It will be good for my hurts, also. Maybe someday, I too will see my son."

A short time later, Juan Diego took Stone into his oficina, the room where he conducted his business. He walked behind a massive, hand carved desk, then pointed to a stout, horsehair-padded chair.

"Be seated, Señor Stone. I trust my daughter was gracious with her hospitality."

"Most gracious. She's a fine lady."

Juan Diego looked at Stone, then nodded. "That she is. Her mother's daughter, that's what she has become." Juan Diego was silent for a moment, then got down to business.

"You know why you are here. You read my letter?"

"Yes. President Lincoln showed it to me. I'm sure it's no surprise that we had some doubts. You were convincing, though. That's when I became this preacher person."

Juan Diego smiled. Stone sensed he was relaxing some.

"The blue-eagle thing. What is it?" Stone asked.

"About five years ago I was taken captive by the Apaches. They had been relatively friendly up to then, but something turned them. They had me staked out by a large anthill in the sand. They had poured sand in my eyes and had my mouth held open with a sharp stick. They had smeared my face with honey, and I soon had ants all over me, even in and out of my throat.

"Some say that one treated this way dies from their mind going crazy. I agree. When near that point, I thought I heard gunshots. Then, I saw this thing standing over me. It was big and blue. To me, in my condition, it looked to be an eagle. A big, blue eagle.

"It turned out to be a U. S. Cavalry sergeant. He got me out of there. He saved my life. It is for this, and all the other times the Union soldiers helped me, that I now make this donation. I have more than I will ever need. If I can help save the Union—"

"Where is the gold?" Stone asked, hoping he wasn't being too bold.

"That would not be good for you to know at this time. I know, my wife knows and so does Miranda Maria. I think Orlando has a suspicion. He was not here when we ever hid any of it, but he may have talked to someone who was.

"For now, our job, and your job, Señor Stone, is to keep us alive until after this rebel invasion. Then, I will be ready to transfer the gold to wherever Mr. Lincoln wants it."

"After the invasion? You don't want to try and move it before the Confederates get here?"

"There are too many here already," Juan Diego said, shaking his head. "There are sympathizers and spies all over town. I trust the Union will somehow prevail. To try to move it now would increase the chance that it would fall into enemy hands. That would embolden them to move on and might well change the outcome of the war.

"I do not believe that either Mr. Lincoln or Mr. Davis grasps the true significance of what's about to happen here. If these rebels get into Colorado, they will go all the way to the Pacific. Then, they will sweep back through Mexico. They will control over five times the land and twenty times the minerals of the Union.

"The Union will exist no more if we do not stop these invaders here. This gold cannot help with that now. For that it is too late. However, it can help shorten things afterwards. It will save lives. But now, first, we must somehow stop these advancing rebels."

After a silence of several seconds, Juan Diego spoke again.

"You have any other questions, or is there anything you need, Señor?"

"No. I don't believe I should be seen with you. I'll go back to the church and stay there. Maybe I can find some of those parishioners and spend some time with them. I'll make plans to do what they usually do at Christmas. I've pulled off my role so far. I best not let down now."

"You do the part well. Maybe it has become more than a cover?" Juan Diego asked.

Stone looked into the eyes of this wise old Spaniard. He slightly and slowly nodded his head. Juan Diego smiled, then returned the nod.

"I will have Orlando take you back, then. He will check on you, often. Send word if you need anything, or hear anything important. Orlando is to be trusted."

"I'm most grateful for your hospitality, your daughter's also. My best to your wife."

Juan Diego nodded, then he rose.

"Hasta la vista," he said as he shook Stone's hand. They left the room and went to the portico where Juan Diego summoned Orlando.

Suddenly, Stone felt something tug at his arm. He turned and faced Miranda Maria.

"Come back, Señor Stone. I await the next time we talk. To talk is good for both of us, for you and for me."

"I'll be back," Stone heard himself say, though it was only reactive. His mind remained on this woman who seemed to have the ability to reach way down deep inside of him and touch his heart—his soul. Her smile was infectious and he felt his lips turn upward at their ends, his cheeks slightly rising.

"Vaya con Dios, Señor Stone," Juan Diego said, snapping Stone back to reality.

"Likewise, yourself. You and all your family."

Later that afternoon, Stone walked back to the cantina. He ate a good meal, then he got some scraps and another bone for Dinger. He then went back to the church. He sat and looked at his wooden leg for quite some time. He took out the small mirror he'd bought in DC and studied his face, the age it now showed. He put the mirror away, looked at his leg again, then he slumped to the floor.

He smacked his leg hard with his cane. No woman would want to be part of his life. He was past that. A mere fifty years old, and his life was washed up.

"God," he cried. "What's left in life for me? If you're real, there's got to be something."

He lay stretched out on his blanket for a long time thinking deep thoughts, mostly about Miranda Maria, then memories of Laura. Finally, he drifted off to sleep.

In the middle of the night, and out of a deep sleep, he was awakened by Dinger tugging at him. His mind was slow to become cognizant of his surroundings. Then, he quickly pushed himself up to a sitting position.

The church was on fire.

CHAPTER 16

From the old parade grounds at Fort Thorn, forty miles up the Rio Grande from La Mesilla, Buck Rafter watched the sun set behind the southern tip of the Black Range. He'd expected to be farther north by now, but had been waylaid when Governor Baylor temporarily moved his headquarters here to be nearer the upcoming attack on Fort Craig.

Last night, Buck took his men upriver, where they bumped into a Yankee scouting outfit thought to be that of Paddy Graydon's. There were a few rifle shots fired by each side, a host of verbal insults hurled through the night's darkness, then both sides retreated back their own way.

Tonight, with no orders to go out on patrol, his mind dwelt on Lucinda while he watched the sun paint the sky a brilliant orange. She was less than fifty miles away—yet it might as well be a thousand. He couldn't go see her, not without getting into trouble.

Shortly after sundown, Buck was aroused by voices. "Hey, Sergeant Rafter," came the call from across the yard. He recognized it to be Lacy's voice. He didn't respond until the group of men, four who were often found together, came close to him.

"The night's just beginning. We're going over to that hog ranch up river. Come on along. You need to loosen up."

"The last time I saw the four of you going off together, Sly and Billy didn't come home for days. Then you two—you Lacy and Kirk—don't you remember Mexico? We're pulling out in the morning. Don't give me any cause to get fired up at you. One of these days I just might—"

"You're too tight, Sergeant Buck. You pull a stunt the likes of what you did back yonder in La Mesilla, you go a shootin' your gun off and the like, I'll—"

"You'll do nothing, Lacy. Nothing. Because that's what you are, and all you'll ever be, if you don't straighten out and get serious about something."

"I ran off from my pa when he got to talkin' to me the likes of that. I won't take no such dressin' down from you, neither, be you my sergeant or if'n you was a general."

"Go, run off then. Go on. See how far it is before the Apaches get you, or maybe them Yankee scouts. Go on, Lacy."

"We're just goin' out to have some fun. We'll be back and ready to go in the morning, Sergeant," Billy said. "I ain't gettin' in no more fights with these locals. That wasn't no fun."

"Going out for fun—as with old Rumbaugh?" Buck asked. "Was that fun?"

"Forget we invited you," Lacy said. "We was just trying to help you, and you go and talk to us as if we was something we ain't. Don't ever expect an invite again."

"Sun up. We're leaving at sun up," Buck said. "I hear General Sibley arrived in Fort Bliss two days ago. Surely, that means we'll be making a move soon. We're going to be some important eyes for the main troops. I don't need you boys all whipped up on, or the likes."

"Where are we going, Sarge?" Sly asked.

"Albuquerque. Governor Baylor wants us in Albuquerque; Santa Fe, too."

———

Stone grabbed his cane and quickly pushed himself up to his feet. He used the cane to pull up his blanket, then he grabbed his coat and bag.

"Hurry, Dinger. Let's get out of here."

In mere seconds, the flames climbed the north wall, the wall farthest from the stove area where Stone had been sleeping. The dried pine boards popped and cracked as the temperature in the church rose by the second.

Stone started toward the main, back door in the most direct way, down the center aisle. He got about halfway there when the intensity of the fire on the north side of the building started collapsing that wall. That caused several of the roof timbers to drop to the floor, spreading the fire as if they were huge matches. One of those timbers fell between Stone and the door. Dinger raced back and forth as if looking for a way out. Stone pushed himself down the space between two pews, toward the south end of the building.

Reaching the wall, he threw his bag through the center window. The glass shattered into thousands of tiny shards. Whipping his cane, he smashed out the remaining chunks still held in place by the putty and mullions. He threw his blanket over the windowsill and went through the window headfirst. He used his cane to partially break his fall.

Laying on the ground, he shook his head as he winced from the stabs of pain the fall caused in various parts of his body. Gaining his senses, he pushed himself to his feet, slipped his coat over his shoulders, then grabbed his blanket from the windowsill after Dinger leaped through the open window. He twisted the straps on his wooden leg back in place, then followed Dinger around to the main door in the back of the collapsing church.

Men were running his way with buckets. From up the street came a water wagon. Stone knew all this effort was in vain. The building was made of old, dry wood that was rapidly mutating into billows of thick, black smoke peppered with shards of glowing coals.

"You did me good, old boy," Stone said to Dinger after catching his breath. He was then surprised by a voice.

"You must be the preacher I heard showed up here the other day."

Stone was startled. This voice, in its harsh, accusatory tone, came from a man who'd approached Stone from behind. Stone turned to see who was speaking to him. It was a large man who was a good ten years older than he was.

"What did you do? How did you set our church on fire?" the man continued his inquisition.

"Pardon me. I'm Parson Justin Stone. I was inside sleeping. Dinger here woke me. I slept over by the stove, by the south side. Look, see where the fire really is? It's over to the north. When I first awoke, I smelled lamp oil. Someone set this building on fire. I don't know why, or who, but someone set it on fire over against that north wall."

"Oh…yes, I see what you mean. Yes, you couldn't have started the fire from the stove area. My apology for my accusation. I'm Frederick Mills. My wife and I are, well, we practically built this church. I guess I took this a little too personal."

"Who would want to burn it?" Stone asked, as he took the hand Frederick offered in friendship.

"Wouldn't have any idea."

"I only arrived the day before yesterday, that night, really. I have no known enemies here. I think they knew I was in there, but I don't think they wanted to kill me. If they would have, they'd have started the fire closer to me, not across the building. I think they just wanted to scare or intimidate me. Any idea who'd want to run me out of town before I do anything?"

"We haven't even met here since Reverend McCoy left 'bout six months ago. I don't understand this at all," Frederick Mills said. "For sure now, you need a place to stay. When this is over, come home with me, Parson Stone. My wife, Mary, will be glad to meet you."

It took several hours for the building to burn down to a host of glowing coals and spot flames. Many people came over to Frederick Mills and Stone to express their sadness and dismay that this had happened. Stone scanned the crowd for anything suspicious. He knew that the perpetrator of a crime such as arson often mingled in the crowd, watching the fulfillment of their act.

Several times, through the smoke and flames, Stone saw a short, squat man wearing a badge who seemed to be staring at him. He figured this to be the town marshal, or a deputy. Stone figured he'd want to question him. That would be a natural part of his investigation. When all the fire was gone, along with most of the people, Stone started home with Frederick

Mills. He was somewhat surprised that by then the man with the badge was also gone.

"That man with the badge who stood across the way, is he the marshal?" Stone asked Frederick Mills.

"Huck Malone. He runs this town, alright. I don't know anyone who votes for him, yet he wins every election by a few votes. I stay clear of him anytime I can."

"He was looking at me every time I looked his way," Stone said. "I thought he'd be over and ask me some questions."

"Too many people around, I'd say. That's why he left you alone. He prefers to do his work in private. He'll most likely be hunting you up in the morning and have plenty to ask you then. Maybe he wanted to see things in daylight first. Don't think any more about it. Come, I'm sure Mary will have the coffee pot on. I know she made a maple-iced, apple strudel earlier. I can taste it now."

Stone met Mary, had some strudel and coffee, then he went to bed. Mary gave Dinger a bowl full of meat scraps, and, from outside his window, Stone could now hear him chewing on them.

The bed was soft, softer than any he'd been in for months. Still, he was unable to sleep much.

What was this about? Why the church?

He had a gnawing fear down in his gut that someone planned to use this against him. It had something to do with the gold. Someone suspected he wasn't what he claimed. But who? He'd hardly talked to anyone here. Might there be a spy among Juan Diego's friends? That could be true. Juan Diego might be the last to see that. Then, there was Marshal Malone, who'd studied him so intently when at the fire.

Stone slept in short, restless spurts the entire night. Shortly after sunup, he heard a knock at the home's front door. Then he heard Frederick talking to someone. When he heard the visitor leave, Stone rose and went to the kitchen where he found Frederick and Mary talking.

"Good morning," Mary said. "I do hope you got some sleep. This has to be ever so difficult for you. I suppose you'll have to make a report to your leaders and tell them about this."

Stone nodded his agreement as he picked up the cup of coffee Mary had poured for him. "I'll go over to the church and see if I can find any clue of what happened," he said.

"We, ah, we had a visitor," Frederick said. "Marshal Malone was here. He wanted to talk to you. I told him you were my guest, that you were still sleeping. I assured him you're not going anywhere, and he could come back later."

"He's only doing his job," Stone said. "Maybe I'll see him over at the fire-site. I best get over there before someone else gets to removing evidence."

"Not before some more strudel, some eggs and ham, too, you're not. I know how you men are. You'll go all day without eating enough to keep up your strength, then you get down sick, and it's we women folk who have to take care of you. You eat up now, Parson Stone."

Half-an-hour later, Stone stood near the area where the fire had started. He looked for a container that might have carried the lamp oil he'd smelled when first awakened by the fire. Using his cane, he lifted a piece of the roof tin that had fallen across the foundation stones. There lay a heat deformed, blackened jar against the foundation rocks. Stone started to reach out his cane for it when he heard his name being frantically called.

"Señor Stone," Miranda Maria called out. "Oh, I was so worried about you when I heard of this." She had left her carriage and was approaching Stone at nearly a run. "I came as soon as I heard this awful news. I so wanted to find you. I prayed for your safety, that you hadn't been harmed. God, in his mercy, has saved you."

Miranda Maria reached Stone, then threw her arms around him. Stone responded by closing his eyes and wrapping his arms around her. Their cheeks touched and Stone shuddered slightly.

"Nothing must happen to you," Miranda Maria said softly. "It would be our fault. You are here because father asked for you. If something happened—"

"Nothing is going to happen to me," Stone assured her. "I'm fine."

Stone released his hold and moved slightly away from Miranda Maria's grip. He looked over at the Francisco coach. It was empty.

Where was Orlando?

Suddenly, Stone saw the driver come from behind him, moving toward the coach. Stone kept him in his sight until he was back in the driver's seat.

"You must come to our home tonight. It is Christmas Eve. I am preparing a meal, much more than we will eat. You must come, I insist." Miranda Maria looked at him with pleading eyes.

"I'm staying at the Mills, Frederick and Mary. Maybe you know them. I don't know—"

"I know them. They are fine people. I shall go and invite them, also. Then you will have no excuse. None will do, Señor Parson Stone." Miranda Maria then became very serious.

"Please. Do not consider me a forward woman—I am not. With Mother, and what her illness has done to our family… It would make me happy if you come."

"I will gladly come," Stone said, his mind, for the moment, was far from the church fire, his preacher cover, the gold, the Confederates, Buck and all else that had consumed him for months now.

"Sundown then. I shall go invite the Mills right now." Miranda Maria again drew Stone's cheek to hers, then turned and went to the coach. Stone watched her leave, then he stepped back to the tin and lifted it again. The jar was gone. He'd had his back turned, and he'd certainly been distracted. Anyone there could have taken it—anyone.

Stone was still staring at the spot where the jar had been when someone behind him spoke to him.

"You're that preacher who was in here when the fire started. How did you start the fire?"

Stone turned to face marshal Huck Malone. Stone extended his hand. Malone ignored it.

"Parson Justin Stone, Marshal. I was here alright, but over on the south side by the stove. It is obvious the fire was started on this side. That's where the first wall fell in and where the flames first went through the roof. Anyone who was here can tell you that. Whoever set this either didn't know where I was in there, or they just wanted to give me a scare, throw some fear into me," Stone said. "What do you think, Marshal?"

Malone raised his eyes and his head tipped back slightly. He hadn't expected that reply from Stone.

"Got any proof of what you say?" Malone asked. "I say you set it yourself. Don't know why. I got no proof you're even a preacher. I say you come down to the office and we talk about all of this."

"Is that an order?"

"Look, Preacher. I don't want to make a scene in front of these people, but I'm telling you, I want you down at my office to answer some questions. Oh, and bring anything with you that might show just who you are. I run a tight town here, Preacher. I don't need some firebug running around."

"I'll be at your office in an hour," Stone said. "Just where is it anyway?"

"Behind the church on the square, you know, that big Catholic Church. Guess it's now about the only one left in town. 'Course this one here never was much, anyway."

"You ever been in it, Marshal?"

"No! I mean, well I just never had the time, my job and all."

"So you didn't know where the stove was, where I'd be sleeping."

"Hey. One hour, my office, or I'll come lookin' for ya."

Stone went over to the stable. The marshal's office was farther than he wanted to walk, and he'd need his buggy to go to the Franciscos' later. He had just reached the stable door when Frederick Mills drove up in his carriage.

"Need a ride somewhere? I believe you're responsible for Mary's and my invite to the Franciscos' tonight. That will be a treat. I came looking for you. So, are you going somewhere?"

"The marshal's office, but I need to get my bag from your house."

"Come on, then. We'll go by my house, then off to the marshal, then to the Franciscos' tonight."

Stone retrieved his bag, then climbed back up to the buggy seat. Frederick started the carriage forward.

"Let's stop a minute. I want to show you my identification and other things. I don't know what Marshal Malone has in mind, but just in case these things come up missing, I want you to have seen them."

"You think Malone is out to get you?" Frederick asked as he stopped the carriage and perused Stone's papers. "He won't get away with anything such as that."

"I'm just being safe," Stone said. After Frederick perused Stone's papers, he put them away, then they again started down the street.

"I'll wait out here for you," Frederick said once they'd reached the marshal's office.

"No, please don't. If I don't make it back to your house, I'll see you at the Franciscos' later."

Stone entered Malone's office. Huck sat behind his desk, his feet propped up on it. He motioned for Stone to take a seat across from him. He looked at Stone for a moment, then he dropped his feet to the floor and leaned toward Stone.

"Tell me, Preacher-man, why are you here?"

"You asked to see me."

"In town! Why are you in my town?"

Stone spent the next several hours answering this and many similar questions. Finally, Huck rose, walked over and opened a cell door, then directed Stone inside.

"When you got something good to tell me, I'll be here," a frustrated Marshal Malone said. "Don't ask me how, but my gut tells me you ain't no preacher, and you're up to your ears in this gold thing. Let me know when you're ready to talk. However, you know what I really want. Tell me where all that gold is, or I'll pin this church thing on you. Cut me in, or I'll hang you."

CHAPTER 17

Stone sat in his cell, reading his Bible until the light got too dim. He then took off his spectacles and put them in his vest pocket. Through his small window, he heard Dinger whining for him.

"Wait for me, old boy. I'll be out as soon as someone comes for me," he called out through the bars of the window.

He dreaded disappointing Miranda Maria by missing her Christmas meal. She'd understand, of course, however, he really wanted to see her tonight. Frederick Mills knew where he was. He'd tell the others.

Did Malone have full run of this town, or, was there a balancing force? He didn't have long to get an answer to his question.

The sun had hardly set when Juan Diego burst through the marshal's office door.

"Señor Malone, what is the meaning of this? You have insulted this man of the cloth, this man of God, this—"

"Save your words, Juan Diego. I know your game. If you didn't have three quarters of this town thinking you're almost God yourself, I'd have you in here with this charlatan. I'd make you tell me all about that gold you're holding out on us."

"Gold, Señor?"

"Yes, gold! You know full well what I'm talking about, you rich, old Yankee-lover. When we take over, and find your precious gold, you'll wish you'd have turned it over to our cause right now. Maybe I should bring in that daughter of yours. Maybe she'd enjoy spending Christmas in the hoosegow with this would-be-preacher here. Maybe then you'd talk."

"That would not be a good move on your part, Señor Malone. I will ask you one more time to turn my friend, the honorable Parson Justin Stone, over to me. He is to be my guest on this Christmas Eve. We are waiting dinner for him."

"Get out of my sight, old fool. Don't come back."

Juan Diego turned and left without another word. Stone sat on the hard bench and looked out through the small barred window at the now star-filled sky.

Mere minutes later, the door flung open again and Juan Diego stepped back through it, followed closely by another man. Huck Malone suddenly jumped to his feet.

"Mr. Mayor, sir. What are you doing—?"

"Shut up, Malone. You're interrupting my Christmas Eve dinner with my family and some very important people. Have you gone completely mad? Holding a traveling preacher? If he's not out here in two minutes flat, I'll be back with the army, the whole division from Fort Union, if I have to. One more stupid stunt such as this and we'll run you out of town. Understand?"

"But sir—"

The mayor and Juan Diego turned and exited before Malone could argue his case. Stone heard Malone mumble to himself. Then, he heard him take the ring of keys from the hook on the wall.

"This ain't over, Preacher. Not by a long shot," he said while he unlocked the door.

Stone picked up his bag, then turned to Malone.

"Marshal, if I were you, I'd resign and get out of town. I believe things are about to change, and not to your liking."

Malone just stared at Stone without comment. Stone stepped through the door, out into the cold, night air. Dinger was there to greet him with tail wagging.

"Come on, get up here," Juan Diego called to him while Orlando drove the carriage up beside Stone. "Dinner is waiting. My daughter is worried."

Stone climbed up into the back and sat on the softly padded seat.

"Thank you," he said to Juan Diego. "I didn't want to spend the night in there."

"Malone is trouble. Foolish enough to try something, again. Not against me, for I have many influential friends here, as you have seen. It is you who he will again come against. We must be on guard for him. A foolish man makes for a dangerous man. Such is the marshal. You are in danger here, Señor Stone."

Stone nodded. "Please take me by the stable first. I'll not spend the night here in Santa Fe. Later tonight, I'll start back to Albuquerque."

"After you eat dinner at my house first. I'll have it no other way. It is the season of Christmas. It is only fitting that all who believe in the savior, Jesucristo, celebrate such an important time. Nothing more will happen with Malone tonight."

Stone agreed. He'd stay for dinner. He was hungry, but more than for the food his stomach craved, his heart yearned to see Miranda Maria again, to hear her voice. For a fleeting moment, he could feel the warmth of her cheek against his the way it had been this morning. He longed, yet in some way feared, to hold her close again tonight.

––––––––

"Must you leave in the middle of the night? Must it be so?" Miranda Maria asked.

139

"I'm an easy target here," Stone said. "Malone, and whoever he is associated with, might try to use me to get to your father's gold. Somehow, they suspect I'm not really this man of God I'm claiming to be."

"Ah, but, you are a man of God," Miranda Maria said. "The Holy Father has sent you to us in this time of turmoil. Just as he sent that soldier when the Apaches were torturing Father to death, so, God has sent you to us now. Do not sell yourself short."

"But I'm not—"

"Hush. It is not for you to determine what you are. That is up to the Holy Father. It is not fitting, I say to you, that you leave here at this late hour. Where will you sleep?"

"By a fire," Stone said. "This buffalo robe your father gave me as a present will keep me warm as toast. I'll be fine."

Rosa reached over and took Stone's hand, then laid her head against his shoulder. Stone felt shivers pulse through his body.

"I must go," he said after several moments of silence.

"Stay. Por favor, for me," Miranda Maria softly said.

"Look at me," Stone said as he gently pushed Miranda Maria's head off his shoulder and turned to face her. "I'm a broken down, worn out, old man who can't even use my own name. I fear that any feelings I had to be close to someone were used up years ago. My only worth now is what people, such as Abe Lincoln, can use me for."

"So you say. God is making you into a new man, Parson Stone. When He is finished with you, with this new phase of you, you will not be as you say you are now."

"I'm not very sure about God, and me. Actually, this whole God thing still scares and confuses me greatly."

"Talk to Him," Miranda Maria said. "To know Him, one must talk to Him, as it is with you and me. How would we ever know the other if we never talked? We ask questions to get answers, so it is with Him."

Stone sat in silence, staring into the dark, calming eyes of Miranda Maria.

What are you doing? You don't have time for any of this. Besides, you're only going to get hurt. There's no way...

"Return, soon, Señor Stone. We must talk mucho time once more," Miranda Maria said. "Go now, if you say you must. But if you should think of me later tonight, as you lay on the hard, frozen earth, be assured that I too shall be thinking of you. Praying for you, also."

Stone stared into those magnetic eyes, then he nodded slowly.

"I shall think of you later tonight," he said. "And every day until we can be together again."

With that, he walked to the door, pulled his hat down tight on his head, and stepped out on the portico's tile.

"Do your best for your mother, and father, as I know you are. I'll be back when it seems prudent. I shall look forward to seeing you again."

"As I you, Señor Stone. Soon, do come back soon."

Stone nodded, then turned and started out to his buggy. Orlando had it harnessed and had fed Stormy. Dinger loped along at his side.

"Look at you, Stone said to his dog. You've only been in this town a few days, and you're getting fat."

As he left town, he heard a group of carolers singing Christmas songs. He stopped and listened for a while, then took the road south out of town.

Stone rode through the crisp, starlit night for several hours on the road south toward Albuquerque. He came upon an often used campsite with a good supply of wood. He started a fire then sat close to it. Though it was now well after midnight, he wasn't sleepy. Thoughts and questions about Miranda Maria were the main cause. However, other things also occupied his mind.

He took out his Bible, dug out his spectacles from his vest pocket, then he opened the old book up to the beginning of Luke, where he knew he'd find the birth of Christ story. Somehow, being out here alone under the multitude of flickering stars seemed to be a proper setting to read and ponder on this story. He pushed himself around so the light of the fire lit the pages. He started reading out loud.

"Listen to this, Dinger. This is what this Christmas thing is all about, at least how it got started. Tell me what you think. 'And so it was, that, while they were there, the days were accomplished that she should be delivered. And she brought forth her firstborn son, and wrapped him in swaddling clothes, and laid him in a manger: because there was no room for them in the inn.'

"That sorta sounds similar to you and me sometimes, doesn't it old boy? In the story, nobody had room for this baby. I was going to say nobody wants us either, but I guess maybe that's not rightly so. That Miranda Maria lady, what does she see in an old broken down man who hasn't been anything but morally and mentally bankrupt for years? Maybe I'm reading her all wrong. Maybe she's just out of character with her mother being sick and all.

"Listen now, let me read more to you. 'And there were in the same country shepherds abiding in the field, keeping watch over their flock by night. And lo, the angel of the Lord came upon them, and the glory of the Lord shone round about them; and they were sore afraid. And the angel said unto them, "Fear not for I bring you good tidings of great joy, which shall be to all people..."'" Stone stopped at that point.

Fear not. Fear not...

"You afraid, Dinger? Probably not. To be forthright, I'd have to admit that I am. I've never admitted the likes of that to anyone before, but I'm telling you now. 'Spect deep down, I'm afraid of meeting Buck; I'm afraid of not completing what I was sent out here to do; and I'm scared silly about my feelings for this Miranda Maria lady. Where's one of them angels to tell a man to 'Fear not' when he needs one?"

Stone threw another log on his fire, then curled up in his blanket. He lay looking up at the stars for a long time.

When you think of me, I'll be thinking of you, she'd said. Was she really thinking of him now?

———

Two days later, Stone reached Albuquerque. He went straight to the central square. In the last two days, he'd passed several columns of Union Troops going north, but had thought little of it. Now, judging by the scurrying and running around town by the remaining soldiers, obviously something was happening. Stone walked over to the quartermaster's office.

"Sergeant," he greeted the quartermaster. "I've come down from Santa Fe. I passed some of your men going north. What's going on?"

"Ain't you heard? We're pulling out, Preacher. We're all going to Fort Union to set up a final defense there. If them rebels get past Fort Craig, up there will be our last stand. I gotta get all this gear and such out on the street and put a fire to it. I'd prefer to just burn the whole blamed building, but that would set the whole street on fire. The captain don't want that. Anything you need, Preacher, just take it. It's all gonna burn anyway."

"No, I best not be seen with any Union issued products on me," Stone said. "I have to try and stay uncommitted in all of this."

"Wish I could. The rebels say we want to tell them what to do. Well, someone needs to tell them. Anyone who has slaves and treats people, so they be darkies, anyone who treats them the way they get treated on some of them plantations needs to be told how to treat others. It's just an outright shame we have to go to war and kill one another just to stop them from abusing those who ain't got the wherewithal to do for themselves. God have mercy on the souls of them I gottta kill, if I have to," the young quartermaster said.

"Where's the telegraph office here in Albuquerque?" Stone asked.

"Ain't got here yet," the quartermaster answered. "Back up in Santa Fe is the closest one. Once this war gets over, real quick like, I expect Albuquerque to become an up-to-date place. It'll have all them modern things such as the telegraph, the railroad, too.

"Where you goin', Preacher?" the young man asked. "You should be goin' back where you came from. Ain't nothin' south of here safe for you.

Fella can't stay here. Come on with us. We got plenty of grub. 'Spect we could use a good sermon or such."

"I have to move on south," Stone said. "I promised the men down at Fort Craig that I'd come back. I'd prefer to get there before they're attacked. I'll be starting that way in the morning."

"You're either mighty brave, or darned foolish," the quartermaster sergeant said. "Them rebels will shoot you as quick as look at you. I hear they got some real sharpshooters, so I do."

"I'll be careful."

"I best get this fire going. Maybe I'll see you on the trail up yonder, sometime, Preacher."

———

Later, Stone watched the last of the Union troops leave Albuquerque as the sun set behind the western mesa. He felt a sense of fear and helplessness among the remaining residents. They were defenseless against the advancing enemy. Even the children sat sullenly and watched the smoldering fires. None played the usual child's games. He'd learned they planned to only march a few miles out of town tonight, but planned to get an early start in the morning.

Stone rode toward the church. It was cold. He planned to wait until morning to start on south. When he approached the door, Dinger let him know they were not alone.

"Easy, old boy. Got company, do we? This is getting to be old. Maybe it's just another cold traveler, such as myself."

Stone slowly swung open the church door. He couldn't see anything as he looked into the very dark building. He stepped inside. Then he felt the all too familiar gun barrel jamming his ribs.

"Hold it, Parson. You got some explaining to do. Just turn around slowly and go back out the way you came in. Get on that buggy and go where we lead you. That way you won't get any trouble from us. There's three of us here, so we've got you well covered."

"That's so comforting," Stone said. "It's nice to know I have the option to be treated civil."

"Save your mouth for preachin' and answerin' questions for the sergeant," the young man who acted as the spokesman said. "We've been watching you. Got us a headquarters downriver about a mile. Come along peaceful like, now. The sergeant will be glad to have a good talk with you."

"If you boys have a fire and some grub, this seems to be a better deal than spending the night in a cold church anyway. I take it you're with the Confederate side of this conflict?"

"Just get up on that buggy seat and come along with us. You can talk later."

It took about half-an-hour to reach the abandoned house these rebel scouts had taken over. When Stone drove into the front yard, it looked dark inside. Coming around to the back he saw the meager flame of one candle flickering in the kitchen. Stone slowly got down from his buggy, then was directed through the low, back door.

"They're all a runnin', Sarge," the first man through the door announced. "All the Yanks be runnin' north. We got us a victory without even firing a shot. This'll make the Governor happy.

"Picked up this here preacher fella we've been hearin' about. Saw him talkin' real friendly like to the Union quartermaster. Figure he's up to no good. 'Spect you'd want to find out what he's about, Sarge."

"Sit down at the table, Mr. Preacher-man. I've heard some tales about you," the sergeant said to Stone without rising from his chair in the darkened corner of the little room. "Tell me, what's your name?"

"Parson Justin Stone."

"And your business with the Union quartermaster, Parson Stone?"

"He was about to destroy a lot of food and other things the poor need. I begged him to let me give some of it to the needy," Stone said.

"So, did he give you any?"

"He seemed to be as suspicious of me as you are."

"Suspicious? Yeah, I'm suspicious just why some traveling preacher shows up somewhere where there's a ton of trouble brewing and there's supposed to be a lot of gold hidden here-a-bouts. I hardly think you're a Yankee spy—I know for sure you're not one of ours. Just who are you, really?"

At that, the sergeant rose and walked over to the table opposite Stone. Then, he leaned over the candle and got his face real close to Stone's. For the first time Stone saw his face. His heart leaped and he jerked slightly forward. That face... It had to be. It had been so long, but the likeness of that little boy waving goodbye flashed through his mind. Stone's heart now pounded and he bit his tongue.

"Who are you, really, I asked?"

"I'm..."

I'm your father! Stone wanted to yell out.

"I'm Parson Justin Stone..." He went through his usual reasoning for being here. Buck kept his face close to Stone's, trying to intimidate him into saying something incriminating.

"You can ask Governor Baylor about me," Stone went on. "He knows me. So does Simeon Hart. I came across much of Texas with Captain Dumont's men. Surgeon Frans Mauer knows also me. I don't know why you think I'm something else."

Buck slumped into a chair, but kept his eyes on Stone. Stone wanted to reach out and take his son into his arms. Instead, he kept his expression solemn and stared right back at Buck.

"Start at the beginning," Buck said. "Tell me who you are, and why you're here. Tell me it all, once again."

This had the makings of being a long night. Stone no longer cared. He was with his son, and Buck was alright. Now, he had to try and keep him that way until his mission was completed.

"I'm Parson Justin Stone…"

———

In Santa Fe, Miranda Maria and Juan Diego sat at the bedside of their mother and wife. The fire in the fireplace burned full blaze—yet the atmosphere was icy cold.

"Mother—hold on, Mother. Just a little while longer and we can go back to the warm sun by the mine. Things will be better there, Mother."

Beside Miranda Maria, Juan Diego sat weeping.

"Go get Father Baca," he told Orlando. "Tell him to hurry."

"Mother," Miranda Maria cried. "Oh Mother," she said while gently squeezing her hand.

CHAPTER 18

Two hours had gone by since Stone had entered the little house south of Albuquerque. He'd been quizzed over and over with the same questions, but now, Buck went in a new direction with his interrogation.

"Are you a member of the Knights of the Golden Circle?"

"No."

"Know them?"

"I know a little of the KGC. I attended one of their meetings at Simeon Hart's house in Franklin, but that's my only association with them."

"Who spoke at that meeting?" Buck asked.

"A man called Judge. That's all I remember. I don't know the rest of his name."

"Have you seen Judge since?"

"A few days later, in La Mesilla. There was a man killed and Judge showed up there."

"A man? I heard it was a run-a-way slave," Buck said.

"He had emancipation papers."

"You believed him?"

"The papers seemed to be in order. He told a good, consistent story," Stone said.

"If Judge walked in here today, would you recognize him?"

"I think so. Yes, I'd recognize him."

"Did you see him in Santa Fe?" Buck asked.

"No."

"Did you hear anyone talk about him? Anyone tell you he's missing?"

"Missing? No one has told me anything about that," Stone said.

"Have you heard about a lot of gold in Santa Fe?"

"Rumors. Lots of talk. Speculation, I'd say. Wishful thinking."

"Did anyone talk to you about that when you were in Santa Fe?"

"I'm a preacher. I'm the last person anyone talks money to. Everyone thinks I'm after all they have. I will tell you this: Governor Baylor offered me a tithe, that's ten percent, of any such gold I help him obtain. I've made no effort in this. I'm more than silver and gold, young man."

Buck seemed exhausted, about ready to give up. He glanced around the room. Several of the men were sleeping. All the others looked exhausted.

"Alright. That's enough for tonight. I don't know what to believe. There's just something about you, Parson Stone, that doesn't sit right with me. I'm leaving for Fort Thorn in the morning. I'll be gone about a week. I'll leave Lacy and Kirk with you until I get back. I'll talk to Governor Baylor and see if what you say is true. If he vouches for you, then you can go your way. If not—I'll see what then."

"So, I'm your prisoner?" Stone asked.

"Guest. We have lots of food. There's lots of wild game around here and the water's good, too. It's warm and dry. What more could you want? We'll even feed that ugly mutt that shadows you everywhere—your horse, too."

Stone nodded. This would keep him in touch with Buck, but out of touch with everyone else. Right now, he didn't care.

Buck pulled his watch out of his vest pocket. When he did, a tiny wooden horse fell into his lap. He picked it up and slid it back into his pocket. Stone's eyes bulged when he saw this. He recognized the horse. He'd carved it and given it to his small son before he'd ridden off to Mexico, over fifteen years ago.

"I don't want to tie you up or anything like that, Preacher. But if you leave, we'll just find you again and bring you back, and then tie you up. Behave, and you can have as much freedom as you need here. I'll see you in about a week."

"I won't be any trouble, Sergeant. You'll find that what I told you is true. I'm who and what I say I am."

Buck nodded. "Take the preacher to that back room. He can have that bed."

"Ah, Buck, that's my bed," Lacy said. "Where am I gonna sleep?"

"Look, Lacy, he's an old man with a wooden leg," Buck said. "You gonna have him sleep on the floor? He's a preacher, too, I guess. Ain't you got no respect?"

"Don't see you giving up your bed, Buck. What about you?" Lacy asked.

"It's called being the sergeant. Just do what I say. You can use my bed while I'm gone."

————

After Buck and most of his men left the next morning, Stone spent much of that day sharpening his knife on a flat slab of sandstone. The following day, he found a good, straight-grained piece of apple wood. He started carving and by the fifth day he'd completed his project: a nearly identical horse to the one he'd made fifteen years ago.

As he'd carved at a slow, diligent pace, he'd often thought of Miranda Maria. When he did, something seemed to tell him things were not going well for the Francisco family.

On the seventh day, Buck and the others returned. Stone again sat across the kitchen table from his son.

"Guess you're telling us straight. That, or you've got everyone else fooled. There's still something about you that doesn't satisfy my mind, but I can't pin it down. You're free to go, Preacher. It's just that—" Buck hesitated a moment. "I ask that you help us, if you can. You see a lot of things out and about. People tell you things, I know. If you'd come and tell me anything that would help our cause—" Buck paused for a moment. "Well, go on now. I've nothing more."

"I'll get my things," Stone said, then went to the back room. Listening through the door, he heard Buck telling Lacy and Kirk that the Confederate troops were to leave Fort Bliss in full force the next day. They could be at Fort Craig in as few as ten days. Stone placed the newly carved little horse on the pillow of the bed, then slipped out the side door.

Dinger greeted him and seemed anxious to be away from this place. He ran up the road a few hundred feet and sat waiting while Stone harnessed up Stormy to the buggy. When Stone started forward in the buggy, Dinger ran well ahead, leading the way down the road.

Several hours later, Lacy went into the back room to reclaim his bed. He found the horse and took it to be the one he knew Buck carried in his pocket.

"Hey Sarge, here's that token horse of yours. It was on my pillow. How'd it get there?"

"Blamed if I know," Buck said as he glanced at the horse Lacy lay in front of him. He reached into his vest pocket and was startled to find his horse still there. He took it out and compared the two. They looked nearly identical.

"Didn't know you had two of them," Lacy said.

"Ain't never had but one," Buck said. "This one is just the same as mine. This is spooky. This ain't natural. I knew there was something not right with that old preacher. He's trying to rattle me, or tell me something."

"He can't be too far," Lacy said. Let's go get him. We'll make him talk."

"No. Let him go," Buck said, still staring at the two horses. "We'll see him again. Don't hurt him, understand? Nobody does anything until I find out what this is all about."

"Whatever you say, Buck. I still say we shouldn't take any chances with him," Lacy said. "I'll make him talk."

"He's harmless—I think. He must have seen my horse. He must have. He's just sending me some silent message. Maybe he knows now I won't hurt him. I'll bet he's just buying cheap protection."

Stone pushed hard, arriving at Fort Craig around noon three days later. Waived on through by the guards at the sally port, he headed directly toward the officer's quarters. He approached the Officer of the Day, identified himself, and asked to see Colonel Canby.

"Parson Stone," the Colonel greeted him excitedly. "I feared you'd been detained by our enemy, or otherwise fallen on tough times. Come, come in and have some coffee. Tell me what you've been up to."

"I've been all the way to Santa Fe, Colonel. And yes, up until three days ago, I was detained by some rebel scouts in Albuquerque. I learned from them that the Confederate army was to leave Fort Bliss two days ago. They could be here within the week, maybe a little longer. Are you prepared?"

"If only they would wait another month. I believe we'd have troops from California and Colorado to reinforce us by then. Now, well, our few regular troops are as good as they come. The Territorial Militia seems ready, though totally untested. This mass of volunteers I've accumulated, well, I fear they've come here for their own safety and for some food in their bellies. We've fortified the walls, what we call walls, and deepened the trenches. We've set the cannon to present the most effective defense,"

Colonel Canby then changed the subject. "What shape is Albuquerque in? If they get by us, can we stop them there?"

"Colonel, Albuquerque has been abandoned, Santa Fe also. Almost all the men have gone to Fort Union. To stop this invasion, you must stop them here, or they walk through Albuquerque and you also lose the capital.

"Without help from Colorado, Fort Union is in worse shape than you are, Sir," Stone continued. "For the Union, this is critical. Unless you stop them, or at least cripple them badly, I believe the Confederates are on to Colorado, then to the Pacific. Sir, this could be the war. Right here in these next few days could decide the fate of the entire Union war effort."

Colonel Canby buried his head in his hands. He didn't look up for several moments. Stone sat silently. The Colonel finally spoke.

"My wife is in Santa Fe," Colonel Canby said. "It' up to the Lord to protect her, now. I guess it always is, anyway. Parson, I believe the only thing that will give us victory is a miracle. I trust you will be praying for such. I know you claim neutrality, but I also believe that in your heart you know the Union is on the right side of this."

How? How did one pray to a God he didn't know for something such as this?

The Apaches… Remember the Apaches?

One day led to another with the troops frantically trying to prepare for the worst. Captain Graydon, and the other scouts, sent reports back daily. Time dragged on and it seemed as if the Confederate war party was having trouble getting things in order to attack.

Several weeks went by. Word from Captain Graydon's men came that General Sibley was waiting for warmer weather. Later, the reports once again confirmed the troops were getting closer. Then Captain Graydon showed up himself. Colonel Canby invited Stone to sit in on a strategy meeting.

"You know as much as any of us, Parson. You've seen what's up north. None of the rest of us have," Colonel said.

"They're close," Captain Graydon said. "They could hit the day after tomorrow. They just need to bring up their artillery and much of their supply train. The main body of men is only ten miles downriver. I say we show them a little Yankee ingenuity."

"You have a plan, Captain?" Colonel Canby asked. "Something to disrupt the enemy?"

"Yes, something to put some fear into them. I say we attack them at night. Give me forty men and I'll have them running back down the river shooting at their shadows."

Colonel Canby shook his head.

"I don't have the men to spare. If things should go badly, it could destroy our entire defense. We cannot go on the offensive. We are destined to defend only."

"But Colonel, what if they choose to go around us? I've heard rumors of such," the Captain said.

"Go around us? You mean not attack the fort at all? I don't know. I just don't know what I would do then. My orders are to stop the rebels here at Fort Craig. I just don't know."

"You must develop a plan, Colonel," Captain Graydon said. "We must know what to do if that happens."

Stone could tell this upset Colonel Canby greatly. The colonel seemed to believe he didn't have the men, or artillery, to defeat the Confederates in an open field battle. Stone, who'd watched the men drill off and on for weeks now, figured the colonel was right.

"I shall try, Captain," Colonel Canby said, "I shall try to develop such a plan."

"They're in battle formation, Colonel. About two miles south. They're readying their artillery to pelt the fort. What do we do?" asked the young sergeant who'd brought back the scouting report.

"Nothing, Sergeant. We stand firm," Colonel Canby said. "I'm not going out to their ground, they must come to mine."

"But, Sir, Captain Graydon—"

"Captain Graydon what? Go tell the good captain I want to see him in my quarters, pronto."

"Yes, Colonel," the sergeant said, then he saluted, spun his horse around, and headed for the road south.

"Come, Parson. We'll await the captain in my quarters. The game is about to be played. May God see fit for us to be the winner."

An hour later, Captain Graydon was let in by the Officer of the Day.

"Come, have a seat, Captain," Colonel Canby said. "The parson and I were waiting for you. What do you see out there?"

"They're ready. All indications are they plan to cross the river tonight, all those fit to, and then go up the other side. I hear they're afraid to attack. Sibley is willing to let you sit here, isolated, and go on to Fort Union. He believes if he takes Fort Union, you will starve out."

Colonel Canby sat in silence. He slowly nodded, then replied.

"He's right, you know. I can cut off his supplies through here, but he can receive them up the Pecos. However, we'll have no way to survive, except possibly supplying from California, a doubtful proposition at best.

"If we don't fight now, we might as well surrender," the colonel continued. "Why won't he take up the challenge? Is he afraid of a good fight?"

"He doesn't think he needs it, Sir," Graydon said. Then he was silent for a moment, before continuing. "Sir, my plan to attack at night. Tonight, sir. I'm inclined to disrupt them tonight. With your permission."

"How many men do you want?" the Colonel asked.

"None, Sir. Just my regular men, and two mules."

"Just two mules?"

"Dynamite, Sir. I'll load them down with dynamite, then lead them into the pack train with the enemy's mules. Then, we'll light the fuses and run like the devil on Sunday," Graydon said.

"You've thought this through?" Colonel Canby asked. "It's been done before?"

"Never before, Sir. You'll get credit for it, Sir. If we disrupt them, and put fear into their bones, then we can whip them upriver."

"Upriver?" Colonel Canby asked. "You're that sure they're not coming in? All my preparations…"

"Permission for the mules, and the dynamite, Sir,"

"Of course, Captain. At this point, we must do something."

Around three in the morning, Stone was awakened by a distant blast, followed by another. At daylight Captain Graydon and his men rode into the fort. Colonel Canby greeted them out on the parade grounds.

"Did it work, Captain?" he asked. "Did we scatter their supplies?"

"Darned fool mules," Graydon said. "No, it didn't work. We led those two mules up to within a hundred yards of their pack herd. They were a tuggin' on their ropes to go join the others. We lit the fuses and hightailed back toward the river, and sure as I'm standing here, them fool mules turned came a runnin' right after us. About killed us all, so they did. I'll never put my trust in such a stupid animal again. I shoulda used horses. They would have charged right in. The only thing we did was kill two good mules and make fools of ourselves."

"What about the enemy?" The colonel asked. "What is he doing?"

"Crossing the river, Colonel. If you want to fight them, you'll have to do it when and where they come back down to the river. I believe that's gotta be Val Verde."

Colonel Canby made no comment. He turned and started for his quarters. Stone went over to a fire and poured himself some coffee. Word spread quickly around the camp of the failure of the mule attack. Graydon would surely take a good ribbing for that, but Stone doubted if the Captain would care much. He seemed to think little of what anyone else thought, or said, about him.

About noon, Colonel Canby called for Stone to join him.

"I've decided to move out our main battery, McRae's battery that is, tonight along with most of our troops. We'll set up a defense at Val Verde. Those rebels will be thirsty by tomorrow. I'm believing they won't get much of their supply train through the deep sands on that side. I'm counting on them having to leave up to one half of everything there. They've already lost some wagons crossing the river, I'm told. They left some supplies over here without even trying to take them through the water. I'm going to send one troop south to try and capture as much of their supplies as they can— destroy everything else.

"Maybe if we can't beat them militarily, we can starve them out. That's a sorry way of winning a war, even cruel some would say, but that may be our only way of stopping them. You can tell that I have little hope that our line at Val Verde will hold," Colonel Canby said. He sat in silence for a minute, then went on.

"I'm leaving the fort dangerously under protected by doing this. Should the enemy circle back, or do some other maneuver and come directly at us, we're done. The fort could be taken over by a few hundred men.

"However, I see no other way to go. I'll put up our battery of Mormon Cannons. The men have carved and painted those logs well. They'll have to

152

get real close to see they're not the real thing. I must do my all to hold this section of the Rio Grande Valley for the Union."

Stone could sense the agony with which Colonel Canby had made these decisions. He wished he could do something to help, but knew of nothing.

"I'll stay here at the fort until I'm sure it won't be attacked, then I'll go north to engage the battle there. Tomorrow will be a deciding day in my career, this army of New Mexico, and the Union. God bless the Union. May God bless our efforts tomorrow."

All through the night, men and artillery moved out of Fort Craig and defenses were set up four miles upriver at Val Verde where the rebels would surely try to re-cross the Rio Grande.

Before sunlight the next morning, the first shots were fired. Through most of the day, word kept coming to the fort that the Union was holding the thirsty rebels, their horses and mules, away from the water. Word also came that most of the volunteers, the local farmers and villagers, had run off and left the fighting to the regulars and the Territorial Militia.

Colonel Canby left the fort and took over the command late in the afternoon when he felt sure there was no possibility of an attack on the fort. He'd gotten word that the large quantity of supply wagons that had not crossed the river down south and at least thirty such wagons stuck in the sand across the river had all been stripped of their cargo, then destroyed. Colonel Canby considered this the beginning of a shaky victory.

With less than an hour of sunlight left, a report came to the fort that the rebels had gained the river in several spots. Worse, they were making a charge for McRae's big guns.

A stab of fear pierced Stone. If those guns fell, so might the Union.

CHAPTER 19

Buck Rafter watched the battle below from his lofty sniper's perch up on the cap rock of Black Mesa. He'd come back south from the Albuquerque area over a week ago and had nosed around Fort Craig, trading a few shots with Captain Graydon and other Union scouts. Today had been the longest day of his young life. Since sunup this morning, he'd watched, and occasionally participated in, the back-and-forth, bloody battle below.

Now, while the sun lowered over the snowcapped Black Range, Buck sat in silence and disbelief. Far out across the river, in the heart of the turf held by the regulars of the Union, he watched a handful of brazen, young rebels charge right up towards the heavy ordnance of Captain McRae that had kept them at bay all day long. One of these guns was a legend to the Union Troops. When its projectiles exited the barrel they pierced the air with an eerie whistle, thus, it was nicknamed the Blue Whistler. All day long, twelve pound balls and canister shot had howled at them from this big gun, as well as similar from the smaller guns in the battery.

His mind flashed back to earlier when he'd watched swarms of Confederate troops, armed only with lances, charge in waves against the mighty muskets of their enemy. It had been a suicidal charge to gain position—none had been gained. The bodies of these young men, along with scores of others from both sides, now littered the field of battle.

Now, with this desperate charge against the strong, six-gun battery of the enemy, it appeared the Confederate fortune could change. Suddenly, one young rebel soldier charged right up to Captain McRae and thrust his pistol at the gunner's chest just as McRae did the same with his pistol to the young rebel. Buck saw the pistols both jump and spew smoke from their barrels. Captain McRae slumped over his powder caisson—the young Texan fell back toward the river. Neither made any attempt to rise.

Buck shuddered. Twice, earlier in the day, he'd watched balls from his own long-barreled musket drop young men into heaps of lifeless flesh. Even in the heat of the battle he asked himself why? For what did he do this? What was the gain for him that he would so willingly take another's life?

Shouts of joy now filled the eastern battlefront as possession of the Union guns changed sides. Smelling victory, the young confederates rotated the guns and wheeled the caissons facing west. A wave of confusion swept through the Union lines.

Shortly after the first of the Union guns rained shot upon its own men, the sun disappeared and the fighting ceased. Now, only the moans and cries of the wounded and dying pierced the air.

A white flag was raised from the Union ranks, followed quickly by one from the Confederacy. Then men, who only moments before had been hurling insults and lead balls at each other, lay down their arms and started gathering the wounded.

"Come on, men," Buck said. "Let's get some shovels and start digging. This is over for today. May I never again see the likes of this."

His men's response was silence. All the talk of killing Yankees was nowhere to be heard. It was quite dark when they reached the front line. It seemed that everywhere men were carrying bodies back away from the river.

"Give me a shovel," someone yelled.

"They were all in the wagons we left out in that sand. I hear the Yanks pillaged those wagons, then sent them up in smoke," came the reply from a sergeant, who had his arm in a sling. "Hey, all you Yankees. This here's Johnny Reb over here. You got any shovels you can spare us? Beings you stole or burned all of ours, and I doubt you want to bury our boys. How 'bout some shovels?"

Within minutes, a wagon appeared containing nearly two-dozen shovels. The driver had a note from Colonel Canby. Buck took the note and read it aloud.

"'May I suggest you take your wounded to Socorro, the next sizeable town to the north. There you can set up a field hospital. I suspect you are short on medicine. Send word from your surgeon and we will try to accommodate your needs.' It's signed, Colonel E. R. S. Canby, USA."

"Just like a Yankee," Lacy said. "They burn and steal our medicine, then offer us their leftovers. I say we tell them to go to—"

"You ain't wounded," Buck cut in. "The wounded deserve whatever we can give them, no matter where it comes from."

"Old Colonel Canby seems to be sorta a right decent fella," Sly said. "Heard 'bout his wife helpin' our boys up in Santa Fe, too. That's a whole bunch more than I can say for our leader. Look at him." Sly pointed to a small mesa now outlined by the rising moon. "Look at him sitting up on that hill in that coach with a hospital flag over it while he sucked on a bottle all day. Some leader the great General Henry Hopkins Sibley turned out to be."

"I hear he's sick," Billy said. "Could be true."

"And the rest of us ain't sick in our bellies, and all else, too?" Sly replied. "We'd have won this hours ago if'n he'd a led us. Most of us ain't never been in battle before. Look how many died here who might not have if that skunk had done his job. Who needs him?"

"Get to work, Sly," Buck said. "It doesn't do any good to talk our leaders down this way."

"Just listen around, Buck, I ain't the only one who thinks this way," Sly said.

Later that night, Buck took a wagon full of wounded to Socorro where the Catholic Church had been turned into a hospital. The first rays of morning sunlight warmed the air as he arrived back at Val Verde.

"Hey, Sergeant," Sly said to Buck, who stood looking at the carnage from the day before. "A bunch of us here, well, we've been more than talkin'. You're the best sniper any of us knows. We got up over a hundred dollars, so far, if you'll do it."

"Do what?" Buck asked.

"Put a bullet in old General Sibley."

Mass confusion reigned at Fort Craig that night and well into the next morning. Some ran around claiming victory, others, who'd seen the fall of their key artillery, knew any talk of victory was hollow. Stone saw a light glimmering in Colonel Canby's quarters every time he got up that night. In the morning, the Colonel summoned him.

"You want to see me, Colonel?" Stone asked, while standing in the doorway.

"Yes, do come in. I want to thank you for the comfort you've brought to me and my men these last weeks. I expect for the enemy to turn back south and attack us, any time now. They must know that without our main artillery battery, we're nearly defenseless. I have no viable plan to defend an attack. Blackened logs may fool an enemy from a distance, but once they rush us, they will see how woefully unprotected we are. I have decided that to save as many lives as I can, convinced that with all things considered, we cannot win an attack by the enemy. When the attack comes, I shall surrender the fort. It is the only humane decision I can make."

Stone said nothing. He knew how hard it was for any commander to make the decision to surrender. Given the circumstances, though, Stone believed it was the right decision. The two men sat in silence for some time. Then, from outside they heard some commotion and the Officer of the Day stepped to the doorway.

"Sir, I have a letter from the enemy. They have approached the gate under a truce flag, Sir."

"Well, give it to me," the Colonel said. He read it in silence, then handed it to Stone. It called for the surrender of the fort, or it would be attacked. Stone looked at Colonel Canby. The Colonel nodded his head slowly. Suddenly, a burst of life entered the defeated mind of Colonel Canby.

"They could be bluffing," he said while he stared out the door across the parade grounds. "There is that chance, ever so small, but this could be a bluff. Why not just attack?" He paused in deep thought for a moment.

"Come, Parson. I'll deliver this message in person. It will be good for the morale of the men. I'll surrender to an attack, not some bluff."

The two men walked to the sally port where the dispatch of six Confederate men awaited an answer. Stone tried to keep up, but fell twenty, or more, steps behind. Colonel Canby walked right up to the young sergeant in command, pointed a finger at him and spoke loud enough to be heard across much of the fort.

"You tell my old friend, General Sibley, that we gave him shovels and medicine last night but that's all he gets. This fort is not up for the taking. It's ours. Go tell him that if he wants it, to come and try and take it. You tell him to come and try."

A cheer went up from the men of the fort. Colonel Canby turned and strode back to his quarters at such a pace that again Stone couldn't keep up. He arrived a moment after the Colonel and found him sitting in his chair, laughing.

"You might as well enjoy this moment with me, Parson. We may not have anything to laugh about for some time. But really, why don't you get out of here? You're not one of us. Ride on out, on up to Fort Union. We did half-a-job anyway. We surely did a work on their supplies. With God's help, that will be enough."

"I'll take your advice, Colonel. I'll get out ahead of these troops and go to Santa Fe, at least."

Walking out onto the grounds, Stone whistled for Dinger. As the dog came running, Stone headed for the stable to get Stormy and his buggy.

"Parson, my name's Hector Moore," a young man interrupted Stone as he slowly walked along the path. "I ask you, beg you, please come talk to my brother. He took a bullet yesterday. Be in powerful pain and mighty down in his thinkin'. I know you can encourage him."

Stone was silent for a moment, then slowly nodded his head.

"I'll go see your brother," he said. He spent the next four hours encouraging the wounded men. When asked to read the Bible, he turned to the Psalms.

"Yea though I walk through the valley of the shadow of death..." he read over and over. When he was finally able to leave, he realized there had been no attack. What was General Sibley waiting on? Probably hoping the Colonel would pursue him up river. Hoping to draw the troops out into the open, away from the fort.

Stone rode up to the battlefield. He smelled it before he saw it. The lingering sulfur of the gunpowder, the decaying blood and flesh, and the foul smell of human waste was everywhere. Over on the Confederate side, he saw men still digging graves. He nudged a nervous Stormy over that way. Dinger lagged behind them on the road.

"Hey Parson Stone. Good to see you. It's me, Zach Faulk, remember?"

"I surely do, Zach. How are you?"

"Got a little hole in my left arm. Got it tied off, though. I'll be fit to fight again. Next is Albuquerque. I hear there ain't nothin' left there, really. Them Yanks done all run off. Santa Fe be ours, too. It's on to Colorado, fast as we can get there."

Stone remembered how Zach planned to be home for Christmas. Now here it was, February, and he was still in central, New Mexico Territory.

"You best get that arm looked at," Stone said to Zach. "Is Dr. Frans Mauer in Socorro?"

"Surely is. He'd fancy seeing you, too, I'm sure. He's most likely a fearful mess by now. You know how he is when things get bad. He ain't never really seen bad 'til this." Zach then got a really serious look on his face. "Maybe this will all be over, and we can go home, real soon. I surely do hope so."

"Miss your folks, Zach? That old farm looks pretty good about now?"

"Yeah. I miss them a bunch. I never thought it would be this way, never. I wrote Pa a letter just last week tellin' him I'd be home to help with the plantin'. I surely do hope that's the truth."

Zach suddenly dropped to his knees and started sobbing.

"I killed a fella yesterday, Parson. Shot him while he looked wide-eyed right at me. I'll never forget that look in them eyes. I know I'll burn in hell now for sure. I'm thinkin' of just runnin' off and never facing anyone ever again."

"Easy, Zach. This is war. It's not as if you killed that fellow for no reason. He would have shot you. From what I figure, God doesn't hold things such as this against us. He knows you're sorry and that you had no choice. Don't be so hard on yourself."

"I'll try, Parson. It ain't gonna be easy. Especially if'n I have to do it again."

"This is war, Zach. It's never easy."

———

"You'll be a hero, Buck. You'd be doin' a big thing for Texas," Sly said.

"Hero? Then you do it. You be the hero. I ain't no murderer."

"Seen you drop a fella dead in his tracks, yesterday," Sly said.

"On the battlefield, an enemy soldier. Ain't real proud of that. Kill my own General? I'm not your man."

This talk had gone on for hours with Buck not budging. Finally, he left the group of disgruntled men, then climbed up to the perch where he'd spent most of yesterday. Sitting up there alone, he thought about what the men were saying about General Sibley. The General had spent the day in a wagon under a hospital flag, and never was active in leading the battle. Now, today he refused to attack Fort Craig. It seems to be the consensus of the junior officers that there would be little Union resistance left, and they could easily capture the fort. Was the fact that Canby and Sibley were old friends a factor?

If they couldn't go south and take the fort, most of the young officers then wanted to advance northward as quickly as possible. Instead, General Sibley ordered them to regroup and re-organize after the battle.

Buck looked down at the area where the fresh mounds of dirt covered the unfortunate. To his surprise, he saw that old preacher. The one he'd interrogated in Albuquerque.

What's he doing here? Who is he anyway?

Buck reached into his pocket and took out his wooden horses—both of them. He watched while the buggy carrying the parson crossed the river, then started up the wagon road toward Socorro.

Buck thought of going to Socorro himself. However, being around all that pain, blood and death kept him out here, not that those things weren't here. He also wanted to be away from people. He'd wait for orders before he went anywhere. Besides, he didn't know where any of his men were. Some old hog ranch most likely, trying to forget yesterday with a bottle or loose woman. Right now he didn't even care. If only he could go see Lucinda. Just to be able to hold her, talk to her for a few minutes.

He again thought of running off, but knew that really wasn't an option. He knew about all he could do was sit here and fret over the carnage below, or close his eyes and think of Lucinda. Buck closed his eyes.

As Parson Stone rode north, up the sandy road, he thought of the battle behind and contemplated the battles ahead, maybe near Santa Fe and Fort Union. Suddenly, Dinger barked and chased after a jackrabbit. That brought Stone's mind back to what he was doing.

Later, nearing Socorro, it was getting dark. He saw several fires blazing off to the west of the road. Each had a handful of sullen Confederate soldiers crouched silently around it. Stone felt for these men. They were far away from home, and things were not what they'd anticipated. Stone knew that not a one of them wouldn't want to be back home with their families.

If they would have decisively lost here yesterday, they probably would have gone back home, at least for a time of leave. However, since they seemed to have won some sort of victory, they now had to go on farther and farther from east Texas. Now, it might be years before they ever saw home again.

The men knew all this, too. The Confederacy may have taken some ground, but personally, the men lost greatly by winning. Stone knew this was a factor in the declining morale he sensed among these young Confederates. He believed this was a point General Sibley was missing, or ignoring.

Stone rode on in to Socorro and the temporary Confederate hospital. He went inside and soon found Frans Mauer.

"Parson Stone," Frans greeted him. "Do I ever need to talk with you. You warned me. You did your best, but I still—this is overwhelming. So many have died. I know more will. We have so little medicine stock. What the Union gave us is nearly gone. What are we doing?"

"Tell me, Doctor, have you eaten yet today?"

"Eaten? Why, no, I don't think I have."

"Then come, before you collapse and are put in one of these beds yourself. I'll buy you a steak. I've been told of just the place to find the best one in town."

"These men. To leave them now…"

"Doctor, they will all be here when we return. Come."

Frans said no more as he left those recovering and those dying in these beds and on the blankets on the floor. He said nothing while he rode across town with Stone. When the two men sat waiting on their food, Frans started   talking.

"The men, they blame General Sibley for not leading them to a quick, decisive victory. He's getting blamed for losing the wagons and everything. Maybe they're right. Sibley waited for months to gather up all those supplies, all they needed for a campaign all the way up to Colorado, even Utah. Then, they go and lose two-thirds of them at the first battle. That does appear to be poor planning.

"I hear the grumbling of the men," Frans continued. "However, I've treated General Sibley. His kidneys are awful. When he gets an attack of those stones, such as yesterday, it's debilitating. Of course, his excessive use of alcohol doesn't help. I've told him he should resign and go home. Maybe he could recover there. He never will get any better out in this wilderness living the way of the wolves and coyotes."

Their then food arrived at the table and the two men ate with little conversation. When they were finished, Frans leaned back in his chair.

"Thank you. I didn't realize how much I needed that. I should know by now, there is little I can do for most of those men back there. You probably can do more than I. Come, it's time for me to insist that you do something. You must talk to as many of these men as you can."

Stone started to protest, but something stopped him. He slowly nodded his head.

"Alright. I'll do that, then stay at the hospital tonight. However, I must leave in the morning. I must get back to Santa Fe. I believe I'll go by way of

Anton Chico rather than Albuquerque. That way should be safer." He picked up the steak bones for Dinger, then Stone followed the doctor outside to his buggy.

Back at the church, Parson Stone went from bed to bed. As he'd done for the Union men back at the fort earlier, he often read a Psalm. Some just wanted him to lay his hand on their heads. Some wanted to talk of family or other things back home. Some cursed everything. It was way past midnight when he talked to the last man. Frans was asleep on a pile of dirty blankets over in one corner of the floor.

Stone looked around and found a small room where the priest kept some of his things. He found a candle, lit it, then went inside and sat on a crude, wooden bench.

He thought of what he'd just done—done all day, really. He knew he hadn't helped anyone physically, but had he helped emotionally? Even spiritually? There was something deep inside him that hoped so.

Then, in his state of exhaustion and frustration, for the first time in his life, he bared his soul before God.

"God—I've never been one claiming to be yours. Oh, I've been acting the part here now for months, but you know that really... Well, I always thought I could make it on my own. Except maybe that time down in Mexico, I did call on you then. Yeah, with those Apaches out here, also. Maybe somewhere else, too, that I don't recollect right now." Stone paused in thought for a moment.

"Look, if I've made you mad by pretending to be a preacher, Elias Crump sure figured you'd be mad, then I come asking for your forgiveness. I've read enough of this here old Bible to know it says you do forgive people who ask you to. Guess I'm asking for you to forgive me for all the downright, no-good and evil things I've done. That's a whole passel, I know. I've surely been a scoundrel.

"And, while you're at it, I'm asking for a chance to do things up right. I've always just been puttin' me first. I did it with Laura—Buck too. I've had me a life full of exciting times. Now all of that seems mostly meaningless, empty, even hurtful. Here I am now. I've got nothing to show for it all. I don't even have a name I can use.

"I know I don't deserve anything—nothing good anyway. I've read of others who seemed to be 'bout as bad as me, and you gave them a second chance. That Moses fellow, and king David, too, they were both killers. Figure I'm no different than them, and others in your book. It seems that even some of your favorite people had their backs up against the wall at one time or another. Some of them were scoundrels, such as me. You say you're not beholding to one person over another, no matter how low down a fellow gets." Stone paused for a moment again.

"I guess what I'm asking, God, is that you give me one of them second chances, those new lives you talk about. As I said, God, I know I ain't nothing and don't deserve anything good from you. However, I 'spect with you leading me, I could make something out of this old life yet. Otherwise, I might just as well die right now.

"Guess that's about all I can think of. If there's anything else, I reckon you know all about it all, anyway. Oh, maybe you could help these hurting fellows here, the ones at the fort, also. Yeah, and take care of my boy, will you God? I only got one son. You know how that is."

CHAPTER 20

Five days later, Stone arrived in Santa Fe. He'd taken the mountain roads well east of any troops or conflict. Now, he moved across the town cautiously, knowing he still faced danger. He figured Malone and his friends would be more anxious, more desperate, each day to find the gold. Still, he had to be here.

He went straight through town and out to the Francisco Hacienda. He stepped down from his buggy, leaned on it to ease his pain and to get ready to walk, then he started toward the door. Suddenly, it flung open and Miranda Maria rushed through it. She reached Stone in seconds, then wrapped her arms around him and squeezed him tightly.

"Señor Stone! Oh, Señor Stone, you are safe. You are safe, and you have come back. Ah, I am so glad to see you. I have prayed for you many times these many days."

"I wanted to, and needed to come back," Stone said. "Your mother? How is your mother?"

"Oh, Señor, she has gone on. We buried her in this icy, rocky soil only days after you left. It was the fault of these evil, rebel fighters. My heart, it is so hurt. I see them to be almost as bad as the Apaches who killed my husband and took my son. These aggressors have no thought of all the lives they are destroying. They do this so they can buy and sell those unfortunate people for their pleasure, and profit. How can it be so? My heart is hard against them.

"Someday I shall forgive them," Miranda Maria continued. "I know I must. However, today is not yet the time. I loved my mother so. Father did also."

"I'm so sorry. I don't have any words to say. Your father, how is he?"

"Quiet. So very sad. I have never seen him so withdrawn. This has been hard on both of us. Father won't say anything, but I know he is also angry. Come, it will be good for him for you to talk to him. He is in his oficina."

Stone entered the hacienda and warmed himself by one of the large fireplaces while Miranda Maria went to tell her father that Stone was here. Father and daughter returned together.

"Señor Stone, come," Don Francisco said, as he came through the archway to the room where Stone waited. "Tell me what has gone on. Where are the rebels?"

"My sympathy to you for your loss, Juan Diego," Stone said. "This has to be the worst of times for you."

"Sí, nothing will bring her back," Juan Diego said, closing his eyes and lowering his head for a second. "I must move on," he then said, raising up his head and looking into Stone's eyes. "The world moves on. So," he continued, "talk to me about the war. I've heard differing stories about what happened at Fort Craig. Tell me, were you there?"

"Yes, I was there. It was indecisive, but certainly no victory for the Union. However, the Confederate supply train has been severely diminished." Stone talked on for about an hour, telling about the battle at Val Verde, the loss of the Union ordnance, and the Confederate failure to attack Fort Craig.

"General Sibley is moving very slowly. I believe he is quite ill," Stone said. "So, tell me then, when will the invaders be here?" Juan Diego asked.

"Well," Stone said, "there is really nothing between Socorro and here to stop him, or even slow him down much. His junior officers want to move quickly. They may prevail. He could be here in a matter of days, or, it could be as long as several weeks. However, to be safe, I believe you should prepare for them to be here soon.

"Please tell me, what is going on with Marshal Malone and his group?" Stone asked.

"Not much, really," Juan Diego said. "I have seen him watching me. He is one to stay away from. Once the rebels take over... much trouble, Señor. However, I do not think he will do anything until then."

"And about the church burning?"

"Not one word. That would be up to Marshal Malone to investigate and, well, most people here who I talk to believe he is the one to set the fire. I have many friends here, Señor Stone. They protect me. They will keep watch over you also. However, you must be most diligent."

Stone nodded. "I will be. It is you, you and Miranda Maria, whom I am more concerned about. I've come to make sure you get hidden safely. As you know, there are many rebel spies here already. The sooner you leave, and the fewer people who know anything about it, the better. I wouldn't even tell Orlando."

"Orlando? Surely, you do not think—"

"The Confederacy has been very successful in making promises of money and power to people who may be drawn in by such. They are using the KGC and all its resources."

"Sí. I have read of the KGC. In fact, I have been told Malone and his friends have what they call a 'castle' here."

"I'd relish knowing who belongs to that group. Every one of them is our enemy. Is the telegraph working?"

"No, Señor. The Union soldiers, they cut it somewhere when they left for Fort Union. I do not know if that was a good thing."

"It wasn't, but it's too late now. Somehow, I need to get word to Lincoln. I may have to go to Fort Union. That wouldn't be a good place for you, though. Where can you hide for the next few weeks?"

"Hide? Sí, I have a trusted old friend down at Galisteo. He will let us stay on his ranch. He has many places we could hide."

"Good. You and Miranda Maria prepare to abandon this place. Can you hide any of your art and silver, other things of value?"

"Sí, there is a hidden cellar. No one will find it. We shall make ready to put the most valuable of things there. I will wait until Orlando is in town. He does not know of the entry to this very hidden place."

"Good. Can you be ready by this time tomorrow?"

"Sí. In the morning I shall send Orlando to town. Miranda Maria and I, we will hide our things. When Orlando returns, we will leave for Galisteo."

Stone nodded his approval.

"Here's what I suggest. You leave Orlando here to look after things. You dress up in Orlando's clothes. Then, you drive the carriage as if you are a servant taking Miranda Maria somewhere. I will follow slightly behind. Once I know you are safe, I plan to go on to Fort Union and contact President Lincoln."

"Sí, this is a good plan," Juan Diego said. "We leave here about this time tomorrow then?"

"Yes. Tonight, when I leave here, I'll go to the Mills' and spend the night. I trust them, but still won't tell them, or anyone else, of your plans."

"That is very good," Juan Diego said. "I shall see you tomorrow, then. Vaya con Dios, Señor Stone."

Stone and Juan Diego walked out of his office, then down a long hallway. Suddenly, Stone heard the voice he hoped he would before he left.

"And where do you think you go?" Miranda Maria asked as she stepped out of a room behind them. "You will not get out of here without a home cooked meal, Señor Stone. I've been saving some good bones for your dog, also. How I wish we had time tonight to talk. I can see that is not to be. Soon, soon we will spend mucho time together. My heart so desires. May it be so with you."

Stone turned and looked at Miranda Maria. Their eyes locked. Slowly, he nodded in agreement.

———

Stone parked his buggy beside Frederick Mill's small barn, then tossed Stormy some of the dry hay he'd carried in the back of the buggy. After unharnessing Stormy from the buggy, he hobbled him, then tied the halter to a buggy wheel. He then knocked on the back door of the house. Mary came to the door.

"Come on in, come in. My, we've been concerned about you. Have you talked to the Franciscos?"

"I was just out there," Stone replied. "I am saddened to learn about Mrs. Francisco, though I expected such."

"Frederick, come see who has come back to bless us," Mary called, but Frederick was already entering the kitchen.

"Parson Stone. What a relief to see you. Please, come on in the parlor. You must tell me about what is going on down south. I heard the rebels got around Fort Craig. Are they coming here for sure?"

"I see nothing to stop them. They'll come when General Sibley is ready. That could be in a few days, maybe a week, or even longer. It's been hard to anticipate his moves," Stone said, then changed the conversation. "I may not be in town for long. Stormy's tied out by your barn. Not wanting to bring any trouble on you, I waited until dark to come here. I may go to Fort Union tomorrow."

"Do what you must, Parson, but you know you always have a place to stay when you are in Santa Fe," Frederick said.

"I appreciate that, I really do. I've slept many nights out in the cold. However, I have to admit, I'm not able to handle that as well as I used to."

"Nor should you," Mary said. "Who ever heard of a preacher having to sleep out on the trail in the middle of winter? I'll not be any part of that. Let me warm up some of the roast we had earlier in the evening. I've saved some of the gristle and a big bone for your dog, also, hoping you'd come soon."

"Oh, I must pass on that, for myself," Stone said. "I ate well out at the Franciscan's. Maybe tomorrow."

Stone slept late the next morning. After breakfast he watched the streets until he saw Orlando in town, then he quickly went to the Francisco hacienda. By the time he arrived there, Juan Diego and Miranda Maria had already stashed their prize possessions and were anticipating him. Dressed in peasant garb, Juan Diego looked the part of a servant as he hitched up the carriage.

"All is in order, Señor Stone. I have left written instructions for Orlando on what to do until we return. Shall we go?"

"Go? Ah, yes, of course." Stone had been watching Miranda Maria. She moved with such grace and looked so elegant in her long, woolen-blanket coat. Stone helped her up into the carriage.

"How so I wish you could come with us," she said, as she longingly looked at Stone.

"I have to make contact with President Lincoln and really need to follow how things go here. Besides, I could give your hiding place away by going back and forth."

"Sí, that is so," Miranda Maria said. "I wish for it all the same."

"I'll follow well behind, in case there's trouble. I can then get help, or do something myself. Juan Diego, if you are stopped, and they should take Miranda Maria and not recognize you, you must continue on. I don't believe they will hurt her, only try to use her to get to you. You must not give yourself up. I will follow to where they take her and get help. Is that clear to you?"

"Ah, Señor. That would be a difficult thing to do. Having just lost my dear wife, if my daughter—"

"I won't let anything happen to Miranda Maria. I promise," Stone said. "So, no matter what, you must go on into hiding. I'll get her there, later."

"Sí. What you say is as it must be."

They rode out the old Santa Fe Trail for several miles and just where they were to turn south, they were stopped by a group of men. Stone stayed far back, hidden from the activity ahead. He watched through his field glasses.

Confederate scouts.

He watched while they took Miranda Maria from the carriage and put her on a buckboard of theirs. Juan Diego turned the carriage around and started back toward town, then he stopped once the scouts with Miranda Maria were out of sight. He turned around, then continued on his journey to the ranch out at Galisteo.

Stone followed the trail of the buckboard that had taken Miranda Maria. It led down a road toward the southern edge of town. Dinger suddenly stopped in the middle of the road. He lowered his head and growled at a cluster of cedar trees. Two men then stepped out in front of Stone.

"Hold up there," the larger of the two men said. "Hey, Preacher, you lost or something?"

"As a matter of fact, I am. I was told some people by the name of Baker lived out this way. They're Methodists and I'm trying to get up a meeting at the Mills' home. You know our church burned and—"

"You're the fella Malone told us to look out for," the big man said as he turned to look at his partner. "Come with us. You're the second prize we've caught in the last hour."

"You know the Baker family?" Stone asked.

"Just come with us. Ain't no Bakers here-a-bouts that I know."

Stone was led to a house well outside the city. It appeared that at one time it was a farmhouse, but now seemed to be abandoned. The buckboard, that had been used to take Miranda Maria, sat out front.

"Don't' go too far, old boy," Stone said to Dinger as he slowly climbed down from his buggy. "I don't plan on being very long." Stone looped Stormy's reins over the rail, then was led by the two young men through the door.

"Look who we got, Sergeant Daley. This is that preacher fella Malone told us about. Fancy we found him," said the larger man, the one who'd done all the talking.

"Hear you're called Parson Stone, right?" Sergeant Daley quizzed.

"That's correct."

"Heard also that you talked to Sergeant Rafter a while back."

"We've met."

"I've got strict orders not to harm you. He wouldn't say why, but he put the fear of God, no offence, in me not to harm you at all," Daley said.

"He's a wise man," Stone said.

"You got something going with him?" Sergeant Daley asked. "Your being back here now makes me wonder."

"Look, there's no time for games," Stone said. "I'm after the gold. You know about that, I'm sure. Governor Baylor offered me a ten-percent tithe on all I turn over to him. Rafter wants a piece of it first. There's plenty for all of us, if you don't mess things up any more than you already have."

"What does that mean?" Sergeant Daley asked, leaning forward in his chair.

"Old Juan Diego is gone," Stone said. "He's in hiding somewhere. Probably where he has all that gold hidden. I was all ready to pick up his daughter from that servant when you took her. She won't talk to you, but she will to me. I can promise her things you can't."

"Well, she ain't doin' us no good," Daley said. "She won't speak no English and none of us knows enough Spanish to even get her to tell us her name."

"I'll take her back to their hacienda. You can keep an eye on me there. I can't get around without my buggy." Stone thumped on his wooden leg with his cane. "If my buggy is there—I'm there. I don't care if you watch me day and night. I'll get the gold location out of her, then we go from there. I get my ten percent, Rafter gets his, and whatever else happens before Baylor gets it, I don't care. You realize, though, this has got to happen before any more troops get here."

After pausing in silence for several minutes, then looking at several of his men, Sergeant Daley spoke. "What have we got to lose?" he asked. "Go, bring the woman," he said. "You cross us, Preacher, and we'll find you. Then I've got no accounting to Rafter. I'd have to take things into my own hands."

"I'm sure you would. You want to do something to help? Patch up that telegraph line. I'm expecting a wire from one of Juan Diego's ex-laborers who claims to know where the gold is hidden. He helped hide some of it. However, he can't get word to me without a telegraph line."

"We're ahead of you on that one, Preacher," Sergeant Daley said. "We patched up that line this morning."

Miranda Maria came into the room, railing in Spanish for the men who led her not to touch her. When she saw Stone, she instantly became quiet.

"I'll be in contact," Stone said to Daley. "Is this where you'll be?"

Sergeant Daley nodded. "We'll be watching you, Preacher."

Stone turned to Miranda Maria. "Señora Francisco, a su residence," Stone said to Miranda Maria. She pushed away from the man who'd brought her into the room. Stone and Miranda Maria started out to his buggy with Sergeant Daley following.

"I'm trusting you, Preacher. But I won't tolerate being crossed."

"I'm one old man. Look at me. What am I going to do?"

"Malone said not to trust you."

"Maybe you shouldn't trust Malone," Stone said. "He's counting on getting his information from Orlando, but Orlando doesn't know any-thing."

Stone jerked the reins and backed Stormy up, then turned the buggy around. "Eh ahh," he then yelled to Stormy. He and Miranda Maria started back up the trail.

"We've got to get out of here and get hidden somewhere before they figure out I told them one big windy," Stone said. "I've got to leave my buggy at your hacienda, so they think I'm there. Who in town can hide us? The Mills would be suspects, and I won't bring trouble to them."

"Father Baca," Miranda Maria said. "He will surely help us. Tonight, when it is dark, we will go to the church."

"Alright. Your father did good. He should soon be safe at that ranch. No one here will know where he is. I believe it's going to snow tonight, so his tracks will be covered, ours also."

Stone and Miranda Maria went to the Franciscos' hacienda. Stone turned Stormy into the stable. Orlando was very cold to them, but agreed to take care of Stormy until Stone returned. Stone still wasn't sure the servant was working against them, but his instincts told him that was likely.

At dark, Stone and Miranda Maria started out slowly across the snow-covered streets for the Catholic Church. Stone slipped several times in the snow, but Miranda Maria caught him each time before he fell. His hip and lower back were thumping painfully when they finally got to the church. Both were cold and exhausted.

Once greeted by Father Baca, Miranda Maria explained their circum-stances. He readily agreed to take them in. He took Miranda Maria to a room often used by young priests in training, then showed Stone to a room next to the one he lived in. The old priest then had a meal prepared for them and engaged them in talk about things other than the eminent war. He retired early, allowing Stone and Miranda Maria to talk alone for several hours.

"I saw Buck, my son," Stone told her. "He held me captive for a week. I left him a surprise. I'm sure he won't harm me until he can talk to me sometime again. I'd expect to find him up here shortly—if he's not already here. He always seems to be out in front of the main body of troops."

"That is good. Buck not see himself in you?"

"I don't think men are as good as women at things such as that. He knows something is strange about me, though," Stone said, then changed the subject.

"I have to sneak out of here tonight and get to the telegraph office. I must contact Lincoln. If he can get troops from Colorado to Fort Union in the next few days, maybe we can surprise the Confederates. Those poor boys must be in rags by now. All are surely ready to go back home. They had little food left weeks ago and there were scant supplies along the way."

"You must be ever so careful. I should go with you," Miranda Maria said.

"Absolutely not. You're not to show your face around here until this is all over. I promised your father nothing would happen to you."

"With you in charge, I believe nothing will, Señor Stone," Miranda Maria said.

A short time later, Stone slipped out through the side door, leaving Dinger inside with Miranda Maria. He worked his way across the town's side streets toward where Rosa told him the telegraph office was located. He stopped and studied the line of commercial buildings in the darkness, finally locating the one containing the telegraph. Just as he stepped towards it, he heard a rustle behind him, then a voice.

"We meet again, Parson Stone. You've sure got some explaining to do. Come. There's an empty building back this alley."

Using his cane and good foot, Stone carefully turned himself around in the freshly fallen snow. There stood Buck, not ten feet away.

"I don't want no trouble, honest, Preacher. But something ain't square in what you tell me. You need to come clean with me," Buck said while he shifted his weight from one foot to the other, then back again, staring intently at Stone.

"This isn't the time," Stone said.

"I'll determine that," Buck said, looking around to see if anyone was watching. "Come on, now. It's cold and I'm getting edgy."

Stone nodded, then started down the alley.

CHAPTER 21

Stone cautiously made his way down the narrow, snow-covered pathway, passing the back doors of several buildings to one where Buck ordered him to stop.

"To your right, this building," Buck said. "Go on. Open the door and go in. There's a fire going in the stove. Go on in and sit down."

Stone did what he was told. He slid a chair over near the fire, then sat with his back to the heat. The flickering fire made an eerie backdrop against the rough adobe walls. Weary from a long day, Stone was glad for the warmth of the fire.

"I'm alone," Buck said. "My men are staying over at one of the buildings the Yankees vacated. This belongs to one of our people here—Marshal Malone. I believe you've met him."

"We've met," Stone said.

Buck stared at Stone for a moment, as if he didn't know where to begin. Then, leaning forward, he started with a statement.

"I know you've got Governor Baylor believing you, and I know about all the others, but I also know in my gut there's something that doesn't set right about you. I'm not leaving here—we're not leaving here—until I have all the answers."

"I can't tell you anything but what I already have," Stone said. "I have some questions for you, though. Why did Malone burn the church?"

"Malone? Burn that church? You're crazy," Buck said. "Why would he do that?"

"That's what I want to know. I'm responsible for these churches out here, so when one is burned to the ground—"

"Yeah, yeah, I've heard all of that," Buck said. "You've heard, too, I'm sure, that there's a large cache of gold here. We need that to go on into Colorado, and beyond. Look, Malone is after that gold. Is that what you're about? Are you part of that gold thing?"

He doesn't know about my encounter with that other group of spies earlier today.

"The Methodists sent me out here to keep an eye on our churches and help our people," Stone said. "It's common consensus that Malone burned this church. I need to know why, and what he's going to do about it?"

"I... You're twisting this all around. You're here so I can ask you questions. Don't try to confuse me." Buck looked at Stone, then reached into

171

his vest pocket and pulled out the two little wooden horses. He held them out in his hand, sticking them right in front of Stone's nose.

"What about these? What message were you sending me? You must have seen the one I always carry, then somehow you duplicated it. But, what were you trying to tell me?"

Stone stared at Buck, but didn't respond. Buck clutched his fingers around the horses, then he shook his fist in Stone's face.

"Talk to me!"

"I carve little animals," Stone said quietly. "I saw your horse when you took out your watch. I made one similar to it for you. I had lots of time to kill, remember? Maybe there's no message."

"But there is," Buck said. "Do you know where my horse came from? You carve the same way. All the lines are the same. They're nearly identical. Did you learn to carve down in Mexico? Did someone there teach you?"

"No."

"Did an American officer teach you how to do this?"

"No."

"Did you think that you'd make me so curious by duplicating my horse that I'd try to keep you alive? Is that why?"

Stone paused for a moment, then he responded. "Maybe that was it. I hear you did put out the word to protect me."

"So I did. So why? Tell me what this is all about." Buck's questioning went on for several hours. The fire burned down. Stone wrapped his buffalo robe tighter around his tired body. Miranda Maria would be worried about him. He had to get to the telegraph, then back to the church.

Buck stirred the fire, then he threw on a small log, one that would burn down in a short time. He stood by the fire, looking at Stone. Suddenly, a rage came over him, and he kicked a chair out of the way and drew his gun. He then shoved the barrel under Stone's chin and cocked the hammer.

"Tell me who you are, or I'll kill you. I swear it."

Stone had seen many men under intense pressure, usually those being interrogated, but sometimes, such as now, it was the interrogator who lost control. Stone knew Buck had reached his breaking point. He had failed to break down the old veteran spy, and he was losing control of his thoughts, thus his actions. Stone slowly nodded his head.

"Alright," he said. "Put that gun away."

Buck slowly let the hammer down, then slid the gun into its soft holster on his belt. He grabbed his chair and jerked it back to the fire, then sat down.

"Start talking," he said.

Stone looked at his son, not knowing if this would be the beginning of something good, or, the failure of all his missions—both government and personal.

"I'm Tyrone Rafter," he said, staring intently at Buck. "I'm your father. Really, Buck, I'm alive. I was a prisoner in Mexico for seven years. Lost my leg there. No one came to rescue me. Then, I escaped and made it home to find that everyone thought I was dead. Your mother had remarried and moved to Texas. I saw you there, her too. I was so hurt I ran back into Mexico and for years took my anger out on anyone I chose. El Pata Fantasma, the fearful locals called me. I..." Stone couldn't say anything more at the moment.

Wide eyed but silent, Buck sat and stared at him. Stone tried to read his son's reaction by his expression, but couldn't. Finally, Buck leaned forward and spoke. "I don't believe you. My father is dead. I waited every day for years for him to return, but he never did—never! My father died in Mexico." Buck re-drew his revolver and again shoved it under Stone's chin. The two men stared at each other in the fading, flickering light of the dying fire. Then, Buck jumped up, stuffed his revolver in its holster, picked up his chair and smashed it over the table. He kicked over another chair, then yanked open the door. He stepped through the doorway, then slammed the door behind him.

Stone sat there, alone, for several moments.

See what you've done now, Abe Lincoln? All I have left is my son. Now, look what you've done. You're no help either, God.

Stone then rose and left the building. Daylight was coming soon. Cautiously, using his cane to steady himself in the fresh snow, he made his way out of the alley, and back to the buildings where Miranda Maria had told him the telegraph office was located. Suddenly, he heard someone calling his name.

"Señor Stone, come. This is the one." It was Miranda Maria who was pointing to one of the buildings. Stone moved as quickly as he could in the fresh, slippery snow to get to her side.

"What are you doing here?" he asked her.

"It was much too long," Miranda Maria said. "I became so worried that harm had come to you."

"I was waylaid, but that's over. Inside, quickly, before anyone sees us."

Once inside, Stone struck a match and found the telegraph key. He checked the batteries and found everything in order. Rosa lit a small candle and kept it near the floor where it wouldn't be seen from outside. Stone started tapping out his message to the contact in Philadelphia, to be relayed on to Lincoln. He started off: Urgent from the Blue Eagle...

"Someone is coming," Miranda Maria whispered. Stone kept tapping the key. "A man on foot leading two horses," she continued. "He is coming this way."

Stone kept on tapping out his message. Miranda Maria blew out the candle. The man tied his horses, then stepped up on the boardwalk and came to the door of the building they were in. The man quietly opened the door and stepped in. Stone stopped tapping his message.

"Miranda Maria? Where are you?" the man asked. "From way up the street, I saw you come in here. This is Raul. I come from the ranch where your father now is. He sent me to try and find you. I am to take you to him. Is that the Señor Parson Stone who is with you?"

"Raul, I am here," Miranda Maria said, then she struck another match and re-lit the candle. Sí, this is Señor Stone with me. Come over here. Close the door."

Stone instantly began tapping out the rest of his message.

"How is father?" Miranda Maria asked. "He made it to the ranch safely, sí?"

"Other than being worried sick about you, he is fine. He is safe. You will be also when you come with me."

"No, Raul. I cannot leave Señor Stone. Father must understand. Tell him—"

"You must go," Stone said, finishing his message. "I will go back to the church and to Father Baca. This place, this whole town, will not be safe once the rebels come here in full force. They will be starving and in rags. That makes for dangerous men. Go now. I will explain to Father Baca."

Miranda Maria stepped over to Stone and in the darkened corner of the room, they held each other for a moment before he again told her she must go.

"I'll be safe here. I'll get my buggy, then I may go on to Fort Union. I've asked for emergency troops from Colorado to be sent this way, immediately. Lincoln will know how important my plea is. They will come—will they be in time is the question. Go now."

Miranda Maria again put her arms around Stone, and they embraced.

"Nothing must happen to you," she whispered in his ear.

Stone nodded. "I'll be safe. Go now."

"Señora Miranda Maria, hurry, we must leave now," Raul said. "I fear if we wait—"

"Raul is right. Go now," Stone said. "Your father needs you and I would worry greatly about you if you stayed here."

Miranda Maria nodded, then spoke to Raul.

"I must speak alone to Señor Stone. I will only be a moment. I will join you at the horses, then."

"Ieeh—"Raul said, shaking his head. He opened the door, then went out into the cold, mumbling softly to himself.

"Father would want me to tell you about the gold," Miranda Maria said. "If something should happen to us... Sí, you must know. The gold is in small ingots. Each one is hidden inside one of the adobe blocks in the north wall behind our hacienda. We brought the ingots from the mine each year, then made more adobe blocks and kept building on to the wall."

"The Confederates will surely move in and setup part of their headquarters at your hacienda. Might they find the gold?" Stone asked.

"I believe not. Not unless there is an attack, or such, on the hacienda and someone starts to destroy the wall. I believe God has his angels posted there and the gold is safe from harm."

"You must go, now, please," Stone said. "Go, be a comfort to your father. I will come to you, as soon as I can. That I promise. Then—well, we'll talk when we meet again."

Miranda Maria let loose her hold on Stone, then nodded. At the door, she turned and looked back through the darkness at Stone. Then, she stepped out into the icy winter night.

———

In the morning, Stone told Father Baca what Miranda Maria had done, then he went for a walk. It was a risk to do so, but he needed to get a feel for what was happening. Running into one of the scouts from yesterday, Marshal Malone, or even Buck could be trouble. He took Dinger with him.

His heart saddened as he saw the tattered Lone Star flag of Texas flying over the Palace of the Governors on the square. The first of the regular Confederate troops had arrived and the young men were as ants, scurrying to and fro, seeming anxious to do something other than marching up the road and scrounging for food.

"Hey Parson, Parson Stone. Over here. It's me, Zach. Hold up. I'm comin' to ya." Zach ran over to Stone and grabbed his hand. Stone flinched at the touch of Zach's icy fingers.

"Don't you have a coat, Zach? You'll freeze out here."

"We're gonna make it soon, Parson. I hear there's new clothes, uniforms maybe, waiting for us in Colorado. We just gotta get there. We're a tough bunch, Parson. Texans, you know.

"There wasn't hardly nothin' for us to forage all the way up the river," Zach continued. "We found some left behind Yankee grain and the like, but most of what went in our bellies, well, I know it ain't right, but most of what we ate, we stole from them local farmers and such. We had to, Parson. There wasn't nothin' else."

"What about those farmers and their families?" Stone asked. "How are they going to make it through the winter?"

"Yeah, I know it wasn't right. But, when a fella's belly been empty for days…"

Stone looked around and shivered just looking at the state of the ragged clothing he saw on these young men out in this cold, high elevation of Santa Fe. Some of the men had only rags wrapped around their feet in the fresh snow that came up to their ankles.

"Gotta get back to work, Parson. Maybe I'll see you later."

"Yeah, I'll see you later, Zach," Stone said.

Stone slipped away from all the activity and walked up a side street. He wanted to see the Mills. When he turned the corner to their street, he was surprised to see Stormy and his buggy. Dinger ran over to Stormy, who lowered his head and muzzled the now frisky dog. Mary answered the door and invited him in.

"There's someone here who wants to see you," she said. "I was hoping you'd come by."

"I came to warn you," Stone said. "I don't know what all will go on here, but this could turn really ugly. These poor men have very little left," he said to Mary, then he went into the parlor. He was greeted by Frederick, and Orlando.

"Señor Stone. Forgive me for what I have done that might have brought harm to you," Orlando said. "I was so much foolish. Sí, me listened to the wrong people. I drank in the poison talk of Malone, and such others. I was even ready to betray my old friend, Juan Diego. You knew, but you did not come against me. You are a true man of God. Por favor, Señor Stone, tell me, are Juan Diego and Miranda Maria safe?"

"Safe as they can be. I'm glad you brought my buggy from the hacienda. I'm sure the troops will take that over by tomorrow. It will be the officers, those with their personal slaves and private supplies of food and lots of warm clothes who will settle in there. They'll not want to be around those they recruited into this mess, those boys freezing down on the square.

"I believed my buggy was being watched, and I didn't know how I could get it and Stormy out of there. Thank you for bringing them to me, Orlando."

Orlando nodded. "Now, is time, me must return to the hacienda. Never do I want to bring trouble to these fine people here. Did so hope and pray to find you here, Señor Stone, so that I might show my sorrow and to ask you to forgive me for my foolishness. The Holy Father and all the angels be with you, Señor Stone, and to your household, Señor Mills. When this is over—"

"It will be, Orlando. Pray that it be soon," Stone said.

Once Orlando left, Stone turned to Frederick.

"I must get my buggy away from here. I don't want to bring trouble to you. I'm at the Catholic Church. The Franciscos are out of town and should be safe. I'll see you when I can."

Stone went back to the church, hid Stormy and his buggy in the church stable, then he spent the rest of the day talking with Father Baca.

"It is good to have someone else here. You bring me comfort. Surely God will protect the two of us together, Parson Stone," the old Padre said.

Well after dark that evening, there was a knock at the rectory door. Father Baca answered it. In stepped a young man so full of fear he told Father Baca he was considering desertion, or suicide. He asked the Father to pray for him.

"Many of the able men are here now, Father. But, there's a whole bunch of fellas who are worn out, many wounded also who are still hobbling up the road. I hear the supply wagons, the few we have left and what little they still carry, are due in sometime tonight. Word is they have orders not to stop until they see the square of Santa Fe. Last I saw, them poor mules looked 'bout as bad as most of us boys do.

"Everyone talks of what's waitin' for us in Colorado. We ain't gonna make Colorado, Father. We're whipped. Old man Sibley done let us down, but good. Ain't none of us got much fight left in us."

The priest prayed for the young man who then left in a little better frame of mind. Stone went to bed early, but tossed for hours. In the morning, word came that the supply train did indeed arrive during the night. An advance party, going out to get ready to plan out the attack on Fort Union, had also left early that morning with many of the healthiest of the men.

Stone spent most of the day in the church. An hour past sundown there was another knock at the rectory door.

"Can you help me, Father? I'm looking for Parson Stone. Figure you might have an idea where he might be."

Stone recognized the voice.

"I'm in here, Zach. Come on in."

"It's just awful, Parson," Zach said. "We just got word that our boys who went out this morning ran into some Yankees, and they whupped us but good. It's got most of the boys all full of fear. Some be sayin' we should all turn and run for home. Others even sayin' we should surrender, that the Yanks would at least fill our bellies and give us clothes.

"I thought maybe you'd come and talk to some of the boys," Zach continued. "You always do so much good for me when you talk to me. Please, Parson."

Stone didn't relish the idea. It wasn't wise to leave the safety of the church at night. Still...

"I'll get my buffalo robe." In minutes, he followed Zach to some of the other young soldiers and found things to be as Zach had described. Fear had swept through the camp from one fire to the next. After an hour or so, Stone put his hand on Zach's shoulder.

"I'm exhausted, Zach. I must go back to the church. I can't do much here, anyway."

"Thanks, Parson. If our bellies were full, and we was nice and warm, it'd be a whole bunch different," Zach said. "I hear we're going to wait for the last of the men to get here tomorrow, then give it to them the day after. Maybe by then things will be a mite better."

Stone left the town square and started toward the back of the church rectory. As he turned up the alley, he sensed someone step out of the shadows onto the path behind him.

"Game's up, Preacher, or whatever you are."

Stone slowly turned around and looked at who threatened him this time.

"Well, no wonder I didn't recognize your voice. Never did hear you say much but your name. Lately, a whole lot of people have been pointing their guns at me and threatening me. What's your problem?"

CHAPTER 22

Stone quickly surveyed his situation. It wasn't good. He was in a dark alley with no one but this gunman in sight.

"My problem? You killed Judge."

"The Apaches did that."

"I don't believe you. I found his grave. I found something you obviously didn't. I found his vest that the coyotes had dragged off several hundred feet. It had a letter in it. One he never mailed. He'd written it to me. He told all about you. How you convinced him you were working for Jefferson Davis and all that foolishness. He believed you—then you killed him."

"Look, I know from back on the train that Judge was your card-partner and—"

"He was my brother. My only brother. He was father's favorite—I was the black sheep. However, Judge and I took care of each other. Now he's dead. You killed him. So, now I'm gonna kill you."

"Look, I'll go out there with you, and we can dig up his body. It's only under rocks. You can see for yourself what the Apaches did."

"And they just let you go unharmed, right? How stupid do you think I am? If the Apaches killed Judge, they'd have killed you too.

"I showed Judge's letter to Governor Baylor," Tuck continued. "There's a one thousand dollar bounty on you, alive for questioning by the Governor. I don't much care about that money. I just want to see you lying out cold, as it is with my brother. Then, I'll drag your carcass out into the desert and sit back and watch the buzzards and coyotes pick your bones clean."

"It was Mangas Coloradas, some of his men. There was a woman captive named Esther with them. There was a boy. He only had one leg. I made a leg out of wood for him. That's why they let me go. They thought I was a mystic, or something."

"A lot of people have thought a lot of things about you, but I've got you figured out. You want that gold—we all want that gold. Only I'm the one who's going to get it, and I don't share, not with the likes of you."

Stone slowly turned his head off to the right slightly and stared that way as if looking at someone behind Tuck. He slightly nodded his head as if responding to some signal, or some direction from someone.

Tuck jerked his head to see what was behind him. Before he could react to Stone's bluff, Stone whipped his cane across Tuck's head sending him sprawling in the snow. His gun went flying into a darkened yard, burying itself in the snow.

Stone turned and started down the alley toward the rectory as quickly as he could. Suddenly, his cane slipped and he crashed to the ground. He rolled over in time to see Tuck back up on his feet. Stone watched helplessly as Tuck drew a knife from his belt. Looking toward Stone, Tuck staggered forward. Still flat on his back in the cold snow, Stone readied his cane to strike at the knife he knew Tuck would be thrusting at him.

Without warning, from up at the end of the alley, there came a gunshot. Tuck stopped, stiffened his body, closed his eyes, then he slumped into the snow at Stone's feet. Stone quickly pushed himself up on one elbow to see who had fired that shot. He saw a man on a horse as it spun around, then he watched it head off into the darkness. It was Buck's horse.

———

Stone spent the next day in the Catholic Church. He was sure it was Buck who'd saved his life. What did that mean? Had Buck been with Tuck? Or, had he been following one of them? Did God have any part in this? He finally went outside for some fresh air and paid a teenage boy two bits to get some hay and water for Stormy. He gave some table scraps to Dinger.

Stone slept little that night and was up early. From a window, he watched the columns of men head out of town. He waited until all the men and the last of the wagons had gone before going outside. He then hitched up his buggy and rode over to the Mills'.

Frederick greeted him heartily. "They're gone. Thank the Good Lord for that. I haven't slept much since they got here. I sat up all last night with my old scattergun. I had to chase several of them away. One tried to come right in through the kitchen window. I know they're nearly starving, and if they'd surrender, I'd help all I could, but when they come here to take what little we have... Oh well, what do you think is going to happen today, Parson?"

"I believe it will all depend on how many men, if any, have made it from Colorado. Just remember, if these Confederates are defeated, they'll come right back through here on their retreat. They'll be in worse shape than when they left."

"I'll be ready," Frederick said. "What kind of leaders push young boys to such lengths, anyway?"

"You've never been a soldier, I'd say."

"No, Parson, I never had to take up arms."

"War is what you see here," Stone said. "On the home-front, the newspapers report the big battles and such, but there is always so much hardship and hurt that one never knows about. Trust me, the Union would push its boys just as hard if it had to."

"I don't understand," Frederick said. "I don't understand the southern cause at all. Then, to push it this far…"

"I'm going on up toward Fort Union," Stone said. "Either way this goes, I need to be there for the men, the survivors, those on both sides."

"Do be careful, Parson. Come back as soon as you can."

Stone followed the trail left by this morning's troop march. The snow was packed into a hard ice in many places, and Stormy stumbled often. About an hour later, Stone came upon a small group of formerly wounded men who just couldn't go on.

"It's no use, Parson Stone. I just don't have anything left," one of the men said. The others weekly nodded in agreement. From that point on, the road was dotted with stragglers, some slumped in the cold snow, their bodies completely spent.

Rounding a bend in the trail, Stone came upon a young man staggering back toward Santa Fe. He recognized him as a friend of Zach Faulk's. Stone had heard Zach call him Buster. The young man held up his arms and headed toward Stone.

"Parson… help me, Parson. Oh, I need some water. Been eatin' snow, but that don't lift a fella's thirst."

Stone handed his canteen to the young man.

"You carrying a message, or something?" Stone asked.

"Goin' home, Parson," Buster said. "I'm a runnin' out on this Confederate thing. I ain't gonna make it, I know. Got nearly nine hundred miles to San Antonio, fifty more to home. All I want is one more mess of Ma's chicken and dumplin's, just one more Sunday supper before they bury me.

"Just done that fer Zach," Buster continued, tears suddenly flowing down his cheeks. "Yeah, my old friend Zach Faulk. Close as kin we was. He took it early this mornin'. Me and Billy Joe dug him a hole in this miserable, icy dirt. Both cried like babies when we pushed in the dirt on top of him. Gotta go home now and tell his ma and pa what happened.

"'Course, I know if the Rebs don't get me fer desertion, most likely them Apache or Comanche will tan my hide," Buster said. "I just ain't got no fight left, Parson. I can't do it no more."

Buster slumped to the hard packed snow, then wiped his face with a filthy, tattered bandana. Stone sat in silence, deep in thought.

Zach… This simple farm boy had wanted to take some of the ocean home to his mother. Now, he lay buried in this forsaken, frozen, rock infested dirt. Then, a thought crossed Stone's mind: what about Zach's soul? What about the souls of all of these young men buried out in this forsaken desert? This war would end, but, he feared the torment for many would never do such.

Buster slowly rose to his feet. He took another drink, then handed the canteen back to Stone.

"You come see me sometime, Parson. Be good if'n you could go see Zach's folks. Zach talked about you all the time. Wrote home to his folks about you, too, I'm sure. He surely did put high stock in you."

The young man looked back toward the noise of the battle, then turned and started the other way again.

"Pray for me, Parson," he said as he turned his head back over his shoulder. "Only the Good Lord can get me home."

Stone slowly nodded his head.

"God be with you, Son. God be with us all."

———

About midday, Stone came upon a fork in the road. The wagons had all gone down into a canyon, but the bulk of the men had marched onward down the high road. Stone noticed there were but a few horse and human footprints alongside the narrow, steel-tired, tracks of the wagons. He took the high road, up the canyon ridge. After about ten minutes, he stopped to give Stormy a break and to listen to the cannon and small arms fire coming from not too far up ahead.

He stood up in his buggy and looked down into the canyon. What he saw shocked him. There, all in one small meadow, was the sum of the Confederate supply train. He counted fewer than a dozen men guarding the wagons. Stone's heart leaped. This could be the battle—maybe the war. He dropped to his seat and shook the reins.

"Come on, Stormy. We've got to find some help." He raced forward, toward the sounds of the battle, when suddenly, he came over a rise and nearly ran into a column of mounted men. Dinger growled and barked. Stone reined Stormy to a stop and quickly studied the leader. Here was a large man, his full beard and piercing eyes created a commanding presence. He intently stared back at Stone. Then he pointed at him.

"You're that Parson Stone fellow I've heard so much about. Claim to be a Methodist preacher. I'm a Methodist Bishop myself, been around a long time. Have to say, until recently, I've never heard of you. What are you doing here, anyway?"

"Colonel Chivington, I assume. You're the Pike's Peakers from Colorado. Thank God, Lincoln got my message. You're here to save the day, to save many lives. Come, follow me back the trail. I'll show you the sum of the Rebel supply train, what little they have left. I was heading to the battle to find someone who could commandeer this poorly guarded train. Come," Stone said as he shook the reins and gave the command for Stormy to start backing up to turn the buggy around.

"Not so fast," Colonel Chivington said. "How do I know you're not leading me into a trap?"

"No trap. You're here at this time to stop this invasion. Come," Stone said, reining Stormy forward, back down the trail. Reaching the spot where he'd seen the wagons in the canyon below, Stone stopped and slowly got down from his buggy.

"Over there, Colonel," Stone said. "Crawl over to the edge and look into the canyon below. Tell me what you see."

Colonel Chivington took two of his officers and they crawled to the cap rock's edge. Pulling out his field glasses, he looked into the canyon below.

"Mercy," Colonel Chivington said in a coarse whisper. It's just as you said. It's a gift, a gift from God to end this carnage."

Chivington crawled back from the ledge, put his field glasses away, then started quietly giving orders. It took less than an hour for the men to get into place and to start their descent down the rocky ledges. When their gunfire started into the encircled camp it wasn't long before there was a white flag flying atop one of the wagons. Being greatly outnumbered, tired, cold and seeing no way to win, the Confederate guards stacked their arms and waited for the Pikes Peakers to reach them.

One by one the wagons were looted, then set ablaze. Soon, the smoke was thick, dark and pluming way into the clear, blue sky. Knowing there shortly would be a rush of Confederate help arriving, Colonel Chivington rallied his men, gathered his prisoners, then marched up the road and off to the high ground above.

Stone had stood most of this time in his buggy and had watched the whole episode from his lofty perch on the upper road. He knew in his heart that he was witnessing the end of this invasion by the Confederacy into the far west. There would be no great Texas Empire going all the way to the Pacific.

"Well old boy, this much is done," Stone said to Dinger. "Now, I've got to do something about that gold, and Buck. Then too, maybe something about that Miranda Maria woman also."

Buck and his men were some of the first to arrive at the scene of the burning wagons. It was too late to save anything by then. With virtually nothing for hundreds of miles to their north, going on would be impossible. However, now the question on everyone's mind was: how would they ever get back to east Texas?

"Sergeant Rafter," he heard his name called. He spun around to see his captain pointing up on the eastern ridge.

"That man, Sergeant, that deceiving preacher fellow is responsible for this. Look at him perched up there as an eagle against the blue sky. I've seen how you shoot. That man is the enemy. Kill him, now. Now, Sergeant.

I'll not let him gloat over our defeat. I order you to shoot him, immediately."

Buck picked up his long-barreled musket, adjusted the sights for the
distance, then took aim.

"Now!" the Captain said. "Do it now."

Which leg is it? The left, no, the right. He was sitting facing me and...

Buck lay the fine-bead sight on his target, then squeezed the trigger.
Buck watched Stone catapult out of his buggy, as if hit by cannon shot.

"Nice work, Sergeant Rafter. That, Sergeant, will get you a medal," the
captain said.

———————

The sun was down and the moon was high and bright. Buck eased his horse
up to the high road. With nervous apprehension, he eased forward. There
sat the buggy.

Where is he?

Buck stopped and looked around. He dismounted and walked slowly
forward.

Grrrrr.

"Hush, Dinger," came a voice from behind a piñon tree. "Over here. I
was hoping you'd come. I figured it was you who took out my leg. Nice
shooting."

"I—I didn't have any choice. It was an order. To kill you, really."

"No loss. It was just a piece of old Mexican door-post I'd carved out
down there in prison. I guess they figured as long as I was doing that I
wouldn't be thinking of escaping. However, I did that anyway. I only had
the leg half done. I took it with me and finished it later.

"Frans Mauer—do you know him?" Stone asked. "He's to be making
me a much lighter one. One that actually has a knee that will bend when I
sit down. Won't that be something?"

"You're not mad at me?" Buck asked.

"Why should I be? I figure with today, and the other night, that makes
twice you've saved this old dead-man's life."

Both men were silent for several minutes. Then Stone spoke.

"So, tell me, what are your plans now?

"Plans? I don't know. We're done here. I don't even know how we'll
get back to Texas. It didn't seem to be such a big deal leaving Fort Craig
untouched when we did. Now, we have to go right back down the river and
right past it. We weren't ready for something this big. We didn't know what
we were in for. Maybe with different leadership..."

Again, there was silence for a moment. This time Buck broke the silence.

"What about you? What are you going to do? Actually, what are you anyway? You sure played that preacher thing well. I'd always heard you were the best, that you could take on any role. I believe it now. Man, that had to be hard faking being a preacher."

"Hardest cover I ever had. Yeah, I was faking it. Then about a month ago, I knew it wasn't fake anymore. I knew God really wanted me to become what I'd been pretending to be. Imagine, me a preacher..." Stone shook his head for a minute, then went on.

"Well, I've got a lot of learning to do. I want this more than I can explain. It's more than a want. It's a must thing, really. It's birthed deep inside of me. A place I didn't know existed until recently."

"From every story I've ever heard about you, this surely doesn't fit," Buck said. "I've heard some bigger-than-life things."

"And you tried to live up to them all," Stone said.

"Maybe I did, sometimes," Buck said.

"What would your mother think about my becoming a preacher?"

"Ma? I don't know. She sure missed you. She talked about you all the time. That made old man Roe so mad and..."

"I made a big mistake by not telling her I was alive when I first came back," Stone said, looking off into the darkened canyon below. "I figured with her being married again, and me with my wooden leg and all—well—I guess I figured wrong. All those years in Mexico feeling sorry for myself, and being meaner than a desert rattler, didn't do anyone any good.

"I didn't know the life you two had," Stone continued. "I'm glad I can tell you all of this. How I wish I could tell it to her. There're many things I'd love to say to her."

Stone was quiet for a moment, then, while staring off into the stars above, he spoke seriously to Buck.

"I've been given a new life. I'm a new man now, Son."

Father and son talked on until the sun was breaking into the eastern sky. Buck stood to his feet and looked toward Santa Fe.

"I've got to go. They'll be looking for me. The sooner we get out of here and back down where it's warm the better. Then, there're all those miles and miles across Texas. Don't rightly know about going back to east Texas. Guess you heard about me and old man Roe. Then, too, this worn out nag will never make it halfway."

"Take Stormy," Stone said. "He's a good one."

"I can't do that. I'll make it to wherever I have to go, somehow." Buck tightened his saddle cinches, then swung up into the seat.

"So, when and where do we get together again?" he asked his father. "We've got some catching up to do, I'd say."

"Might not be until after the war. I've got lots of business to wrap up. I still have one major part of my mission to complete. That will take some time. Then, there's this lady… I don't know about that, but maybe." Stone paused for a moment. "Tell me where I can contact you."

"Las Cruces. Cantina de la Palma. There's a—well, her name is Lucinda. Thinkin' I might settle down there. Once this war thing is over, that is."

"May she be as good as your mother."

"You'll fancy her. I know. Look, it's time, I really gotta go," Buck said as he spun his horse around.

"Stay hidden for a few days. Remember, Father, you're supposed to be dead—again."

Stone looked at Buck, then nodded his head.

"The old Tyrone Rafter really is now dead, Son. By God's grace, I've got another chance, and I'm more alive than ever. I'm forevermore to be known as Stone. Parson Justin P. Stone.

ABOUT THE AUTHOR

Robert Mowry is a longtime resident of New Mexico, where much of this story takes place. He is a student of the area's rich history with firsthand knowledge of most of the settings and locations depicted in this story. *Adobe Gold* is a realistic, though fictional, depiction of historic events.